Murder at Myrtle Hill Plantation

A Dane Hunter Mystery
By Robert Ray

dragon
tree books

Published by

1620 SW 5th Avenue
Pompano Beach, Florida 33060
(954)788-4775
editors@editingforauthors.com
dragontreebooks.com

Prologue: A Hot, Stormy July Night in Camden Grove, South Carolina

Black clouds tumbled together, racing from Georgia toward South Carolina's piedmont area. They blotted out the shine of the moon and stars, leaving only the street lights and the occasional glow from a shaded window to ease the darkness. Lightning crackled and popped like static electricity, with the rumble of thunder following seconds behind as the storm approached Camden Grove.

The water of the Saluda River bubbled, rolling over the sand, shale, and boulder shoals as it rushed toward the earthen dam built to harness it, creating power for the textile mills and surrounding area. The dam-controlled run-off slowed the water to a gentle meandering for the river's next stretch ending in Lake Murray near the state capitol.

Once a booming textile mill-town, Camden Grove marks time as the Saluda waters race by the cozy southern hamlet its presence helped create in 1902. The years and economy have not smiled on the town, especially after the Bowen Textile Mills finally closed their doors in 2002.

Since the mill closing, jobs are scarce. The Chapman Farms, part of Myrtle Hill Plantation, became the largest local employer. While a model organic-produce farm affiliated with the Clemson University's College of Agriculture, Forestry, and Life Sciences, the farm only offers fifty full- and part-time positions, about a hundred seasonal jobs, and intern and field study positions for students. Even though the cottage businesses the Farm promotes touch every household, many residents drive to surrounding towns to find jobs, and helplessly watch their children leave for careers and better opportunities in bigger cities.

Only 638 families remain.

Downtown, the theater, YMCA, and train station on the town square have the windows painted and doors chained. Only the mayor, police department, volunteer fire department, two lawyers, the drycleaners, and Lucy Aaron's *Lucy's Cafe*, still show some signs of life around what was once the hub of town activities. The Piggly Wiggly, a little book/Hallmark card shop, and a florist remain open in the shopping center two blocks down Main Street. Lone convenience stores/gas stations stand sentinel at either end of Main.

On the surface, there is little to recommend Camden Grove. No stately southern mansions grace tree-lined streets. Only one house in the town proper fits into the "mansion" category, and it stands as an empty reminder of the town's more prosperous days. Six sizeable houses face the avenue that fronts the old mansion, each covering the entire end of a block. Behind the stone fences of these backyards, smaller frame houses and mill row houses built in the 1920s line the residential streets. A handful of more modern, brick ranch houses dot areas around the outskirts.

But, the town has a secret pulsing beneath its streets...a vortex of psychic energy points fueling those who can tap into it. The area at the start of the Blue Ridge Mountains with its crystal-quartz formations are believed to act as a psychic magnet, and it's drawn or provided a home to gifted psychics, clairvoyants, and healers for generations.

Mary Johnston, lifelong resident and most powerful town psychic and healer, sat wide awake in her English stone cottage-style house, one of the six across from the empty mansion. It was almost one a.m., and despite the surging winds, the air was oppressive, heavy as three quilts on a bed. Trees trembled, limbs shook, and leaves held on for dear life with the wind's onslaught. Dry dust and grass clippings from the day's mowing caught in its grasp and swirled about helter-skelter.

The familiar unease that often came with these surprising electric-current–laden storms niggled at the back of her mind. She stood from her kitchen table, walked to the sink, and looked out the window, unable to latch onto the foreboding feelings and give them shape. Something was afoot, and it didn't feel like anything good. She put a kettle on the stove to brew a calming cup of her favorite nighttime tea, chamomile with a hint of lavender.

Two doors down, the new police chief, Dane Hunter, stirred from the restless night before his first-day-in-a-new-job sleep. He almost woke, but instead scrunched closer to his wife, Joan, spooning her; pulling her in tightly as if she might escape. He slipped back into dreams touched by the smell of vanilla and the sounds of stormy weather.

The rest of Camden Grove's residents were mostly sleeping, oblivious to the cresting wave of the storm, except Ethel Chapman Bowen, owner of Myrtle Hill Plantation just three miles northeast of town where generations of Chapmans had lived since receiving a Land Grant in 1769. Ethel already left her body behind on the bed on the first floor of the huge old house built in 1786 on the sloping rise overlooking the curve of the river where she, as every Myrtle Hill caretaker, had been born. Her spirit raced away with the surging winds ahead of the rains that would drench everything in its path.

CHAPTER

ONE

Bright sunlight was already evaporating the signs of the late-night storm, transforming the clean scent that follows the rain into the earthy, muggy smell of the south on a hot day. Dane Hunter had been in the office for just over two hours, busying himself with settling in. It was his first day on the job as police chief in Camden Grove, South Carolina.

He heard the phone ring in the outer offices. His Deputy, Harvey Turner, answered it on the second ring. It didn't take long before his phone intercom buzzed.

"You gotta take line-one, boss," Harvey announced dramatically. "It's Miss Isabelle from Myrtle Hill. She says Miss Ethel's been murdered."

"Is this a joke?" Dane asked.

"Don't sound like it. Nope. Sounds legit. Miss Isabelle's been with the Bowen family forever, and trust me, she ain't much of a jokester."

Dane punched the line-one button and said, "Chief Hunter."

"This is Isabelle Ricks. I already told Harvey that Ethel Bowen has been murdered. Having to repeat myself is wasting time."

"I'm sorry, Ms. Ricks. First, are you in a safe place?"

"Of course I am."

"Are you in the house and sure no one else is there that should not be?"

"Yes."

"Are you sure?"

"Yes."

"Good. Did you see or hear what happened?"

"No."

Dane looked at his watch and wrote the time as ten-twelve on a notepad.

"Where is Mrs. Bowen?" Dane asked.

"In her bedroom."

"Have you been in the room to check for signs of life...pulse, breathing, movement, anything?"

"Don't need to go all the way in. I can see enough from the door to know she's been murdered."

"Are you sure she is not alive?"

"There's no doubt in my mind. She has been shot, and there is no way she could have survived," Isabelle replied quietly. "You are my first call, and I won't make any others until you've been here and gathered up all the evidence you need."

"Ms. Ricks, please don't touch anything, clean anything up, or call anyone else until we get there. We'll take care of all the calls. Please don't let anyone into the bedroom, or for that matter into the house, until I get there. Are you sure you are safe?

"I know you're the smart new guy from Washington, D.C., but don't think I'm stupid just because I'm from the rural South."

Dane smiled at her prickly quip. "I didn't make that assumption, Ms. Ricks. We'll be there as quickly as we can."

"I'll be waiting." She hung up the phone before Dane had a chance to say anything else.

He dropped the receiver back into its cradle and looked up to see Harvey leaning against the doorjamb, lanky and unkempt with a fairly nondescript face, and hair, whitewall short on the sides, curly and untamable mouse-brown on top. If he didn't have bushy-to-the-point-of-almost-creepy eyebrows, he could go unnoticed. Dane somehow already knew that Harvey was not simple, but so used to blending in that he could be forgotten, and had probably been left out of most police activities in the past.

"First murder I can remember," Harvey declared. "Good thing you know all about murders and stuff. Can I come with you? I can tell you all 'bout the Bowens, Miss Ethel, and the senator."

"The senator?" Dane questioned.

"Yup. Senator Bowen is Miss Ethel's son. He's gonna be our next governor, then probably vice president or something. Ronnie's good looking, smart, and got lots of money."

"Okay, Harvey," he said, "we have a few calls to make before we leave, but I do want you come with me and tell me about the Bowens and Isabelle Ricks on the way. Get the numbers for the Piedmont Region Investigation Services, the Forensics Office, county coroner, and the hospital in case we need them. Oh, and get the judge's number; I'd like to have a search warrant before we start. "

"Uh, it'll take me some time to look up the numbers."

"You don't know the numbers?" Dane asked, a note of surprise in his voice. "Hell, just grab your cell phone, and let's go. You can Google any other numbers we need."

"My cell don't Google," Harvey said holding up an old flip phone.

"You have got to be kidding me. Grab the phone book, for now; we'll just have to do this the old-fashioned way. But we're going to get you a smart phone, Harvey."

Harvey beamed as Dane picked up his briefcase and opened it to check for his recorder, gloves, and crime scene tape, all the basics he'd need for the initial assessment of a potential crime scene.

"Why are we calling all these people?" Harvey asked innocently.

Dane glanced at him to see if he was putting him on, and realized that the question was genuine. Harvey hadn't a clue about investigating a murder. "Well, whenever you get a call that someone is dead and the words 'murder' or 'suicide' are used, there is a whole protocol that needs to be followed. Later on, we'll look it up together and go over it. For now, just know that it's in my head. I'll talk you through everything we do, and it's very important that you do exactly what I ask you to do."

Harvey smiled like a kid on Christmas morning. "Sure, boss. This is great. My very first murder investigation."

As they got into the car, Dane asked, "Harvey, you do know where we're going, don't you?"

"Sure, everyone knows where Myrtle Hill is; just go like we're going to Greenwood. It's 'bout three miles out of town."

Dane eased the car out of the parking space, put on the light, and sped down Main Street. "Harvey, first call is to the Piedmont Region Investigation Services. If I remember correctly, it's run by Major Forrest Sikes. You dial; I'll talk."

Harvey looked up the number, dialed, identified himself, and pronounced that the new Camden Grove police chief needed to talk to Major Sikes, and it was urgent. He handed over the phone.

Dane waited a minute before Forrest Sikes came on the line. "Major Sikes, Dane Hunter here."

"Heard we had a D.C. hotshot right here in our neighborhood," Sikes drawled. "Welcome to Carolina. Thought I was going to see you next week."

"Thanks, and yes, we have an appointment next week; however, I may need your help now. You know it's just Officer Turner and me at

Camden Grove. We have a report that Ethel Bowen has been murdered at Myrtle Hill."

"You gotta be shitting me. Ethel, murdered? Ethel's a tough one, but no one 'round here would want to hurt her. She's a legend. She or her parents before her have done something for just about every family in the area. What, with Ronnie running for governor, I think someone is just playing a joke on the new guy."

"We received the call about fifteen minutes ago from Isabelle Ricks. She was adamant that Mrs. Bowen had been murdered. We're on our way over there now. The point of my call is to alert you. Officer Turner's never been involved in a murder investigation. If, in fact, we find Mrs. Bowen dead, this needs to go by the books. I know my stuff, but I don't want to step on any toes or break any South Carolina rules I don't yet know about."

"Let's hope this is a horrible prank," Sikes said in a serious, professional manner, dropping the exaggerated southern drawl. "But if it isn't, call me back, and I'll have a team over within the hour. Don't worry about calling forensics. I'll take care of that and tell them you might be calling back. If it turns out to be a prank, you can expect some ribbing. We'll get a laugh at your expense when you come in next week and probably for a long, long time to come."

"Thanks, I'll be back to you one way or the other," Dane concluded and handed the phone back to Harvey. "Okay, next call, the judge." After setting the search warrant in motion and getting Judge Bradley Ladner's okay to proceed, Dane decided to wait on the other calls until after he knew exactly what they were facing.

"Harvey, I want you to tell me what you know about the Bowens and Isabelle Ricks."

"You really need to talk to Mary Johnston. She knows everything about everyone. Even things nobody else knows. People say she's the head witch in Camden Grove. She don't ride a broom or anything like that, and she ain't ugly, just old, but—"

"Harvey, the Bowens."

"Well, anyway, Miss Mary knows all about the Bowens and the Chapmans. Miss Ethel was a Chapman, born at Myrtle Hill. Land always belonged to the Chapmans since forever. She must be about, let's see, I'm forty-two, the senator is forty-three, he was one year ahead of me in high school," he mused, cocking his head to one side thinking, "and Miss Ethel was probably about twenty when he was born, making her 'bout sixty-three now. She's been a widow for 'bout six years. She and Mr. Bowen fought like two old mules, but when he died, she just ain't been quite right since, with dealing with the mess he left behind from closing the mill, managing her farm, and taking care of Miss Becky, who's sometimes crazy as a loon."

"Who is Miss Becky?" Dane asked.

"Miss Becky is Miss Ethel's daughter. She's four years younger than the senator and was fine till she went off to college. When she came back in her third year, something was wrong, and she's been in and out of hospitals since. Something really bad happened to her, but it was all kept real quiet. She used to be real pretty, but now she just don't look right. I heard they even give her regular shock treatments, hook electric wires right to her head and 'buzz.'" Harvey stiffened and twitched to portray current zapping through his body and said, "Sent the electricity right into her brain to try to make her normal and all. Along with the electricity, I know she takes lots of pills, 'cause I've seen them putting together her prescription bag at the pharmacy. Lord, I could never swallow that many pills. You're gonna take a right just after the next curve. That'll be the driveway to the big house." Harvey directed, tapping the side window with his pointer finger knuckle.

"Harvey, before we get there, tell me about Isabelle Ricks."

"Don't know a lot about Miss Isabelle. She's always been there. I think she's a witch, too, but she don't have anything to do with Miss Mary and her group."

"Harvey."

"Well, she don't," he said, adding with a scrunch of his face, "and she scares the pee-willy-wunk-wunk out of me the way she's always looking at ya like she knows exactly what you're thinking. The story I heard is that her people were so poor they gave her to old Colonel Chapman and his wife, Miss Francis, just before Miss Ethel was born. She's been there ever since as a nanny or a maid, whatever Miss Ethel needed her to do. She's always been in that house 'cept when she went away to school with Miss Ethel when they were young. Never goes nowhere much, but she knows stuff about people, too. I'm telling you she's a witch, so you'd better watch out for her."

Following the point of Harvey's finger and the tap on the window with his knuckle, Dane slowed the car and turned right into the tree-lined driveway. He didn't react outwardly to Harvey's 'witch' talk, a small smile twitching at the sides of his lips, caused by his deputy's descriptions. The trees along each side of the drive were stately crepe myrtles. Dane hadn't known they could get as big as these were, but he knew myrtles bloomed from June through August. It was a spectacular sight.

As they drew near the end of the drive and the view opened to include the house, Dane let out a low whistle. "Geez, it is huge." Myrtle Hill was a sprawling three-story brick structure with the eighteenth-century central house connecting two nineteenth-century wings. A columned, two-story veranda spanned the entire distance between the two wings. Four broad brick steps lead up to the veranda. As they pulled into the circular drive, one side of the double front door opened and a bone-thin black woman with short steel-gray hair stepped out. She walked the twelve feet to stand at the top of the stairs.

"That'd be Miss Isabelle," Harvey said, rolling his eyes theatrically, "and I bet she knows I've been talking about her."

Dane and Harvey got out of the car, and Isabelle immediately said, "Lost again, Harvey? Or are the two of you just slow?"

Harvey turned red. Dane ignored the remark, opened the back door and picked up his case. He sat it on the trunk lid, took out his voice-activated digital recorder, and stuffed two pair of latex gloves into his pocket. He closed the case, walked around the back of the police car, and approached the stairs.

"Ms. Ricks, I'm Dane Hunter. I see you already know Officer Turner. I'm sorry to meet you under difficult circumstances."

"Do you just like hearing your own voice, or is there another reason for your chatter?" Isabelle snapped. "This isn't a visit. I called you because Ethel Bowen has been murdered. Can we just get on with it?"

Dane looked her in the eyes. Neither blinked. After a silent battle of wills, he said, "Ms. Ricks, as I begin the official process of investigating your call regarding the alleged murder of Mrs. Ethel Bowen, let me explain how I'll proceed. When we enter the house, I'll be recording my observations, not because I like the sound of my voice," he said raising one eyebrow, "but because it's important to capture first thoughts and impressions. After my cursory review of the situation, I'll tape off the area where I want to control access for the purpose of gathering evidence. Officer Turner will be accompanying us now. After I determine the next steps, he'll make calls for other personnel to assist us. Do you have any immediate questions?"

"None," Isabelle said peevishly. "Shall we begin, or do you have more instructions for me?"

Ignoring her comment Dane took the gloves out of his pocket, handed one pair to Harvey, and began putting his on. "From this point on, don't touch anything you don't absolutely need to touch, Harvey." He pushed the button of the recorder to voice-activated on. "Dane Hunter, the time is..." he paused, looking at his watch, "ten-forty-seven. I'm about to enter Myrtle Hill Plantation with Ms. Isabelle Ricks and Officer Harvey Turner. Officer Turner and I are responding to a ten-twelve a.m. call from

Ms. Ricks informing us of the possible murder of Ethel Chapman Bowen. In the time between the initial call and now, Officer Turner and I drove from the station, contacted Major Forrest Sikes, head of the Piedmont Region Investigation Services, and Judge Bradley Ladner who authorized a search warrant of the premises in response to the call. We are about to enter the front door."

Dane paused, turned to Isabelle, and asked her to lead the way. She walked to the front door and went in, leaving Dane and Harvey to follow. They entered a spacious central hall that stretched from the front to the back of the house. A staircase curved from the right of the hallway to the next floor, and then continued on to the third floor. Double pocket doors were partially open on either side of the hall, one leading to a parlor, the other to a library, allowing Dane a glimpse into the very large rooms. Beyond those two rooms was another hallway that divided the house between the two wings.

"Ms. Ricks, where is Ms. Chapman's room?"

"Down the center hall here and to the left."

They turned into a left side corridor and into the recorder Dane reported, "I am heading down a hall toward the master bedroom. The main smell in this portion of the house is that of cleaners, mostly lemon and pine."

On the left was another entrance to the parlor; to the right, double pocket doors lead to the dining room. Dane noticed the table and counted seven places set with china, glasses, silver, and all. There was no place setting at the far end of the table. Fresh flowers completed an elaborate centerpiece. Past the dining room was a door into a powder room, and then the hallway ended at another set of double pocket doors. They were closed. "Is this Mrs. Bowen's room, Ms. Ricks?" he asked.

"Yes."

"Was the door open or closed when you found Mrs. Bowen this morning?"

"Closed."

"Did you go in?"

"I believe I already answered that," Isabelle grumped.

"Not really. You said earlier that you didn't need to go all the way in to see that Miss Bowen was dead. I'm assuming that you had to open the door and go in at least partway."

"Yes," she huffed, "I opened the door and entered into the master suite until I saw the bed. I came back out, closed the door, and called you."

The musty, burnt odor of a gun fired indoors, mingled with the almost overpowering scent of Shalimar perfume, the same his mother used to wear, gave Dane a prelude to what he was to see when he opened the door to the master suite at Myrtle Hill Plantation. Even at six-foot three and two hundred pounds, he was dwarfed in the wide hallway with its fourteen-foot ceilings and elaborate crown moldings.

As he began his routine by rote, Harvey was following him so closely that a quick stop would cause him to run right up Dane's butt. Isabelle hovered behind Harvey.

After quickly scanning the room and taking in the gruesome part around the bed, Dane paused to process what he saw before beginning to speak. No matter how many crime scenes he saw, there was always a gut tightening reaction at first glance. His digital voice-activated recorder captured his words when he began speaking. "At the end of the paneled hall, I see a bed to the left. The body of a middle-aged woman occupies the bed, about center. From where I stand, it appears that a portion of the left side of the victim's face and head is missing." The sounds of Harvey gagging interrupted Dane's observations. As he turned to look at him, Harvey doubled over and vomited on the carpet near the wall.

"Jesus, Harvey," Dane barked. "You're contaminating the site. Get out of here until you get yourself under control. I'll finish up myself."

Dane's further observations were delayed by a caustic hiss from Isabelle Ricks. "Harvey Turner, you're a medical miracle, a man standing without a spine. I'm going to have to clean that up, you know."

Harvey suppressed another gag, moaning, "It ain't like the room's not gonna have to be cleaned anyway, Miss Isabelle. Lord, there's stuff all over the wall and the bed. Half of Miss Ethel's face is gone. Who could've done such a thing?"

"Harvey, go on out," Dane instructed. "Call Major Sikes and tell him we'll need his forensics team. Ask him if he wants you to call the county coroner and the hospital emergency team to let them know what we have here, or if he would rather do it himself. Miss Ricks, would you please take Officer Turner someplace where he can make his calls?"

As Harvey and Isabelle left the room, Dane refocused, quietly detailing his observations. "I'm approaching the bed to determine whether Mrs. Bowen is alive." He crossed the enormous room to the queen-sized bed. "Mrs. Bowen is propped against the headboard. She's apparently wearing a medium brown wig. Numerous other wigs lie on the bed around her. Her right arm is angled awkwardly from her body and extending from her hand is..." he paused, leaning over to look at the gun, "a thirty-eight caliber special, wooden-handle, two-inch barrel revolver. It's half on her hand and half on the bed. I'm checking both her right wrist and the undamaged side of her throat for a pulse. There is none. It appears that a bullet may be lodged in the headboard to my right as I look at Mrs. Bowen."

Dane walked to the various entrances to the room, saying, "There are windows on either side of the bed. The first closed but unlocked." Moving toward the other window, he said, "The second is also unlocked. Two French doors stand on either side of a large family painting." After checking them, he records, "Both doors are unlocked." He stepped out and noted a large terrace, pool with six lounge chairs lining the side closest to the house facing a brick and tile wall on the opposite side of the pool with lion heads spouting water into the pool. In the distance he saw a fenced tennis court. Mature, impeccably manicured landscaping and lawns sloped to the river bank. He noticed the water was much slower and appeared deeper than it was flowing through town.

Back inside, he recorded, "Beyond the doors to the outside is a sitting room with two windows. These windows, too, are unlocked. There's an open door into a bathroom. Inside, one window is shut but unlocked. A long, narrow, transom window above the tub is slightly ajar."

He walked from the bathroom back to the bed where he visually counted and reported, "Seven wigs cover the bed, along with a number of combs and brushes. Several large pieces of jewelry that appear to be costume are scattered among the wigs on the bed. Most are made with bright buttons and large fake gems. Blood and tissue spatter the wall above and to the left of the bed. Splatter can also be seen down the left side of the headboard, the left side of Mrs. Bowen's body, and on the bedclothes. Besides the items on the bed, nothing else in the room appears out of place.

"Mirrored closet doors, all closed, cover the entire left wall. All dresser drawers are shut. An ornate wooden jewelry box is open on the dresser.

"This completes my initial assessment. All accessible entry routes to the room—doors and windows to the outside and the door into the main part of the house—are unlocked; the narrow window in the bathroom is the only one open. I've touched nothing in the room except Mrs. Bowen's right wrist and the right side of her neck. I'm wearing gloves. The only alteration to the scene can be found near the bedroom door where Officer Turner lost his breakfast."

Before leaving the room, Dane strung Police Crime Scene tape across each window and door. Walking from the bedroom into the main corridor of the house, he closed and taped the door. He heard Harvey's voice and followed it to the library where Harvey spoke with over-stated authority to the person at the other end of the line, closely watched by Isabelle.

Dane wasn't exactly excited about spending more time questioning Isabelle Ricks.

Joining Harvey and Isabelle in the library, Dane said, "Ms. Ricks, I'd like to ask you a few questions while Officer Turner makes some calls. With your permission, I'd like to record your answers."

Isabelle nodded. Dane sat opposite Isabelle and said into the recorder, "Initial interview with Ms. Isabelle Ricks, who first notified Officer Harvey Turner that Mrs. Bowen was dead." Leaning forward, he continued, "Ms. Ricks, you stated on the phone that you had made no other calls but to the station. I assume that you have not yet contacted any family members," he said placing the recorder on the table between them.

"Does, 'I've made no other calls' mean something else to you?" Isabelle snapped.

"Ms. Ricks, I'm only trying to establish who may or may not know about the situation here. Do any of Mrs. Bowen's children live here in the house?" he asked.

"No."

"Do they live nearby?"

"Yes."

"Would you have their addresses and phone numbers so that we may contact them?"

"Yes."

"Will you provide them to me?"

"You want them right now, or when you finish your questions?" Isabelle asked tightly.

"Ms. Ricks, let's start over," Dane said, taking a deep breath to control his temper. "We seem to have gotten off to a rough start for some reason, and I know you must be very upset by Mrs. Bowen's death. I'll make my questions as brief as possible for now. You've stated that Mrs. Bowen was murdered." Sitting back, he knitted his fingers together and in a more friendly tone, he continued, "I have to ask questions so that we can establish facts regarding what happened here. If I could get the addresses and phone numbers before we leave, that would be great. Does Mrs. Bowen have a pastor or priest we should call to accompany us for family notifications?"

"Father Rhett Leverett. Mrs. Bowen was Catholic, not a Southern Baptist like Mr. Bowen and her children. If you're going to have a minister accompany you to talk to Ronnie and Becky, I recommend you ask their pastor. No matter what Mrs. Bowen tried, they'd never have anything to do with the Catholic Church, even though Mr. Bowen signed the agreement to raise the children Catholic when they married. He rarely kept his word," Isabelle said with a disapproving look. "The children's pastor is Reverend Doug Reed."

"Thank you." Turning to Harvey, Dane said, "Harvey, would you call Reverend Reed and ask him if we could stop by in a little while and talk with him? If he asks the topic, just tell him that there has been a death, and I'd like him to accompany me to notify immediate family members, if he has the time. Don't give him any other information, but explain that I will, when I arrive."

Harvey stepped into the hallway so his conversation wouldn't interfere.

Turning back to Isabelle, Dane asked, "Are there any other immediate family members we should contact?"

"No, Ronnie can take care of the rest."

"Okay. Now tell me about yesterday. Was there anything different about the day? Was Mrs. Bowen in good humor, or was she sad or depressed in any way?"

"She was in a fine mood until dinner. Ronnie, Becky, Ronnie's wife Robin, his son Ronnie Junior, one of Ronnie Junior's hoodlum friends, and Mrs. Bowen's lawyer, Wayne Wenzel, were to have dinner here last night. You probably noticed the table is still set. Mrs. Bowen made Ronnie so angry that he and his family all went away without eating. She and Mr. Wenzel ate their dinner here in the library."

"What made the family angry?" Dane asked.

"She told them that she was changing her will to leave Myrtle Hill to the church as a Catholic Retreat, along with the farm that produces a quite sizeable income each year. She also said she was going to divide a large part of the rest of her money among her charities. She told them their father had left them more than enough to last them a lifetime, so she felt the Chapman money should go to help others who were less fortunate.

She told them Mr. Wenzel was drawing up the new will. That put a bit of a damper on the dinner party, and I'd been cooking all day," Isabelle said with mock exasperation.

"Was there any argument?"

"Ronnie said he wouldn't stand for it. Robin had already had so much to drink before arriving that she just started crying. Becky said something like, 'and y'all say I'm the crazy one.' Ronnie Junior turned white, and his hoodlum friend just looked at him. That about sums up the reactions."

"Did Mr. Wenzel say anything?"

"Nothing."

"What happened then?"

"Ronnie pulled Robin out of her chair saying they'd come back when Mrs. Bowen came to her senses and not to call him until that happened. Becky eventually just wandered out of the room and never came back. Ronnie Junior and his friend followed Ronnie out."

"What time did all of this happen?"

"They all arrived between five-thirty and six. Ronnie and Robin arrived first, then Mr. Wenzel a few minutes later. Ronnie Junior and the hoodlum came in about ten-of-six, and Becky wandered in around six. They were all having drinks. Am I giving you enough detail, Officer Hunter?" Isabelle asked sarcastically.

"You are doing just fine," Dane replied, flashing his best smile.

"I brought in a platter of shrimp and cocktail sauce at about six-fifteen. That was when Mrs. Bowen began her announcement. The house was cleared out inside of fifteen minutes except for Mr. Wenzel. The two of them ate dinner here in the library at seven. I served them peach pound cake, ice cream, and coffee at eight-fifteen. Mrs. Bowen asked me to show Mr. Wenzel out at nine. She remained here in the library about an hour. During that time, there were two calls, Ronnie and Ronnie Junior. After leaving the library she came into the kitchen and told me she was retiring for the night. I finished cleaning the kitchen and putting away the uneaten food and went to my room at about ten forty-five."

"Did Mrs. Bowen seem upset when she said goodnight?"

"Quite the contrary. She seemed quite content, despite her children's anger."

"How did you know that the senator and his son called?"

"I answered the phone."

"Do you know what they talked about?"

"I answer the phone, I don't listen to conversations," Isabelle said.

"I wasn't implying you did. I thought that perhaps Mrs. Bowen might have spoken to you about why they called."

"It was a family conversation."

"What time did you go to sleep?"

"I turned off my light at about twelve thirty. I didn't go to sleep for some time. If you remember, we had thunderstorms last night."

"Did you lock all the doors and windows before going to your room?"

"None of them have ever been locked, as far as I can remember."

"This was a practice?"

"Again, I do not believe they have ever been locked."

"Did you hear anything else?"

"No."

"As far as you know, no one else came to the house?"

"No."

"Did you hear the gunshot?"

"No."

"Think about it. A gunshot is fairly loud."

"Officer Hunter, in case you hadn't noticed, Myrtle Hill is a large house. My room and Ethel's room are at opposite ends, with a whole floor of rooms in between. Add to that the storm. I may have heard a gunshot and not known it was a gun rather than thunder."

"Do you know if the gun belonged to Mrs. Bowen?"

"I didn't look at it, but there are many guns in the house. While Ethel wouldn't hunt, she knew how to handle a gun and frequently went target or skeet shooting."

"I didn't see a note. Did you?"

"No. I wouldn't think a murderer would leave a note," Isabelle said matter-of-factly.

"I noticed what appeared to be costume jewelry on the bed and the dresser. Did the jewelry box contain any valuable items?"

"No. She has jewels that came down from both the Chapman and the Bowen families, but that is kept in the safe or in the bank vault unless Ethel was going to attend a function.

Looking at her thoughtfully, Dane replied, "Ms. Ricks, thank you for your answers. I have just one more question for now. When you called, you said Mrs. Bowen was murdered. Why would you assume murder instead of suicide? Is suicide even a remote possibility?"

"Mrs. Bowen is Catholic. She would never commit suicide."

"Who do you think did this, then, and why?"

"You said one question; these two make a total of three."

"I know." Dane smiled sheepishly.

Isabelle sat bolt upright, unfolded her arms and cupped her hands in her lap and calmly looked Dane straight in the eyes. "Well, Officer

Hunter," she said, "There are lots of reasons why she wouldn't do this herself. In addition to her faith, she wouldn't be able to physically hurt herself. She has never handled pain very well. There are also reasons someone else would harm a very wealthy, influential, and accomplished woman. I don't see any reason to do your work for you. I'll answer your questions, but I don't think I need to volunteer anything. I've got too many secrets squirreled away from a lifetime with this family and don't want to lead you down any paths you don't need to travel. But don't think I'll let you jump to calling this a suicide just to make it easy for everyone. Come see me when you have something specific to ask."

Dane understood that Isabelle had thrown him a challenge. He sensed that their contact was to be like the game of hot/cold he'd played growing up. If he discovered something, she would tell him if it were pertinent or not, but wouldn't divulge her suspicions until he found clues to things she knew.

The silence was broken by the doorbell announcing the arrival of Major Sikes and the forensics team. Isabelle showed Forrest and his three-member team into the library, but did not accompany him in. Dane quickly briefed him on the actions that he'd taken since their previous conversation.

"I'll take over the site while you notify the family," Sikes said. "We can talk later today about results and where we go from here. My suggestion will be that because this is likely to be a high-profile case, we need to work as a team. I won't leave you out of anything, as long as you do the same."

"I definitely want your involvement!" Dane replied gratefully, adding, "Harvey Turner is very willing; he doesn't have the experience yet. We'll work on that, right Harvey?"

"Yes, sir," Harvey said with gusto.

"I'll provide you transcripts of my initial observations and my interview with Isabelle Ricks. I won't record my family notification visits, and I'll keep the questions minimal, but I'll immediately write up the information along with impressions after the visits. Didn't expect to have to do this kind of work down here," he observed. "I really expected it to be totally quiet."

"This isn't usual in Camden Grove. Looks like it followed you. You know the old saying, 'you can run, but you can't hide,'" Forrest observed. "I've got your cell number; you've got mine. Stay in touch today."

Isabelle reappeared as Dane and Harvey prepared to leave, giving them a listing of the phone numbers and addresses Dane had requested. She ushered them out the front door and closed it behind them without a goodbye. The two left to meet with Reverend Reed, with Dane thinking how much he hated delivering news of a death to family members.

Dane dropped Harvey at the station and got simple directions to the reverend's house.

CHAPTER

THREE

At Reverend Doug Reed's house next to Camden Grove First Baptist Church, Dane shook hands with the pastor and told him about Ethel's death. The two were just about the same height and both with blue eyes, but that's where the physical similarities ended. Doug was prematurely gray, thinnish, but not muscular compared to Dane's muscular frame with just a little extra around the middle. Doug's paleness indicated that he spent too much time indoors.

Dane observed that Doug had the look he used to see in himself—one who'd seen too much bad, but was still fighting to see only the good in people. In Dane's early days on the force, his fellow officers called him Pony Boy because he put a positive spin on everything. They claimed he could walk into a room full of crap and start looking for the pony that had to be there.

Doug quickly agreed to accompany Dane to inform Ethel's two children, Ronnie and Becky, of Ethel's death. He gave Dane good driving directions, but both were silent on the way.

"Take the next left," Doug directed. "The house is on the cul-de-sac." He seemed again lost in thought and finally said, "Ronnie and I have been friends since college. I spent a lot of time at Myrtle Hill during school breaks and know that he always felt he didn't measure up for either parent. His father wanted him in business, but Ronnie wasn't interested. His mother wanted him to do anything as long as he did it as a Catholic, but he couldn't please her, because his father was so against what he called the Pope's 'interference' in his life. Ronnie is going to be devastated. He was after his father died."

The two pulled up in front of the two-story colonial house, home of South Carolina District Ten State Senator Ronald Dee Bowen and his wife, Robin. Together Dane and Doug walked up the sidewalk to the front door and rang the bell. It wasn't long before the senator's sixteen-year-old son, Ronnie Junior, opened the door. His hair obviously hadn't seen a comb yet, and he was wearing shorts and a T-shirt many sizes too big for his thin frame. Dane noticed the wide-open pupils and knew he was high on something.

"Hey, pastor. What brings you over?" Ronnie Junior asked with a disinterested look.

"Are your father and mother home?" Doug asked him, ignoring his rudeness.

"Yeh, man. Mom's in the den with one of her headaches, and I think Dad is out by the pool. Want me to get him, or do you just want to wander out there?"

"Why don't we wait in the living room while you let your father and mother know we're here and would like to talk to them," Doug suggested.

"Sure. I can do that. Don't know if Mom's headache will let her get up," he said, rolling his eyes as only a teen can do, "but I'll tell her and Dad." He left them, disappearing through a door that he closed behind himself.

Doug led Dane into the living room, where they sat silently on the sofa facing the room entrance, waiting.

The senator came into the room just a few minutes later, tanned, muscled, slim, and wearing only swim trunks and a towel draped around his neck. Both Doug and Dane stood up.

"Doug, what a surprise," the senator said, punching Doug's arm in an easy comfortable acknowledgment of their long friendship. He turned to Dane and shook his hand. "From the blue uniform, I assume you are our new chief of police. Welcome to Camden Grove. But seeing the two of you together along with the somber looks on your faces doesn't make me think this is a social call."

"Senator, I'm sorry to meet you under these circumstances. I'm afraid I have the task of telling you that your mother has died," Dane said uncomfortably. No matter how he practiced saying those words, they never came out the way he wanted them to. The senator turned pale beneath his tan, and Dane saw in his eyes the struggle to maintain control. Focused on him, Dane hadn't seen the senator's wife leaning against the doorway. Her gasp made all three men know that she was there.

The senator went over to her and wrapped his arms around her. Dane noticed two things: the squint of her eyes indicated she was sensitive to the light or had a headache, and she tensed at her husband's touch. She pulled away, walked to a chair, and melted into it, her left elbow going to the armrest and a hand to her forehead to prop her head up. Tears rolled down her cheeks.

"Honey, why don't you go and lie down? I'll talk to Chief Hunter," the senator said.

"How did she die?" Robin asked.

"Honey..."

"How did she die?" she asked a little too loudly while looking straight at Dane, ignoring her husband.

"It appears that she died from a gunshot wound to the head," Dane answered, focusing his full attention on her. Robin's right hand flew up to cover her mouth.

"Shot?" the senator asked. "You mean she killed herself?"

"We don't know what happened yet, Senator. Our investigation is just beginning," Dane explained.

"No one would hurt Mother," Ronnie said emphatically. "She hasn't been herself since father died. I think she just couldn't bear to live without Dad."

"Mrs. Ricks believes that your mother would never take her own life," Dane said, watching for his reaction.

Anger shot from the senator's eyes and was as swiftly controlled. "Of course the old lioness would say that. She'll even try to protect Mother's path into heaven. I bet she also told you that we had an argument about inheritance last night. That established a motive for any one of us family members to kill Mother for money." Moving to sit on the arm of the chair in which his wife sat, he picked up her hand and said, "Well, for the record, if you are looking for a suspect, my wife and I came straight home, fixed ourselves dinner since we missed dinner at Myrtle Hill, and spent a quiet evening together."

Dane observed Robin's incredulous glance at her husband before a blank look took over. He knew right away that a lie was out on the table, but also knew that the time wasn't right to pursue the truth.

"Senator, it's too early to look for either suspects or alibis. Let's wait until we get some facts first. Just know that I'm terribly sorry for your loss, and we'll do everything possible to resolve all issues quickly."

"Timing couldn't be worse. The election's just a few months away," the senator mused before again catching himself.

Doug went to where Ronnie and Robin sat and stooped in front of them, putting one hand on each of their legs. "I know you must both be distraught. Ronnie, you know how I feel about your mother. She's always been good to me despite what she called my 'wrong-headedness about religion.'"

His remark brought a weak smile to both their faces as they must have remembered feisty dinner battles of the past.

Doug continued, "You'll both be in my prayers, and know if there is anything I can do, I will."

Ronnie said, "You're a good friend, Doug. But I think we just need to process this right now. God, Mother's gone. I just can't believe it."

Dane could tell that the senator's sense of loss was genuine as the possibility of his mother's death began to sink in.

Ronnie continued, "Gone with angry words between us as our last. It seems like I'm doomed to having unfinished business with my family."

Doug quickly responded, "Ronnie, Chief Hunter still needs to go talk with Becky and let her know. I can stay with you and Robin while you tell Ronnie Junior, if you like, but I think I should go with him after that. We can stay here as long as you need us to, and you know I can come back. Whenever you want to talk, I'm here."

"I know you are, Doug. Robin and I will tell Ronnie Junior. I think I'll take a raincheck on that talk, though. We need to work through this ourselves right now, but I'm sure we'll all come looking to borrow those broad shoulders in the coming weeks. I don't know what kind of shape Becky's in today," he said to Doug, knowing the other man understood the comment. "She doesn't handle turmoil well, and I'm sure last night upset her. Maybe I should come with you?"

"That's not necessary, Ronnie. I'll go with Chief Hunter. You stay here with Robin. Becky's comfortable with me, and I'll call to check on you when I get home," Doug said.

"Senator and Mrs. Bowen, I am truly sorry for your loss," Dane said. "Please know that we'll do everything possible to complete our work quickly, and I'll provide you with as much information as I can."

The senator stood and guided them to the front door, leaving Robin sitting in the living room. The three shook hands before Dane and Doug turned and walked toward the car, the senator closing the door behind them.

Once the car doors were closed, Doug asked, "You don't think that Ronnie had anything to do with this, do you?"

"I honestly don't think anything right now. It's really way too early, and we don't have any facts yet."

"I know how much Ronnie loved his mother, and I know him well enough to vouch for his integrity. This isn't something he could ever do."

"There are no accusations. We don't have any idea what happened at Myrtle Hill. We only know that whatever happened, Mrs. Bowen is dead, and her children need to be told," Dane said patiently as he pulled the car out of the driveway, heading for the stop sign and the first intersection from the house.

"Ronnie is a rising star in politics," Doug said, "but hasn't found the same level of success in his personal life. He has a lot of charisma and loves the spotlight, but Robin isn't a comfortable politician's wife who can easily handle the pressures of constant scrutiny. Ronnie Junior has had a difficult adolescence. It has to be tough when your only child acts out at every chance and gets caught almost every time." Looking absently out the car window, lost in thoughts, Doug continued, "I also know that Ronnie's been disappointed that his mother hasn't thrown herself behind him, especially this past year in his bid for governor. Ethel carries a lot of weight around here. Sorry," Doug paused, "I can't think of her in the past tense yet." He was silent for a while, and Dane did not interrupt his thoughts.

"At the sign, you're going to take a left," Doug instructed. "I'm probably out of line, but I just looked at Ronnie and Robin through your eyes a few minutes ago and saw problems that I've been ignoring. I just don't want you to have a bad impression of them. They're both good people struggling to handle what life throws at them. It isn't always easy, even if you do come from a family with money and privilege. That sometimes complicates things even more."

Changing the course of the conversation Dane said, "Before we get to Ms. Bowen's house, is there anything you can tell me that I should know before telling her about her mother?"

"Becky is very fragile," Doug replied. "She's had severe depression and other psychiatric problems since she was twenty-one. She has a live-in companion who takes basic care of her, ensuring she takes her medication, eats, and doesn't hurt herself. Becky tells me she hears voices that tell her, at times, that she must be punished. She's done some pretty horrible things to herself as a result."

Dane said, "As you can probably tell, I'm not good at delivering bad news. Any guidance would be much appreciated."

"I don't think many people are good at delivering bad news. You're direct, and that's good for most people. Turn right at the next light," Doug said, adding, "if you don't mind, though, let me gauge how we go with Becky. Sometimes it's better to give things to her in bits, letting her take each as she is able to. It might be that we start with something like, 'There has been an accident.'"

"I'm perfectly comfortable with your taking the lead," Dane told him as he noticed that they were on the road that he had driven to and from Myrtle Hill earlier. "Does Ms. Bowen live near her mother?"

"Actually within a mile," Doug answered. "She lives in a small farmhouse where the crop manager used to live before Ethel built the Chapman Farms complex on down the road. You just go to the driveway beyond the entrance to Myrtle Hill. The house is about a half mile down the next dirt road."

Following the directions, Dane turned, and as the house came into view he recognized it as one of the standard southern farmhouse layouts, two rooms wide separated by a central hallway, with a covered porch wrapped around three sides of the house. There was an addition on the back. While modest in size, the house was beautifully maintained, with a manicured lawn surrounding it. Flowerbeds blossomed everywhere, evidence that either Becky or her companion spent a lot of time gardening. As they pulled to a stop, they saw a woman Dane assumed was Becky in the porch swing, swinging back and forth at a steady pace. From a distance she appeared young, with long blonde hair parted in the middle.

They got out of the car, and before they reached the porch, Becky said, looking at Dane, "I wondered when you'd come. Didn't expect to see you, Doug. Come up and have a seat. You're the new police chief. I saw your wife while you were interviewing for the job. Your wife's people are from Camden Grove. You belong here, and your daughters will bloom here. You'll forget they ever had problems."

Dane knew his face had to show the surprise he felt. He didn't know that anyone was aware of his twin daughters' issues. He was also taken aback at how much older Becky looked up close. She looked leathery, with far more wrinkles in her face than someone under forty should have, even if she had been a sun bunny her whole life. The heavy eye make-up and foundation that stopped at her neckline rather than blending added a hard edge to her look. Despite this, she was attractive, dressed in a skirt, knit blouse, socks, and brown loafers.

"Doug, don't give me that look. You know I speak my mind and don't know sometimes that I shouldn't say what I know. I know Mamma is gone, too. Don't ask me how, but I know. She left us early this morning, and she's at peace."

Dane supposed the surprised look on Doug's face was a mirror of his own.

"Becky…"

"I'm okay, Doug. Mamma hasn't been herself lately, but she didn't want to talk about it. I was expecting something bad to happen. Now she won't hurt anymore. I hope I don't have to leave my house. I can't remember if Daddy gave it to me or if it's still part of Myrtle Hill. I'd hate for the Catholics to have my house. I don't care as much about the big house as Ronnie does, but I don't want anyone to have my house. I hope Daddy took care of that. Maybe I should ask Mr. Wenzel. I guess I should know if I have any money left from Daddy. If Mamma's not leaving us money, I may have to find a job. I don't know what I'll do, but I'm sure I can do something to take care of myself. Don't you think so, Doug?" she asked, continuing without waiting for an answer. "Where are my manners? Can I offer you gentlemen some lemonade?"

Becky called for her companion, Charlotte Kirk, and turned back to Dane and Doug. "How about some cake? We can set up a table in the garden and eat cake, drink lemonade, and visit before I take my nap."

A hundred questions were in Dane's head, but he held them all, taking his cue from Doug's response. A stocky woman, probably in her late fifties, early sixties came out the front door.

"Good afternoon, Charlotte. This is our new police chief, Dane Hunter," Doug said.

"Nice to meet you, Chief Hunter. Can I get you both some lemonade?"

"None for me, thanks," Dane said, noting that Charlotte appeared to be about the same age as Becky, a little heavier, and without any make-up whatsoever. Even her hair was cut short in a low-maintenance style, and she was dressed casually, as a friend, rather than as a nurse. "I can't stay long."

Doug added, "I came with Dane, but I'm sure he wouldn't mind if I stayed if you'd be able to get me back to the church when Becky takes her afternoon nap."

Charlotte responded, "Of course. We need a few things from the store anyway."

"That okay with you, Dane?" Doug asked.

"Absolutely. When you get home, though, how about giving me a call to schedule a time to finish our conversation?"

"You're not telling all our secrets, are you, Doug?" Becky asked, smiling sweetly. "Chief Hunter, don't believe everything you hear about me. I prefer to call myself eccentric rather than crazy. Ladies in the South are allowed to do that, you know. I'm just out of place and time and have my feet in too many worlds for my own good. It was so lovely to meet you. I hope your wife won't be afraid to pay me a call," she said in her young-woman, breathless, melodious speech. "I know we could be friends, and we both need a friend. Tell her I'll look forward to lunch real soon."

Not knowing exactly how to respond, Dane just said, "I'll tell Joan, and Ms. Bowen, I'm terribly sorry for your loss."

She held out her hand, briefly touching Dane's, and then turned all her attention to Doug. Dane could tell a dismissal when he saw one and knew that he was already forgotten as Becky and Doug became engrossed in conversation. Charlotte walked Dane to the car.

"Becky had a very bad night," she confided. "Storms make her edgy. I don't know what you believe, but people around here believe in all sorts of things. I know that Becky has some psychic abilities. I found her wandering outside in the rain. I'm not sure how she got out of the house without me hearing. I'm usually a light sleeper. I guess with the storms, I just slept through it. I also don't know how long she was out. She told me early this morning that her mother was dead. How did Mrs. Bowen die?" Charlotte asked.

"She was shot," Dane replied.

"Oh, my God!" she almost choked on her words. "Becky is deathly afraid of guns. I know there is no way she would have gone over to her mother's without telling me. There's no way she could've done anything. I would stake my life on it."

"We don't know what happened yet. The investigation is just beginning," Dane said, adding, "I'm sure we'll talk again. I have the number, and I'll call before coming out."

"I'd appreciate that. That way I can let you know what kind of day it is, and whether it would do you any good to drive out here. Some days she can't make any sense at all. On others, you'd never be able to tell she is a troubled soul, bless her heart."

Dane shook her offered hand, got into the car, started it, and backed to turn around. Before starting forward, he looked at the porch swing and both Becky and Doug waved. As he drove down the driveway and out of sight of the house, he called Forrest Sikes to check and see if he should stop back at Myrtle Hill.

"We've just about finished up here," he replied. "Let us put together a preliminary report this afternoon and plan to meet at your office early tomorrow morning when we have more organized information. We may be able to get them to do the autopsy this afternoon. On the surface, we didn't find many prints in the room or footprints outside the windows or doors to the room. If someone went into the bedroom, they did it from inside the house, unless it rained after Ethel was shot. Let's wait for a time of death and then decide where we are."

"I'll go ahead and write up my observations from talking with Ms. Ricks, the senator and his wife, and Ms. Bowen and her companion. I haven't talked with the senator's son, the son's friend, or Mr. Wenzel yet, but I think I'll wait until after tomorrow to do that. If you need me, you can reach me at the office or on my cell," Dane said before disconnecting the call.

Driving back to the office, he began organizing the day's revelations to ready himself to capture all the details and impressions of people, places, and events on his computer. He mentally ticked off his first list of the case, capturing everyone he'd need to talk to, based on what he learned since beginning that morning: Mary Johnston, Wayne Wenzel, Father Rhett Leverett, Doug, the senator and his wife, Ronnie Jr. and his friend, Becky, Charlotte, and Isabelle Ricks. He had no idea how many more would be added to the list as the investigation unfolded. For now, though, it was just reports from the day that loomed before him. He could only hope to get lucky and have all evidence point clearly to suicide. But for Isabelle Ricks' firm belief that it was murder, this might have been possible from the scene. With her allegation, though, he was afraid that a full investigation would be necessary.

Dane's mind was shifting into detective mode.

CHAPTER

FOUR

Before Dane realized it, it was seven-thirty, his reports were mostly done, at least in draft form, and he was already very late for dinner. He was surprised that Joan hadn't called, and realized that she, too, must have gotten lost in unpacking and setting up the house. He picked up the phone and called home.

Joan answered on the third ring. "Oh, Dane, I'm so glad you called. I have the most amazing news. I wanted to call you right away, but Mary told me you were investigating a death, so I knew not to bother you. But, oh, Dane, it's so amazing. I don't want to tell you over the phone, I want you here as quickly as you can. It's so amazing. Hurry home, love!"

He had to smile. Everything just felt better since their move to Camden Grove.

Dane reflected on the journey from their house on Highland Avenue in Arlington, Virginia, the day their lives took a turn toward South Carolina. At thirty-eight, after fourteen years as a detective in the nation's capital, he had lost faith in humankind. His work life was often filled with shifts of rapists, murderers, and thieves who would as soon shove a knife into your heart for the five dollars you had in your wallet as look at you.

It had been getting more difficult for him to remember that all most people really wanted out of life was to belong somewhere, do something meaningful, know somebody cared, and at the end of the day, know that they'd made a difference. It didn't seem to be a lot to ask.

He had reached the point that he was carrying his work home with him in the evening. He was a physical and mental wreck, and all the pressures, both at work and the self-made ones at home, were affecting his marriage.

Joan and he had wanted a large family, and unlike most of their friends, had never practiced birth control. But for more than eleven years, they had remained childless despite the doctors' assurances that they were healthy, fertile, and perfectly capable of producing a child the old-fashioned way. They had been ecstatic when they finally learned Joan was pregnant, and over the moon when the found they were having twins.

The births had been easy, even though Julia had entered the world head-first and Rose had presented her butt to the doctor before any other part of her anatomy. The nightmare hadn't started for a long time. The girls seldom cried, but that didn't concern Joan and Dane.

From the beginning, the girls couldn't stand to be apart. They crawled and walked at an early age, but never even attempted to talk. Many doctors and many bills later, they had two perfect specimens of health who were physically capable of speaking, but who rarely even uttered a sound in their parents' presence. Dane felt shut out every time he looked at them doing everything in unison without a word spoken. They just knew what the other would do. He fought to hide his frustration as their big blue eyes obviously took in everything he said, but never let a response pass their little lips. They were in their own world. At the recommendation of one child psychologist, they separated the two to see if it would cause them to communicate, but that only lasted three days during which neither of the girls ate anything. They decided not to take more drastic measures, but to wait and hope that the girls would naturally progress.

It had been a Friday morning when Dane looked at the mountain of paperwork stacked on the corner of his desk and felt the futility of his current job. It wasn't enough to get the criminals off the street, but each required reams of paperwork and months to get to trial, and the end result was usually that they went free to start the whole process again. In that stack of paper, a single, yellow sheet stuck out from the rest. Pulling it out, he was surprised to see it was a job announcement. They weren't normally sent around, just posted on a board by the personnel office. He crumpled it up, threw it in the trash and went for coffee.

After having the same conversation with his coworkers about the lack of impact they had because of the system, it hit him that he needed a change. Back at his desk, he pulled the announcement out and smoothed it flat. It was a police chief position in Camden Grove, South Carolina. For some reason, he folded it up and put it in his pocket. The phone rang, and his day was off and running.

He had since found that change had been brewing in Camden Grove. Police Chief Danny Bader had decided it was time to retire and move to Florida. Officer Glenn Yarborough, who had only been forty-three, had a heart attack and died while eating his meatloaf, parsley potatoes, and snap peas. And the third member of the three-man police department, Officer Turner, knew that he did not want to take on any additional responsibilities, even if the town would let him. The Town Council met and decided to reduce their department to a force of two, a chief of police and Officer Turner.

After sticking the job vacancy announcement in his pocket, his work day was crazy and he didn't walk through the door at home until after ten. He grunted something like "bitch of a day," and headed into the bathroom to take a shower. By the time he got out, Joan's bedside lamp was off, and she was facing the wall on the very edge of her side of the bed. He put his dirty clothes in the hamper, pulled the towel from around his waist and slid nude between the sheets. He scooted up to spoon her, putting his arm around her. Joan remained rigid, unresponsive, and he knew she was angry.

Joan was a striking woman. He knew from the first time he saw her with her auburn hair, big blue eyes, and wide smile when he was in tenth grade and she in ninth that she was the one for him. Quietly, almost in a whisper, she had said, "I've decided I'm leaving. I'm taking the girls and moving in with my parents until I can decide what I want to do next."

Dane had sat straight up in the bed. "What the hell are you talking about?"

"I don't know what's happened to us. What's happened to you? I don't know where the man I love has gone, but he's gone. I don't know if it's something I've done wrong or something that I should've done but didn't. All you had to do was tell me, and I could've changed it. Instead, you shut me out. You just checked out on me, turning your back on all we've shared and worked for. I don't know how to fight for what we had, and I am just not ready to focus on anything other than our daughters. As a mom, I don't have the option of disappearing into my work."

"Leaving certainly isn't going to solve anything. You want to talk? Let's talk," Dane said.

Talk they did.

Finally, Dane said, "I've been thinking for a long time that we need a change. We need to get out of here. It's almost ironic that we are having this talk tonight. Today, for the first time ... move?"

"Move where?"

"Well, this one is in a little town in the South. Camden Grove, South Carolina."

"You're kidding."

"No, seriously, Camden Grove."

"I didn't mean the name. My parents were talking about Camden Grove last week. I never knew, or didn't remember, that my maternal grandmother was from Camden Grove. She evidently left them a house there that's been rented to the same family for over twenty-five years. The family's moved, and my folks were talking about going down to see what kind of shape the house is in, what the market is like, and possibly getting rid of it."

"A coincidence? I don't know, but if I get an interview, we could do that for them."

"If you get the job, we could have the house."

"Don't jump too fast. The first hurdle is mine. I'll check out this vacancy. We don't even know anything about the town, the house, anything. Don't get too excited, but also, don't give up on us. I'm foolish and stubborn at times, but I love you as much as I ever have. Losing you is a frightening thought. I promise to talk more, to be home more, to be more accessible and in better moods."

"You know I don't want anything to happen to us. Just don't shut me out! For right now, hold me, you jolly giant. Just hold me," Joan said.

Dane mailed his resume the next day, and ten days later he received a call to set up an interview with the hiring committee.

They decided to drive down on a Saturday, spend the night, look at the town and the old house, and drive back on Tuesday. They also decided to leave the girls with Joan's parents. While they were doing better as a couple, they needed some time away, just the two of them.

All it took for the Town Council was his resume and one interview to know they were getting someone over-qualified for the job, but they weren't going to look a gift horse in the mouth. A fourteen-year veteran of the police force in Washington, D.C., and a detective to boot. They had checked him out and knew he was considered good, in fact, not just good, but one of the best. Nobody cared what his reasons were for leaving a job; they would sleep easier knowing that they had a really good police chief between them and any bad stuff that was happening elsewhere in the country.

For the Hunters, it was a chance for a new start in a quiet, charming town with apparently no crime or stress, and with what turned out to be an absolutely beautiful craftsman-style bungalow in mint condition that wouldn't cost them a penny.

The deal was cut, and not six weeks after Chief Bader announced his retirement, Camden Grove had a new chief of police who, with his wife and twin daughters, moved into their family home.

Daydreaming while he drove, Dane found himself already home from the office. As he got out of the car, the back door flew open and Joan raced out of the house, stopped in front of him, and wrapped him in her arms. "Rose and Julia spoke today," she said. "They spoke right there in the pickle aisle of the Piggly Wiggly. They spoke. They spoke in crystal-clear voices. They spoke, they spoke, they spoke," she yelled.

He didn't know what to say. He wanted to ask, "What did they say?" but felt the words wrong for such a momentous happening. He didn't need to say anything, though, because after catching her breath, Joan went on.

"They looked up at an older woman examining a jar of pickles, and Rose said, 'Are you an angel?' clear as a bell. Distinct. Enunciated like she has been talking for years. It turns out that the woman, Mary Johnston, knew my grandmother. Mary said, 'No child, just an old woman who loves children. Now why do you think I'm an angel?' Do you know what Julia said? She said, 'You have white light all around you. You're shiny.' Can you believe it? Can you just believe it? I swear it's true."

No amount of coaxing could make the girls utter a single word while Dane was home. He tried not to get depressed, and Joan admitted that they hadn't said anything else since. Something about what Joan had said in relaying the story nagged at Dane throughout dinner and into the evening as they unpacked boxes. It finally hit him when they were getting into bed.

"What did you say the lady's name was? The woman at Piggly Wiggly?"

"Mary Johnston. She invited me to tea tomorrow. She said that it would have to be around lunchtime, because you're going to talk with her tomorrow morning. She said for me to come at around twelve-thirty and bring the girls. She evidently has a regular group of friends come over and wants me to meet them all," Joan explained.

"Weird. Harvey told me this morning that I needed to talk to Mary Johnston. He said that she knew everything about everyone, but I haven't called her yet. I can't imagine Harvey taking the initiative to call her himself and set up an appointment for me." Another thought popped into his head, "That makes me remember that when I called you, you also said that you knew I was working on a case. Who did you hear that from?"

"Mary told me when she saw how excited I was, and I said I had to go call you right away."

"What time was that?"

"I think it must've been about ten or so. I'm not real sure. Everything's been such a blur today."

"Isabelle Ricks said she hadn't called anyone before she called me, and she didn't call me until ten-twelve this morning. Something just isn't right." Dane knew his mind was going into overdrive and if it wasn't after eleven, he would have called Mary Johnston right then and there. It would just have to wait until morning. He switched off the light, thinking he would be awake all night, but the next thing he knew the light was streaming in through the windows.

CHAPTER

FIVE

It was barely six o'clock when Dane walked into the office. Harvey was already there, and the aroma of brewing coffee filled the room. Harvey loved coffee. He proudly told Dane that he made the best in town and drank only "the best, Gevalia. It carries the seal stating that the coffee is provided by appointment to His Majesty the King of Sweden." Dane sipped the cup of Popayan Columbia coffee Harvey handed him, and had to admit that it was the smoothest coffee he'd ever tasted.

"Harvey, did you set up an appointment for me to meet with Mary Johnston this morning?" Dane quizzed.

"No, boss, you haven't told me yet who ya want to talk to."

"My wife ran into Ms. Johnston at the grocery store yesterday morning, and Ms. Johnston told her I was investigating a death and that she was meeting with me this morning. They had that conversation before Ms. Ricks called us."

"I told you she's a witch. You don't believe me, but I'm telling you she knows everything that goes on, usually 'fore it even happens. I try to never think about her at all, 'cause she knows exactly what you're thinking," Harvey moaned. "Chief Bader used to take her along whenever there was an accident or when someone was burned or such. Miss Mary can talk fire right out of a body so's they don't hurt much and they don't scar much. I watched her do it once up at Doc Martin's office. Scared the shit out of me. Bobby Sanders had burned hisself with a fireplace popcorn popper lid. His mother called the office because Pete, that's her husband, was away working, and she had no way to get Bobby to the doc's office. I took them over.

Why Bobby put that thing up to his lips is beyond my thinking, but he did, and he had a mean old burn on his lips that the doctor said was gonna leave a scar. While he was in with Doc screaming like no tomorrow, Miss Mary came in and sat down without saying a word. When Doc and Bobby came out of Doc's office, Doc looked at Miss Mary sitting there patiently like he just knew she would be there, and told her to do her magic; he couldn't help any. Well, Miss Mary took Bobby and stood him up against the wall and told him not to move," Harvey relayed getting caught up in the story. He began mirroring the motions he described as he continued, moving one of his long, skinny, big-knuckled fingers in front of his lips while saying, "She took her index finger and went back and forth over the area where his mouth was burnt, not actually touchin' him. It was all swollen and red. She was mumbling something the whole time she was moving her finger back and forth. After a little bit, couldn't have been more than a couple a minutes, she stopped and told Carrie Sanders to take him home. She said he'd be okay."

Harvey opened his eyes as wide as he could while saying, "Bobby's eyes were big as saucers, and he'd stopped crying altogether. No wailing, no moaning, just lookin' like a deer in the headlights. Miss Mary told Carrie that the burn would be pink and tender the next day, and all signs of the burn would be gone in three days, and there would be no scar. Doc Martin just said, 'Mary, don't know how you do what you do, but I always appreciate your showing up at just the right time,'" Harvey said, using a different voice to mimic the doctor.

"The Doc and Miss Mary smiled at each other, Doc went back into his office and Miss Mary told me to take them all home. I tell you what, I shore didn't want to be alone in the car with her after we dropped off Carrie and Bobby. I tell you she knows everything, and I sometimes have thoughts I just don't want anyone to know about. Ain't nothing bad, just private-like thoughts."

"Did Bobby have a scar?"

"Course not. Whatever Miss Mary says is true turns out to be just what she said."

Finishing his coffee, and again marveling at how Harvey could tell a story, Dane looked out the window and saw a man opening the lawyers' office across the street. "Harvey, is that Mr. Wenzel?"

"Yes, sir."

"Seems like Mr. Wenzel likes an early start, too. I'm going over to see if I can talk to him for a minute. If I'm not back by eight, how about you calling Mary Johnston and asking her what time she and I are going to meet. No matter what she says, tell her that ten is best for me this morning."

Dane walked across the street, opened the door to the lawyer's office, and found himself in a reception room. "Mr. Wenzel," Dane announced his arrival, followed almost immediately by the lawyer walking out of his office.

"You have to be the new police chief," Wayne said, sticking out his hand.

"What gave me away?" Dane replied with a smile. "I'm Dane."

"I'm Wayne," the five-foot ten, slight lawyer said, adjusting his blue-and silver-striped tie held in place by a gold collar bar. "I was expecting to talk to you today. Didn't expect you quite this early, but I'm glad to meet another early riser. Things always look better early in the morning before the day gets to you, don't they?"

Dane laughed, "How is it that everyone knows what I am going to do before I do?"

"It's really no mystery," Wayne replied with a knowing shake of his head, leading Dane into his office where they sat in leather winged-back chairs facing each other, a small table between them. "I heard about Ethel yesterday, saw today's headline in the newspaper. I knew that you would find your way to my door sometime. I planned to call you later this morning. Please tell me that Ethel wasn't murdered, as rumor has it, and that she didn't suffer. She was such a wonderful, giving woman. I'd hate to know her last minutes were difficult ones."

"Unfortunately, I can't tell you much. I haven't seen the newspaper coverage and didn't expect it," Dane said. "It appears she most likely died from a gunshot."

"Jesus," Wayne exclaimed, leaning to pick up the paper from his desk and handing it to Dane saying, "I had hoped that part wasn't true."

Looking down Dane saw the screaming headline in *The State*, the daily newspaper out of Columbia, South Carolina. The banner headline, big, bold, top story, read Senator's Mother Believed Murdered.

"I think I'll read this later," Dane said. "Right now, I'm really just trying to piece together what her general frame of mind and mood were, along with what went on day before yesterday. Just the typical things you try to come to grips with when something like this happens."

"How can I best help you?" Wayne asked.

"Tell me about what took you out to Myrtle Hill night before last."

"It was a dinner that had been planned for about two weeks. Ethel's been a bit worried about her will lately and had asked me to come out a few times to discuss things she was thinking about changing."

"I understand that the topic of her will brought an end to the dinner party."

"Hearing that your mother's thinking about turning over your childhood home to the church, along with a good chunk of her money, and a very lucrative business isn't exactly the kind of conversation that puts a family in a festive mood. I've seen more families come apart over inheritance than I care to remember, and that's usually when there isn't much to fight over," the blue-eyed lawyer said.

"How did the family react?"

"I'd say the responses were pretty predictable. I didn't handle her husband Harold's estate, but I'd guess that even after closing the mills, Ronnie isn't hurting for money with what his father left him, so it wasn't about that. I do know that Ronnie's always had a passion for the family home. Not so much the Chapman Farms operation Ethel had built over the last forty years. Hearing that Ethel was proposing to turn it into a Catholic retreat didn't make him happy. Nothing much bothers Becky. They're really the only two that count. As the only children, they'd be the ones most affected if Ethel were to change her will."

"So you're telling me that she hadn't changed the will yet?"

"No, she'd just been thinking and talking about it."

"Did everyone know that it hadn't been changed?" Dane asked.

"Yes," Wayne replied thoughtfully, "I think that was pretty clear. While we've had a few discussions, she hadn't yet asked me to make any changes."

"Were family members pretty sure of what the distribution of the estate was to be before any change?"

"Oh, yes. Harold and Ethel kept their finances fairly separate. Both came from old money, but they never combined their family fortunes. Because of the money, they each had wills that left most of their fortunes to the two kids. There were many others named in one or both of the wills, and they left certain items of importance to each other, but the bulk of Harold's estate went to Ronnie and Becky, and Ethel's will was set up along the same lines."

"Who else was to receive anything major from Mrs. Bowen's estate?" Dane asked.

"Ethel believed in independence, especially for women, and wanted to make sure that a few others were taken care of. She wanted Robin— that's Ronnie's wife—to have money of her own. She never had any, has never really worked, and Ethel thought part of her problem is that she has to depend on others for everything. She was leaving a healthy amount to Robin."

"Mrs. Bowen knew this?"

"Sure, Robin knew. Ethel thought it was important to be clear about it so that there were no arguments later."

"Who else is named in the will?"

"Charlotte Kirk, who takes care of Becky, was to get a little money, and Isabelle Ricks would become what Ethel always said was a 'woman of independent means.' Ronnie Junior, as the only grandchild, was also left money in a trust fund that would be managed for him until he was thirty. Those are the main ones. There are others who get small bequests, things or money, and a number of charities that'll receive money."

"As far as you know, would everyone named in the will know what they were to get?"

"Absolutely, for those who would be major inheritors. Probably not for many who may receive personal items."

"But only those at the dinner knew she was planning to change it?"

"Unless she wanted someone else to know. But I'd say that she probably hadn't told anyone. Ethel wouldn't have wanted anyone to try to pressure her or dissuade her from taking an action before she made up her mind."

"Can you give me a list of everyone who'll inherit from the Bowen estate?" Dane asked.

"Sure, but it's now, as always, the Chapman estate. The Bowen estate was Harold's."

"Just out of curiosity, does the lawyer stand to inherit anything?"

Laughing, Wayne said, "Haven't found a client yet who wanted to leave me anything worthwhile. No, I'm strictly a friend and hired help. Ethel's already given me more than anyone deserves to get, so there's nothing more coming my way but a lot of wonderful memories. Most of my life has been lived right here in Camden Grove. My family didn't have a lot of money. I won the South Carolina spelling bee as a kid, and as a reward, Ethel summoned my mother and me to Myrtle Hill for tea. I can still picture how afraid Mom and I were as we sat in the parlor with the lady of the house. No matter what she tried, Ethel couldn't put either of us at ease that day. Just near the end, she asked me what I wanted to be when I grew up. I told her a lawyer, if we could afford school. She told me if I wanted to be a lawyer, then that was exactly what I should be. She said if money was a problem, come back and see her," Wayne said.

"I didn't have to go back. She kept tabs on me all through junior high and high school, and when it came time to go to college, Ethel arranged for a scholarship to the University of South Carolina in Columbia. Just before my senior year at Carolina she again summoned me to Myrtle Hill. She told me she'd followed my progress and felt that I shouldn't go to the USC law school, saying Georgetown was a better place for me. My part was to keep my grades up, do well on the LSAT, and if I didn't get scholarships to cover tuition, she'd take care of it. She was a woman of her word.

I graduated top of my class from Georgetown and didn't have any debt to work off like so many of my classmates, so I could come back home instead of looking for some high-paying job I'd hate. Ethel became my first client putting me on retainer for all the legal requirements of Chapman Farms."

"Was that major?" Dane asked.

"Oh, yes," Wayne replied. "We're talking an annual income in the millions for the farm. Ethel was a phenomenal businesswoman and hugely respected in the agriculture community. She designed the farm to produce year-round income and had the land to make her operation one of the largest in the state. Eighteen wheelers regularly leave the farm loaded with produce going up and down the east coast. Strawberries from March to June; peaches May through August; blueberries, June to August; watermelons June through September; nectarines, June to August; apples, July through November; Christmas trees in November and December; vegetables year round; and honey. In her store she had a place for local ladies to sell everything from canned goods, jellies and jams, to quilts.

"How do you know all this?"

"I review all the contracts for the business. She remains my largest client.

"Is that why you came back to Camden Grove?"

"As strange as it sounds, everything I love is right here. I wanted to be a lawyer, but not anywhere but Camden Grove. I always knew this is where I would live."

"Do you think Mrs. Bowen could've shot herself?"

"Absolutely not. She loved life. She was a wuss about hurting anything living; she respected guns, and I know she knew how to use them, but she was very much against hunting. She was also very strong in her religious beliefs and it would go against her very nature to take her own life. She wouldn't chance missing out on getting into the heaven she believed in. No, I don't believe for a minute that she'd take her own life."

"Why would she have a gun in the house?"

"I'm sure there are probably many guns around that house from generations of people who hunted. It could have been one that Harold or even Ethel's father or someone gave to her because she was living out on her own away from people."

"Do you know if there were any professional jealousies that could have resulted in her death?"

Without hesitating, Wayne answered, "No, I can't think of any. If Ethel was murdered, I only pray that it happened so fast that Ethel didn't know a moment of fear or pain. She was a wonderful woman. I wouldn't want to know she suffered."

"Wayne, I appreciate talking with you this morning. Do you mind if I call or drop in if I have other questions? It seems to me that your view of things might be useful as I try to sort everything out."

"You're welcome any time."

"Thanks. I'm sure we'll be talking again. Can I send Harvey over later for a list of those in the will?"

"Of course. I look forward to working with you. My door's always open."

Dane knew he liked the lawyer from the moment they started talking. There was just something about his intensity and how comfortable he seemed to be with himself. As Dane walked back to his office, he also thought how interesting it was that there wasn't a division among those to whom he'd already talked about whether murder or suicide had taken place at Myrtle Hill, except for the senator's comment.

When Dane walked into the office, Harvey immediately reported that, "Miss Mary said she thought that a ten a.m. meeting would be best for you, and she would have coffee and cake waiting."

Dane smiled to himself, thinking how interesting that meeting would be, and asked, "Where does Mary live?"

"She's your neighbor, although on the opposite end of your street. Hers is the stone house. She also owns the big house, ya know. She was married to Miss Ethel's husband's uncle. He was a mess. When he died after being drunk for years, he left the house to Miss Mary. When her parents died, she moved back into the stone house instead of staying in the big house."

Dane didn't have a response, so he said nothing for a while. He broke the silence by telling Harvey he wanted to see the newspaper before talking with Major Sikes.

"I was afraid you'd ask for it," Harvey said, shaking his head miserably. "I promise I didn't say all the things the newspaper says I said. The reporter called last night, and I didn't want to disturb you, so I talked to her. She was sneaky in the way she asked questions, but I really, really didn't say all she says I did."

"Let me read it, and we'll talk afterward," Dane said.

Taking the paper out of Harvey's clutching hands, Dane walked into his office and closed the door. Laying it flat on the desk, he began reading.

Senator's Mother Believed Murdered

CAMDEN GROVE, S.C.—Ethel Chapman Bowen, businesswoman, philanthropist, and mother of Senator Ronald D.

Bowen (D), was found dead in her Camden Grove plantation yesterday morning. A police spokesman said she was shot in the head while in her bed.

"It was just awful," Harvey Turner of the Camden Grove Police Department stated. "Don't know who did it, but some maniac murderer is on the loose out there. None of Ms. Ethel's doors or windows were locked, but then I guess nobody around here locks their doors. We'll catch the crazy man who did this, but until we do, it looks like people in Camden Grove need to be locking their doors and protecting themselves," Officer Turner said.

An investigation is underway.

Senator Bowen, a candidate in the hotly contested race for the South Carolina governorship, was not available for comment.

Ethel Bowen was the owner of Myrtle Hill Plantation and Chapman Farms, and a well-known philanthropist and supporter of education throughout South Carolina and the nation. A widow of six years, she was married for 43 years to Harold D. Bowen, owner of the Bowen Textile Corporation based in Boston. In addition to her son, she is survived by a daughter Rebecca Bowen of Camden Grove; a daughter-in-law, Robin Bowen; and a grandson, Ronald D. Bowen, Jr.

Funeral arrangements have not yet been announced.

Dane called Forrest Sikes, who answered his phone on the third ring.

"Forrest, Dane Hunter here. Thought I'd touch base before all hell breaks loose."

"I saw the article. What was Harvey thinking?"

"I don't think he was. He's too trusting. He can't be blamed; I should've thought about it and been prepared. Too late to worry now; we are where we are. If my experience is any good, *The State* broke the story, and it will be on every wire. I'd bet that Camden Grove is about to be invaded by every form of media."

"You'll have even bigger problems with the local people. Hell, Harvey told the world that there's a murderer on the loose and that no one locks his or her doors. You won't have time to do any interviews, because you'll be dealing with worried residents and media."

"I've already thought of that. Do you have a good PR person?"

"No. We've one who is good enough for what we usually deal with, but not this. I'm sure that we're going to have our share of inquiries, too, thanks to your officer," Forrest said.

"I can't afford to be mired down in PR. We used a consultant in Washington occasionally. I first met her when she was working for the Washington Metro Authority. Pat Lambe is a real pro. She has since gone out on her own and authored a couple of books. The one I need to get to Harvey is *I Didn't Say That*. I'll figure out a way to bring her in as a consultant, if she's available. I trust her with any public relations nightmare."

"I'd make that call fast if I were you," Forrest counseled.

"Before we go, last night I transcribed my observations from Myrtle Hill, along with summarizing my visits with Senator and Mrs. Bowen, and Miss Bowen. I'll e-mail them to you. This morning I talked with Wayne Wenzel, and I have an appointment to talk with Mary Johnston at ten for background information and to figure out how she knew what I'd be doing yesterday before I even received the call."

"Don't spend too much time worrying about it. I know Mary. We've even used her on some tough cases. She can't always explain what she knows or how she knows it, but you can usually trust her to be pretty much on target. Never used to believe in psychics and such, but, well, she and her friends have made a believer out of me."

"None of my cases to date have brought me into contact with a psychic that was believable, so I'm not sure how to react to one that isn't a whack job. Guess we'll see. I'm probably more comfortable with the facts I can track down. I know, though, that there are times when I go on hunches and feelings that help me make a breakthrough, so I kinda understand. Anyway, I'll let you know if I find anything important. How is it going on your end?"

"There are a few interesting things. First, there was gun powder residue on Ethel's hand that would support the suicide theory, but there was also a spot without any like someone's finger was on top of her finger. I told you yesterday that there weren't many prints. Most prevalent were those of Ethel and Isabelle Ricks, which is pretty much what you would expect. There were prints left by three others that have not yet been identified. Two of the different prints were on the jewelry box, the other in the bathroom. We're running the prints through the FBI. I have an explanation for the wigs, too," Forrest said. "Looks like Ethel's had some kind of chemo recently," Forrest said. "Most of her hair's gone. I thought that was very odd when I first saw all the wigs on the bed, but it makes sense now. Hadn't heard that she was sick."

"Did you ask Ms. Ricks about it?" Dane asked.

"No, thought I'd leave that up to you, since you've already started talking with her. I'm sure you'll track it down and see how it affects this case. Haven't gotten most of the lab work results yet, and I don't believe the autopsy is scheduled until later today. I'll get back with you if I get anything of importance. If not, let's talk again tomorrow, just to see where we are."

"Sounds good to me. I'll let you know if I come up with anything, too. The senator seems to think his mother's been depressed. He intimated, though he didn't actually say, that she might've done it herself. Everyone else I have talked with is positive that she couldn't have committed suicide. I'll get more information on the beneficiaries from her will this afternoon and will continue my interviews. Are you interested in seeing them all or just the ones I think might be important?"

"I'd like to tell you I'll look at them all, but I stay buried in paperwork. How about you just keep the whole file there and let me know what I need to know."

"Can do. How well do you know Senator Bowen?"

"Wouldn't say we're friends, but this area is like one big little town, and Ronnie is a public figure. I'd say I know him casually well. Why?"

"Just one of my gut feelings. When I talked with him and his wife yesterday, he told me they'd gone home and had a quiet evening together after they left his mother's. I have a hunch he didn't stay home, from the look his wife gave him."

"Can't say that I've heard much dirt, but Ronnie's a good-looking, powerful, and rich guy. I wouldn't be surprised if he had a little something on the side. I'd be very careful in finding out, though. He's running for governor, and you wouldn't want to get caught up in the politics," Forrest cautioned.

"Oh, I'll be careful. If it isn't related to the case, I know enough from my Washington work not to bring it up. Anyway, how about I send you just a brief summary of the conversations I've had so far? You seem to know the characters here in Camden Grove, so you can tell me if there's anything I'm missing. That reminds me, I thought I'd have heard back from Doug Reed last night. He went with me to talk to the senator and his sister. I left him out at the sister's house. I'll have to call him later to see how she's handling things."

"Reed's a good guy," Forrest said. "You know how to get me if you need me. If I don't talk to you again today, I'll look forward to talking tomorrow."

"Me, too. See you later."

After hanging up the phone, Dane first called Pat Lambe and got her answering machine. He knew she hated answering the phone, so he left the most urgent message he could and spent the next hour editing his work from the previous day and drafting his thoughts from his morning meeting with Wayne Wenzel. He was reading it one last time when his cell phone rang. "Hunter."

"Hunted. I win, big boy," Pat said with a laugh. "I called as soon as I heard the pitiful sound of your voice. I thought you were getting away from all this stuff."

"Don't get me started! Thanks so much for calling back. Looks like I'm in a bit of a jam down here."

"Darling, you aren't in a jam, you have the whole world about to crash in on you. What was your man thinking when he gave that interview? Let me rephrase that. How could someone bungle a first report like that? I did some quick homework before calling, and your story's already on the AP wire. I can guarantee that you'll have all the major networks picking it up. You have all the ingredients for a national story–wealthy family, political race, small-town America where people never lock their doors. I shiver to think about it."

"I need some high-priced Washington consultant to bail me out and teach us country boys how to work the media."

"First, Dane Hunter, you don't fit the country boy role, and second, I've never seen a member of the media you couldn't schmooze into saying exactly what you wanted him or her to say, and believe that it was all his or her idea. You're a piece of work."

"Truth be told, I need you, but I don't have the budget I had up there to pull you in. How cheap can you be? This is real high profile, and no one can handle it like Pat Lambe can handle it."

"Don't play me, Hunter. I already have my ticket and plan to orchestrate this debacle whether you want me to or not. You're going to reimburse me for my ticket, take care of a place to stay, make sure no one's going to nag me about my smoking while I'm there, and do exactly what I tell you to do, when I tell you to do it. Are those terms acceptable to you?"

"You're going to save my life. Give me orders, oh strong woman."

"I don't know how Joan puts up with you. Tell her I'm coming to bail your ass out. Give me your fax. I have a brief statement I drafted for you to give to the press. Neither you nor your sidekick is to make any statements I don't approve first. Got it?"

"Got it."

"Arrange for a place for the media to set up and call home for the next few days. It needs to have a meeting room so you can hold regular updates.

Make it look professional, not some country café with big-haired southern girls in their country outfits. Got it?"

"Got it."

"I'm flying into Greenville. I have to take one of those shitty little planes, so I've already reserved a limo to get me to Camden Grove, and yes, I know where it is, but God, I never thought I'd be traveling there. Oh, you're going to pick up the tab for the limo, too," Pat said with mock gruffness.

"I'll take care of it all before I go to my next interview. Can't wait to see you. You have my cell, and please don't call Officer Harvey Turner any names when you get here. He means well, he just hasn't been to the Pat Lambe finishing school yet. We'll take care of that while you're here."

"Don't think you're getting in the last word here."

"Think I will. Bye," Dane said with a smile as he pressed the End button on his phone.

He finished proofing his summary, attached it to an e-mail to Forrest, hit Send, and yelled for Harvey to come in. Harvey tentatively poked his head in the door.

"Harvey, you're going to thank me for this later–probably much later. Your every move, every word that comes out of your mouth is about to be organized by a five-foot-two, high-heeled, totally accessorized, bigger-than-life, chain-smoking woman who's the best in her field. Before I leave, let me go over what you need to do."

Dane went over the requirements with Harvey, got a copy of the fax, and called both Mayor Gordie Buckley and Judge Ladner and filled them in.

At about a quarter to ten, he left the office for the five-minute drive to Mary Johnston's house. As he passed his own, he realized he lived in one of the larger ones, though small in comparison to the empty big house across the street that he now knew Mary owned. The house he and Joan moved into had been built by Joan's great-grandfather who had been the town doctor from 1905 until his retirement in 1940. During that time, his office and exam room had been on one side of the first floor of the house, now a family room, with an outside entrance from the wrap-around porch.

He looked at Mary's mansion across the street with new interest, checking to see if disrepair was a reason it stood empty. The house, sitting on probably ten acres of lawns, was a beautiful reproduction of a French chateau. It seemed a bit out of place in this southern town. The chateau had salmon-colored stone walls, a slate roof, slender chimneys, and dormer windows. The tall French windows on the first two floors had gray shutters. It looked perfectly maintained. Joan and he had commented more than once since arriving in Camden Grove that they would love to get a look inside.

He pulled up the driveway of Mary's stone house. It was English cottage style, and while interesting and cozy looking, it, too, appeared a little out of place in the South. He could see how it would be much easier to maintain, and probably a lot more comfortable to live in than the big house across the street.

He didn't even have time to push the doorbell before it was opened. "Chief Hunter," Mary said, sticking out her hand to shake his. "Please tell me you don't want me to call you that. It seems so formal. I know that in time we're going to be great friends, so how about we just move right beyond all the terribly uncomfortable portions and go right to Mary and Dane," she said with a very distinct southern drawl and an open, friendly smile.

"I'd like that. I've already been told that if you say it's true, it has to be so. I'm happy to know that we're going to be great friends. I've never known a witch before," Dane said, smiling at her. He was pleased that she laughed at his attempt at humor.

"I see you've been listening to Harvey Turner. Believe half of what he says, and you'll be closer to the truth. Let's not just stand in the doorway. Would you like to talk out here on the porch, in the house, or in my back garden?" Mary asked.

"Where'd you see us talking when you predicted the meeting?"

"I can see that you've a mischievous streak in you, Dane. I'm going to have to watch you closely. Actually, I keep my crystal ball in the back garden, and it's closer to the kitchen with the coffee and red velvet cake with cream cheese icing I made for you. Why don't we go there? And yes, I know that you've never had a red velvet cake and that your favorite is pineapple upside-down cake."

Dane was sure shock registered on his face.

Mary led him through the house as she explained, "I'm just guessing about the red velvet cake, and your wife told me she was buying ingredients for your favorite cake yesterday." She chuckled at his obvious relief. "Guess you believed a little of what Harvey told you about reading minds after all. He tells everyone the same thing. Some believe him," she said, raising a penciled eyebrow.

Seated on white wrought iron chairs on the patio, a cup of coffee and a piece of cake on the table in front of each of them, Mary became all business. "What can I tell you?"

"Actually, I was a bit worried when I heard you had told my wife I was investigating a death and would be visiting you today, before I'd even been contacted about the case. Made me wonder how you'd have the information before anyone else. Forrest Sikes advised me that you help him with some cases and recommended that I not dwell on how you know what you know."

"Oh, I don't mind your asking; I just don't have all the answers to make you understand.

"For starters, how did you know?"

"Beginning with the hard question first. Let me give you the abridged version, for now, with a promise that sometime we'll have a real deep philosophical conversation. As long as I can remember, I've known things and could do certain things that others couldn't. My mother explained to me that God gave many people gifts and we should embrace these gifts, not be embarrassed by them. She believed, and many people in the South did and do, in healers, fire talkers, people who have visions, people who can transmit or receive thoughts from and to others, and people who can see auras and know when someone is sick or is going to die.

"She also believed that there is a thin veil between here and now and heaven, where our loved ones have already gone. She didn't see any of this as supernatural or something a good Christian should avoid. Instead, she called them forgotten gifts from God."

Seeing Dane leaning into the conversation, seemingly fully engaged, she continued, "Mother explained that over the years, man had decided that some of the gifts shouldn't be used, so they began to disappear. She talked about my Aunt Sarah, who could tell you amazing things about people by touching something that belonged to them. She also talked about her friend, James, who, contrary to the pattern, was a fire talker because his grandmother didn't think any of her daughters or granddaughters were fit to take, use, and pass on her gift."

Taking a sip of his coffee, Dane put both elbows on the table, cup in both hands, engrossed in Mary's story.

"She told me all that to explain things that frightened me. My grandmother had many types of gifts, and Mother had always experienced them through my grandmother, but didn't have any of her own. Skipped her totally, but I was real receptive.

"I believe that there are special energies here around Camden Grove because there are many people like me, and have been for as long as people can remember. Your wife's grandmother was my best friend when we were children, and she and I never had to talk. We just knew what the other was thinking and could carry on whole conversations in our heads.

"The energies often tell me things. I don't always know exactly what's going to happen, or to whom it will happen, but night before last I felt a change in the energy and knew someone had died. That made me know that you'd get a call, thus I could honestly say to your wife that you'd be investigating a death," Mary explained.

"What can you tell me about the actual death?" Dane asked her.

"Very little. And that in itself is surprising. It was as if I could only sense things through a thick fog. I normally know things right away, and a lot more clearly. I'll have a strange feeling hours, sometimes days before something bad happens. But this time, it was after the fact and murky."

"What can you tell me about Mrs. Bowen?"

"I have known her all her life. She married my husband's nephew, Harold, but I assume Harvey already told you that."

Dane again had the feeling that she knew exactly what he was thinking. He really had let Harvey get into his head.

"Ethel and Harold were well matched. Both were headstrong, spoiled, and rich, but deep down good people. When they loved, they loved with a passion. When they fought, it was like two wildcats. They both embraced life and lived it fast and fully. Harold died about six years ago, and Ethel had a difficult adjustment to being alone. It's only been for the past year, however, that I've really lost touch with her. Somehow, our lives have both just been so busy that we've barely had a conversation. You don't really think about it until it's too late," she said sadly.

Changing the subject, Dane said, "In her bedroom, there was only costume jewelry like button pins. Is there a story behind that?"

Mary laughed. "That's been a joke with a lot of us over the years. We told Ethel she collected people."

Dane was sure his face showed his confusion.

Mary continued. "Ethel was famous for doing nice things for people. If people didn't have money for food and Ethel found out, she appeared at their house with a basket of food and charmed them with a steady stream of chatter so that they weren't uncomfortable with the gift. Years ago, one of the women made her a button Christmas tree pin after she had surprised her family with a Thanksgiving dinner. Ethel was seen wearing that pin at church and around town. It became kind of a badge of honor for any of the women she helped to have Ethel wear a pin she had made. Ethel could tell you the name of every lady who had made one of the button pins for her, and she could remember the deed that had earned the pin."

"So they were something she treasured?"

"Oh my, yes," Mary said. "Ethel had jewels that came down from both the Chapman and the Bowen families. When Ethel wanted to be decked out, she had infinite choices. But Ethel often said the handmade jewelry gifts were her most valuable possessions, because they were given to her from people's hearts, and each person she helped here on earth helped ease her way into heaven. She said to me once, 'Just think that if every person you touched in this life said just one little prayer for you when you die, how short your time in purgatory would be.'"

"I don't understand the logic," Dane said.

"You, good man, weren't raised Catholic. Ask Father Leverette when you see him."

Dane took a moment to decide his next question. "Do you think she could've committed suicide?"

"Not Ethel. I don't care how low she would get, she'd always be ready for the next day."

"Do you know if she was sick?"

"Not that I know of. It's been ages since I saw her." Looking him in the eyes, she asked, "What do you know?"

"Nothing for sure, yet."

"You're holding back on me, but I guess you have to."

"What can you tell me about Isabelle Ricks?" Dane asked, not addressing her question.

"You mean besides Harvey's story that her family was so poor that they gave her to Colonel Chapman?"

"How do you do it?"

"That one's easy. Harvey tells everyone the same stories about people, so I know what to expect. Actually, his story is founded in fact. Isabelle's family was dirt poor. Colonel Chapman and Francis were my parents' ages, but childless when at age thirty-eight, Francis discovered herself pregnant. Of course the colonel was beside himself. He wanted everything to be perfect and knew that Francis would probably not be a great mother, since she was often sickly herself. He looked for someone who would be available for the child all the time.

"Isabelle was just the right age. The colonel paid the family to allow him to move Isabelle to Myrtle Hill, and it was the best thing that could've happened to her. I don't believe she ever looked back once she made the move. She was there when Ethel was born and has been more of a mother than Francis could have been. She's been a true and devoted friend. Ethel could never stand to be away from Isabelle for long.

"I know you've already met Isabelle and recognize that she is smart as a whip and always soaked up every bit of knowledge she could. She went away to school with Ethel, and while she couldn't attend classes, she and Ethel worked hard on lessons at night. Learning did not come easy for Ethel, and I'm sure that Isabelle completed much of her degree for her. Ethel's passion was anything to do with the land. Isabelle actually has her CPA license and manages the farm's financials. She has always been protective of Ethel."

To ease the intensity of the conversation, Dane said with a grin, "Harvey tells me she's a witch, too, and can read his mind."

"Harvey sometimes runs his mouth just a little too much," she laughed, then looked reflected and added, "I sense something in Isabelle, but I'm not sure what it is. If I had to guess, I would say that she, too, has special gifts, but I don't know what they are or how strong they may be."

"Tell me about Mrs. Bowen's children," Dane guided the conversation.

"What a pair! Different as night and day. Ronnie was always a hellion and loved attention, any kind of attention. He's too good looking for his own good, and knows it. I'm sure he gave Harold and Ethel many sleepless nights. He turned out real well, though, and that wasn't easy. Harold and Ethel threw hard shadows to live in. Sometimes that drives you too hard. I would say Ronnie is driven, and Ethel used to tell me that he never thought his father was proud of him, or that she was, either. Children just don't understand that parents can't always show or tell them just how proud they are. I think Harold wanted to make sure Ronnie worked for everything instead of having it handed to him. I know Ethel felt the same way.

"Becky was as timid as Ronnie was a daredevil. She, too, was very pretty, very popular, but if given her choice, would have never left Myrtle Hill or Camden Grove for even a day. She went away to Columbia College for Women while she was dating Doug Reed. The two of them ended up in the wrong place at the wrong time, and something pretty horrible happened to them. Becky has never been the same. Her spirit was broken."

"Do you mind my asking what happened?"

"It isn't my story to tell. Only Becky or Doug Reed can tell the story."

"Ms. Bowen knew her mother was dead before I told her," Dane said. "Should I be worried that she may have been involved in the death?"

"No. Becky knows a lot of things, too. She's gifted and doesn't always know how to handle the gifts. She struggles with life and would really be happiest left alone in her little house, tending her gardens."

"Do you think money would be an issue for either the senator or Miss Bowen?" Dane asked.

"Absolutely not. I am sure they each received enough from Harold's estate to ensure they won't ever have to worry about money."

"Would losing Myrtle Hill make a difference?"

"Interesting question. To Becky, no. She'd be happy with her little house and plot of land. Ronnie, on the other hand, has a passion for Myrtle Hill that rivals his mother's. Harold never cared for the place and would've been much happier if I'd just given him the house across the street. Ethel would've never lived in it, and for some strange reason, I couldn't let Harold have it. With all that said, if you are asking if Ronnie would kill his mother for Myrtle Hill, such a thing is impossible."

"How about the farming business?" Dane asked.

"He's never been interested in the farm. I remember Ethel trying to make him learn the business from the ground up. One summer she assigned him to peach picking. Up the first tree, an overripe peach fell on his head and he was done. Nothing could mess with his hair in those days," Mary laughed.

"Can you think of anyone who might want to kill Mrs. Bowen for any reason?"

"No, I really can't. Ethel wasn't the kind of woman you could dislike. She did so much good for people, not just here in Camden Grove, but also in the larger fabric of life. I can't imagine anyone being able to murder her."

"Thus my quandary, Mary," Dane said. "So far everyone but the senator has said that Mrs. Bowen couldn't have committed suicide, and not a single person I've talked with can think of anyone who'd want to hurt her."

They both realized that Dane's cake was eaten and his cup empty while Mary's remained untouched. "I've taken up enough of your time this morning," Dane said. "The cake was delicious. It tastes chocolate, but it's red."

"The red is, of course, dye, but the chocolate is because I put in three instead of two tablespoons of cocoa. The other secret of the moistness and flavor is buttermilk. The cream cheese icing complements the strong flavors."

"I love it," Dane said appreciatively. "You've given me a lot of background to think about. May I come back and discuss things with you when I run up on something I don't understand? Seems like there are many things here in Camden Grove that may challenge me. I might need your insight, and every time I ask a question, the suggestion for background or answer seems to lead to your door."

"I'd like that. I told you, we're going to be great friends for a long, long time."

As Mary showed Dane out the back gate to the driveway, she said, "If I might offer a little advice about Harvey. There is a lot more to him than he shows. Harvey's demeanor is the result of the small town and how they treat scandal. Harvey's mother left Camden Grove with a trumpet player when Harvey was nine. He got cards from her over the years, but never saw her again until his father died five years ago. Small town minds and mean-spirited kids made Harvey pay for his mother's sins. Called him Trumpet Whore Sarah's boy from middle into high school. He doesn't have good social skills and developed a persona to protect himself. A little kindness and mentoring will get you a loyal friend and a competent employee.

"He isn't stupid or weak. His mother, Sarah, showed up at his father's funeral. His father had never divorced her, and at the funeral home when she came in she said, 'Harvey, you look a mess. I'll be moving back in the house and will set things right.' Harvey just looked at her and said, 'No, Momma, that house belongs to me and Daddy. You won't be welcome there.'

"Harvey rented her a nice little house and takes her shopping and to dinner at least once a week. He treats her well, but no matter how much she whines, that is all he is willing to do for her."

"Mary, I promise you I will treat Harvey well," Dane said.

Leaving, he decided to stop at home on his way back to the office. It was wonderful to live five minutes from work. He needed to take advantage of it. As soon as he walked in the door, Joan told him Harvey had called and said it was an emergency. Dane called the office.

"Boss, glad you called. Major Sikes said they've identified the prints from the bedroom. He wants to talk to you right away."

"Thanks, Harvey. I'll call him. Any other calls I need to know about?"

"Pastor Reed called. Said when you're free, give him a holler. Said to tell you he's sorry he didn't get back to you last night, but he didn't get home until late and didn't want to call you at home. Other than that, there are TV trucks arriving, and I've been giving them the directions just like you told me to, and not saying a word except, 'Your questions will be answered at the evening meeting. Sorry it can't be sooner, but we have an investigation to conduct.'"

"In between media visits, what have you been doing to keep busy?"

"Nothing much. Pulled out a couple of detective magazines. Figured I need to learn some of the stuff you know so I can be more help to you."

"That's good, Harvey. Let's free up some time today or tomorrow to look at the kinds of training you've had and what we can do with reading, on-the-job experience, and formal training to expand your knowledge."

"Really? Geez, no one's ever talked to me about stuff like that since after Police Academy. That'd be great. I can learn to do most anything."

"I know you can, Harvey. In fact, have you ever put together a case or crime board?"

"No, Boss. Ain't never made one, but I've seen them on TV shows."

"Why don't you do some research, and it can be your responsibility to create a crime board for this case. We can review it at the end of each day and see what we need to add, based on the day's information gathered. Any questions you have, ask me."

Harvey said, "I'll get right on it. You won't be sorry you gave it to me."

Ending the call, Dane pulled Forrest's personal number from his wallet, added it to his contacts list, and hit call while Joan made him a fried chicken finger sandwich with mayo, chips, and a large glass of sweet iced tea.

"Forrest, Dane here. Harvey said you needed to talk."

"Yeah. We have an ID on those prints in the bedroom. Seems like young Ronnie Jr. and his friend Steve Adams were in the bedroom and left their prints opening drawers and going through the jewelry box. We'll have to see if Isabelle Ricks can tell us if anything's missing. The third set of prints belong to Nathan Webb. His were found on a doorknob and in the bathroom. That makes sense, as he's the local plumber by day. He drives an ambulance in Greenwood four nights a week. I bet we'll find he made a house call in the last few days. I think we need to focus on Junior and Steve Adams. What I'd suggest we do is interview the two separately. I'd like to bring Mr. Adams in here. He has a record. Petty stuff, nothing violent. Couple of minor drug possessions and one car theft from taking a joy ride in his girlfriend's car without permission. How about I have a team pick Steve Adams up and bring him in, and you talk with Junior? I think the senator will be more comfortable with your talking to his son than us formally bringing him in."

"I'd really like to observe Adams's interview and then talk with the senator's son," Dane said. "We don't want them to have a chance to discuss stories, if they haven't already done so, but I'd really like to see how they both react."

"Good. Come here at two. I've sent a car to pick up Adams."

"Okay. I'll see you shortly."

Calls finished, Dane asked Joan where the twins were.

"They're upstairs playing," she said as he sat at the kitchen table eating his sandwich, "Last night I never asked about the case you're working on. I guess I was so caught up in my news that I didn't ask about yours."

"Not much to tell, yet," he said and started to end it there, but caught himself and knew he had to share more with her or they would fall into old patterns, and he was happy with their rekindled closeness. "Ethel Chapman, owner of Myrtle Hill plantation just outside of town is dead. She was shot. Don't know if it was a suicide or a murder. Most of the people I've talked to so far seem to believe it couldn't be a suicide. We'll see. You wouldn't believe the house. It's been in the same family since the seventeen hundreds and added to, over time. It's really an amazing place. I also found out why the big house across the street is empty, and who owns it."

"Really? Who owns it?"

"The girls' angel."

"Mary Johnston?"

"Yep. Harvey tells me she was married to the guy who owned the mills around here. That was his house and he left it to her. They had no children, so he left the mills to his nephew, Harold Bowen, who married Ethel Chapman from Myrtle Hill Plantation. She's the woman who is dead."

"Maybe I should call Mary and tell her we could come some other time."

"I think she's okay. She seems to handle things pretty well, and she told me she's looking forward to your coming over today. She said your grandmother was her best friend when they were kids, so I know she wants to talk with you."

"I'm not the only one who will be there. She said she's having a few friends over, but encouraged me to bring the girls. I guess she knew I wouldn't have a babysitter. Isn't that sweet of her?"

"I'm glad you'll be out of the house for a while. You can't spend all your time unpacking while I'm working. We need to do more of the unpacking together. I never expected to get caught up in something like this investigation so soon," Dane said, finishing his sandwich.

"I'll try not to be too late this evening, but we're having our first press conference. Which reminds me ... I persuaded Pat Lambe to come in and handle the media. How about we have her over and I'll grill something for dinner?"

"Sounds good to me. It'll be great to see Pat again. She always makes me laugh so hard. No one can tell a story like she can. Oh, Mary told me not to bring anything, but I think I'll take some flowers from the garden."

"I think she'd like that."

"I can't wait to talk with her. I hope she has time to tell me some of the family history. Mother didn't seem to know too much about Grandmother's life before she lived in Virginia. I really don't recall ever hearing about Camden Grove until very recently. Isn't that strange?"

"Don't know about strange, but you'll like Mary. Have a great time, and I'll see you this evening."

Giving her a quick kiss, he went up to the girls' room where he found them playing dolls, the two old blind Bichons on guard between them and the door. He sat on the floor without any acknowledgment from his daughters. Winston, their rescued now-sixteen-year-old blind, toothless, three-legged dog crawled into Dane's lap while he watched the girls.

Dakota sat at his side for the few minutes before Dane got up and went back downstairs. He had hoped his daughters would speak to him after what Joan had told him. He left more than a little sad, wondering if he would ever be let into their world.

"Joan, I don't have an appointment until two o'clock, so why don't I walk the three of you down to Mary's."

"That would be lovely."

CHAPTER

SIX

The bell rang and Mary opened the door to Dane, Joan, Rose, and Julia, and Dane said, "I had a few minutes so I thought I would walk them down."

"Well, come in and meet my friends." Focusing on Joan, Mary added, "I'm so happy you were able to come. I hope you won't be too bored spending an afternoon with a bunch of old women, but we've been just too curious about you and your family since your arrival."

"I'm glad to have the chance to get out and meet people. I haven't done anything but unpack since arriving, and this is a most welcome break. With Dane already so involved, it's up to me to start putting down the family roots."

"Well, your family roots are already here. You just have to tap into them."

"You know," Joan said, "I really don't know anything about my grandmother or her family. She died before I was born, and mother never said much about her except that she was eccentric. I'm excited to learn more."

"Come in and let me introduce you to the girls. I know we'll have time to chat some before the afternoon is over."

Walking into the living room, Mary said, "Girls, let me introduce Dane and Joan Hunter and the twins, Rose and Julia.

Before she could begin introduction, Julia immediately looked at one of the women and said, "Your colors are bright."

Mary heard both Dane's and Joan's intake of breath and put a hand on each of their arms to stop them from saying anything. She gently pulled them back and put her finger to her lips to encourage them not to interrupt the conversation. Both girls stepped forward.

Katherine knelt by Rose and Julia. "Let's play the color game. Tell me what colors you see around Lucy here," she said, waving for Lucy to step forward.

Rose said, "I see white, bright green, blue-green, red, and yellow with blue next to it."

Julia finished the statement saying, "I also see pink and gold."

Katherine took a hard look at Lucy. "Those are the exact colors I see." She nodded toward the other women. "Do you know what they mean?"

Both girls shook their heads.

"Let's look at Madeline," Katherine said pointing toward Madeline.

Mary guided Dane and Joan into the kitchen and put another pot of water on the stove, not wanting to interrupt what was unfolding in the living room by going back in for the teapot.

"What's going on?" Joan asked.

"Well, it's hard to explain. Let me start by telling you something of your grandmother. I think it lays the foundation for what is happening in the other room. Lily was my best friend from my earliest memories. Living just a few houses from each other and being the same age, we were inseparable. I know Dane has told you Harvey thinks we're witches. Well, we aren't. We do have what I like to call gifts from God. Your grandmother had at least one such gift. She and I could 'mind talk' without ever having to speak. I believe your daughters do that all the time."

Dane and Joan looked toward the living room to see what was happening.

"I remember the day I last saw your grandmother," Mary said. "It was July fourth, 1935. We were in her room getting ready to go to a big party at the Bowen manor that stands across the street. It was the first big party they'd had since the market crash in nineteen twenty-nine. The Bowens had lost a lot of money and had worked the mills to make some back. It was a special day for your grandmother because she was going to meet Collin Bowen's family for the first time. They'd just been told that she and Collin were to be married. Lily wanted to look and act perfect, so they'd accept her.

"Collin had come to Camden Grove in 1930, when he was eighteen to manage the textile mill the family owned. It was just one of many holdings, and each family member had been assigned one to manage. Collin had it hard because he was so young, but he'd done well over the five years since his arrival. Being young, he spent a lot of time in all our houses for dinner, and he and your grandmother quickly became an item, much to my chagrin. Collin was a beautiful man," Mary said wistfully.

"Long story shorter, the party was a disaster. Collin's mother didn't give Lily a chance. There was a huge scene regarding your grandmother's suitability for Collin that ended with your grandmother saying that they may not be in the same league as far as money goes, but she and her family had every bit as much pride and a whole lot more goodness. Lily was so angry, but walked down the stairs, out of the house, and out of our lives that night.

"After all these years I can still see it all as if it were yesterday. The Bowens' ball never came off. The town never saw the fireworks display that had been scheduled. Lily left town that night to stay with relatives in Washington, D.C., and she never once came back to Camden Grove.

"After Lily's departure, Collin began drinking. He was trying to drown the memories of the way Lily had looked at him, and the accusations she'd thrown at him. He turned to me, as Lily's friend, to try to grab a lifeline. Don't ask me how, but he persuaded me five years later that only through me could he find life. He convinced me to marry him. Lily said she didn't care, but the day we married, I felt a door slam in my head. The link Lily and I'd always shared had been cut off.

"Over the years, I received only a few glimpses of the life Lily led. The final one was just before she died. In her final moments she shared her regrets over our lost friendship and over not seeing her first grandchild born."

"That grandchild would have been me," Joan said. "I was born four days after grandmother died."

"Despite the miles separating us, Lily and I made peace with each other in the end. I linked with Lily who was walking toward a group of people. As she neared, I saw that they were friends and relatives who had died years before, there to help make the crossing easier. Lily was embraced and enveloped in the warmth and moved by the group toward a brilliant, intensely white light, the brightest one I'd ever seen, surrounded the group.

"That was my first experience with a crossing, and it added a new dimension to my abilities," Mary said, wiping a tear from the corner of her eye.

"As much as I am hungry to learn know more about my grandmother, I am having a hard time concentrating on what you are saying," Joan said honestly.

Looking into the other room, Mary said, "I understand. I don't believe it is just chance that brought you here. Too many stars had to align for it to be just chance. That tells me you are supposed to be here in Camden Grove for some reason. Sure, we need your police and detective skills, Dane, but I think there is more of a reason than that. Think about it, our police Chief Danny Bader decided it was time to retire and move to Florida, Officer Glenn Yarborough had a heart attack and died, the tenants in your grandmother's house suddenly decide to move, and your husband decides to apply for a job here. I believe there are two very strong reasons all these events happened sitting in that next room."

"I'm not sure I follow. What do Rose and Julia have to do with any of this?" Joan asked with a puzzled look on her face.

"You said to me that the girls talked for the first time in the store yesterday. Don't you find it a bit odd that speech was so easy for them if they've never spoken?"

"I've been sure they've always been listening when we talked to them. They picked it up, just didn't use it," Joan replied.

"I'm sure that's true, but then when you got home yesterday, did they continue to speak?" Mary asked.

"No."

"And today, did they talk?" Mary pressed.

"No. But…"

"So the only time they have spoken is when I've been around, or now with my friends in there?"

"Yes," Joan hesitantly admitted.

"Would it surprise you if I told you that I was able to speak to them both yesterday just like I did with their grandmother? My mother used to talk to me a lot about Angel Gabriel. She said that he was the ruler of the First Heaven and responsible for selecting souls from heaven to be born into the world. Once he made his selection he spent the time the child was in the womb informing them of all he or she would need to know on earth. Then, just before birth, he pressed his finger on the child's lip, silencing them to all they know until they need it. I think his touch was extra strong with Rose and Julia, because I believe you have two very powerful girls in there who don't know how to deal with what happens to them. We all had help here in Camden Grove. My mother and grandmother taught me how to cope. The only one in the group who didn't come into her gift early is Audrey. But we were here to help her after her accident. I think you are here because your daughters need us to help them before you lose them," Mary said gently.

"I don't know what to say," Joan said.

"Let's go in and see what the girls think," Mary said, putting her hand on Dane and Joan's shoulder as she went to get the teapot from the living room to warm it up. They both followed her.

"Anyone for some more tea and cake," Mary asked. "It'll take me just a minute, but first let me introduce everyone. Joan, going around the room,

Audrey Baquet, Katherine Kiser, Madeline Jones, and Lucy Aarons," she said pointing to each as she introduced them. "While I make fresh tea and cut the cake, why don't you ladies talk to Dane and Joan about what's happening in here."

Dane and Joan sat down, and both Rose and Julia came and stood on either side of them, touching their arms.

Katherine said, "Let me start. When they described colors, I looked to see what I saw. I haven't really looked at Lucy's colors for a long time, because we know each other so well, and with friends, you often don't look because the aura can tell you more than the person may want you to know. But the girls had her colors absolutely correct. Lucy's a healer, thus the bright green moving to the blue spectrum. The bright green shows Lucy's abilities in the areas of empathy and calmness. The red is the color of strong energy. When Lucy's in her healing mode, her reds and greens become brighter. Pink is one of the colors of compassion, very important in a healer, and gold shows a dynamic spiritual energy of one who's comfortable in his or her powers. Rose and Julia were correct with the colors they said they saw.

"Let me tell you about your daughters' colors. They're both pretty much the same at this point. Their first layer is white, the color of truth and purity. It shows that they are cleansing and purifying themselves. There's a lot of red, which indicates a strong awakening of latent abilities and talents. They also have orange, which tells me there's a new awareness of what I call the subtle realms of life, those that most people never see. They both have strong yellows, which indicate awakening of their psychic abilities and clairsentience. They both have blue-green, which indicates an ability to heal. Their blues show me the possibility for clairaudience and development of telepathy. Mary has strong blues, too. They're both developing gold, which tells me that they are beginning to come into their own power.

"Now let me tell you why this is so exciting. First, you don't normally see such strong colors especially, in young children. Second, none of us have all these colors. Finally, they're fast approaching a crossroads right now. All these gifts are sometimes a burden. They need help in sorting out all the things they see. It'll probably be a difficult transition for them because they're so strong. Most children who have talents just naturally learn or are taught to ignore them and end up losing them because they remain undeveloped. Others learn to trust what they call instinct, but never fully realize what their potential could be," Katherine said.

"Katherine spoke of their healing abilities," Lucy began. "I transferred a little calming energy to them because they were nervous with us in the beginning. They learn quickly, because they're now doing the same thing to you."

Dane and Joan both looked down at where the girls each had a hand on one of her arms.

"Katherine used words you may not have understood," Audrey began. "She used two of the three 'Clairs,' clairsentience and clairaudience. Clairsentience is the experiencing of another reality through one or more of our five senses. Since my accident, I am able to do this, as is Mary. You've probably experienced the same thing when you had a strange feeling and the hair on your arms or back of your neck stood up. If you don't learn to take it further, it just feels spooky.

"Clairaudience is taking it further and is the development of a psychic ability that allows us to receive information in the form of words or ideas. It can be through hearing voices in our heads or seeing people talking to us. The third of the 'Clairs' is clairvoyance, which is the development of both clairsentience and clairaudience to enable us to form pictures, like a movie screen in our heads. We can actually connect with spiritual guides, both our own and others, who are always available to help us in our life journey."

"I guess that leaves me," Madeline said. "I have only one little talent. I'm a fire talker, which means that I can talk burns out of people and do enough healing to ease their pain and, in many cases, ensure that their scarring is minimal. I'm not as good as Mary is."

Dane and Joan sat looking at the four ladies before Dane said, "I don't know how to process this information. I feel that I have stepped into the twilight zone and am surrounded by alien creatures."

Mary brought in a tray of cake and a fresh pot of tea, which she handed to Audrey to fill the cups. "The girls have thrown a lot of information at you," Mary said, "and it is too much to process. Let's make a deal. Let's not talk about this for now; let's just see what happens. I promise you that we're not crazy old women, and no harm can come to your daughters through us, but I also promise you that we can help them face the things they are going to have to face into the future. When you're ready to talk further, you can come to me and ask me any questions you may have."

"If you all can see so much, why can't you tell Dane what happened to Mrs. Bowen?" Joan asked.

"You've just asked us the question of the day," Mary said. "Before you arrived we were talking about that and surprised that we have no inkling of it whatsoever. None of us had any specific premonitions, and since the event, it feels like there is a blanket of darkness or complete void every time we try to sort things out. I think we have to depend solely on your husband's skills to solve this case, and I think we're in good hands."

"And I think that's my cue to leave," Dane said, standing. "I have an appointment I have to make, but really don't want to leave. But I know Joan wants to know more about her family, so will leave y'all to it. Ladies," he said to the four women, "it has been...interesting, and I look forward to seeing you again."

He gave Joan, Rose, and Julia each a quick kiss before Mary walked him out.

CHAPTER
SEVEN

Thirty-five minutes later Dane sat with Forrest in the mirrored observation booth to observe the interview with Steve Adams. His first impressions were not favorable.

Detective Andy Garner began, "Do you know why we've brought you in here this afternoon?"

"I never know why one of you decides to harass me, just because I've had some problems in the past. Will it ever stop? What are you trying to pin on me this time?" Steve asked, arm draped over the back of the chair, his legs crossed, left ankle on his right knee.

"We just want to ask you some questions about your dinner the other night."

"What dinner, and what night?"

"Night before last at Myrtle Hill Plantation."

"Didn't have dinner at Myrtle Hill," Steve answered.

"Well, I have information that says you did."

"Your information is wrong, cop."

Andy slammed his open hand on the table, causing Steve to jump. "I have a number of witnesses who say you did."

"Then I'll tell you that you have a number of witnesses who are god-damn liars," Steve barked, putting both feet on the floor and hands on the table facing the detective head on.

"You're telling me you weren't at Myrtle Hill night before last?"

"Didn't say that, and that ain't what you asked. I was there. Just didn't have dinner. Everyone got all hot and bothered, and we all left before we had a chance to eat anything but a couple of cold shrimp."

"Son, this isn't a game. Don't make this harder than it needs to be."

"Don't know what you're talking about. I learned a long time ago to be careful what I answered. I know y'all like to ask trick questions to make me look stupid. Well, I'm not stupid. Do I need to have a lawyer present while you question me?"

"That is certainly your right. But as we told you in the beginning, this is an informal, information-gathering interview. You can stop the questioning at any time you feel uncomfortable or think you need an attorney."

"Shit, I was uncomfortable the minute I opened my door and saw your face," Steve replied emphasizing the word uncomfortable by raising two-finger quotations in the air and making a sarcastic face.

"Are you stating you want an attorney present for this discussion?"

"Naw, it ain't necessary. I'm clean, and besides, I've had enough experience that I won't let you trick me into saying anything incriminating. But I'll let you know if I change my mind," Steve drawled.

"I presume that you knew you were a guest that night of Mrs. Ethel Chapman Bowen?"

"Not exactly. I was Junior's guest."

"Okay, you were a guest of Ronnie Junior at his grandmother's house for dinner."

"Nope. She never served us dinner, just a Coke, shrimp, and a lot of blah, blah, blah until everyone was mad and left."

"Did you leave with everyone else?"

"I left with Junior."

"Did Ronnie Junior leave when everyone else did?"

"Well, that's not real clear. The lawyer was there, his crazy aunt, and the maid when we left."

"This was in the library, right?" Detective Garner asked.

"Yeah. We were in the library."

"Were you in any other room of the house?"

"Nope. Came into the library from the front hall door and left the library and went out of the house through the front door."

"Did you know that Mrs. Bowen was shot that night?"

"Wait a minute. What's this all about?" Steve asked sitting up straight, a twitch starting in his left eye.

"Just trying to find out where you were while you were at Myrtle Hill and what time you actually left," Andy said.

"So the old broad was shot. Are those rich sonsabitches trying to pin something on me? Well, they can't. Junior was with me the whole night. He'll know I couldn't have done anything."

"So what time did you leave Myrtle Hill?"

"Just after Junior's mother and father left."

"What time would you say that was?"

"Shit, I don't know. Didn't think I would have to keep a diary about the night," Steve answered. "Whatever time his parents left we left."

"And you left the house through the front door, you said?"

"Yeh. That's what I said."

"Did you go back into the house once you left?"

"Naw, we just left."

"In that case, can you explain to me how your fingerprints got into Mrs. Bowen's bedroom where she was found dead?" Detective Garner asked.

"Oh, yeah. Junior took me back there to show me something."

"What did Junior want to show you in his grandmother's bedroom?"

"He said that his grandmother had this great treasure chest full of old jewels that'd been in the family for more than a hundred years. He wanted me to see some of them."

"And why'd he want to show his grandmother's jewels to someone who has been arrested for stealing? Is the kid just stupid or was there another reason, like maybe you needed some drugs, and the only way to get them was to steal some jewelry, come into town, and find a place to hock it for cash?"

Steve looked decidedly uncomfortable, allowing all observing the interview to guess that the purpose of the visit into the bedroom had been revealed.

"Shit, man. We went in there to look at the shit. He took me to the box on her dresser and opened it up. And all that was in it was cheap shit. Stuff made of buttons and glass and all sorts of things, but nothing that looked even a little expensive. I had a hard time not laughing out loud at the look on Junior's face."

"How did you get into the bedroom?"

"We went around the side of the house and in through the French doors. Junior said they were always open, and they were."

"So then what did you do?"

"We drove around and picked up a chick, took her back to my place and played the rest of the night."

"Can you give me the name of the 'chick'?"

"Alice."

"Alice what?"

"Alice is all I know. Junior knew her from his fancy private school."

"So what do you consider all night?"

"Well, we blew some weed, that's what you want to know, right? We blew some weed, then I took off my clothes to get things going, and I tried to help Alice out of her clothes. She kept saying no to me humping her. Said she was too afraid I would hurt her. She was really more into Junior, so I figured if Junior would get her going, after him, it would be easier for me to finish things off. Ya want to hear the details, cop? Well, there aren't any. Junior didn't want to do anything with her. He ain't really into girls much. After a while she said she had to go home. Maybe you want to hear what I made the senator's son do for causing me to lose out on a good virgin fuck? Would hearing about that get you excited, cop?" Steve asked, on his feet, hands back on the table between them, glaring at the detective.

"I think that will be quite enough, Mr. Adams," Detective Garner said. "We're going to hold you for a little while for suspicion of possession and dealing in drugs, perhaps a little corruption of a minor. I don't know how old the young lady is, but I believe the senator's son is still a minor, so I assume the young lady will be, too. I forget, Mr. Adams, aren't you over eighteen? You might want to think about contacting that lawyer we talked about earlier. I think you just might be in a little trouble for issues outside our current investigation. Let's get your pretty face photographed and put you in lock-up while we get a warrant to search your apartment and car. By the way, that Rolex on your arm, is that stolen, or did you come into a wad of cash?"

"The watch was a gift."

"Really? Who gives a seven-thousand-dollar gift to a nineteen-year-old punk?"

"How about the son of a certain senator who just happens to be running for governor. He follows me around like a puppy dog."

"You make me sick," Detective Garner said, mirroring Steve's stance, both hands on table leaning in as if ready to come across and take Steve down.

Forrest jumped up to end the interview before it got out of hand and sent a team in to take Steve to the lock-up. He told Dane the detective had a sixteen-year-old daughter named Alice who went to school with the senator's son. Dane was sure the young woman would be answering some questions before the day was over.

Dane left for his interviews back in Camden Grove. He arrived at the senator's home, parked, and walked to the door. It was almost two in the afternoon when he rang the doorbell. Robin Bowen answered, looking markedly different from the last time he'd seen her. She obviously hadn't had anything to drink. Her eyes were bright, and she seemed in total control.

"Chief Hunter, Please come in," she said, opening the door to him and then leading into the living room where they had been on his previous visit. She gestured for him to take a chair, and then seated herself in a matching one across from the one he sat in. "Ronnie's in Columbia today. Is there something I can help you with?"

"Actually, I came to talk with your son."

"Why do you need to talk to Ronnie Junior?"

"I have a few questions about the friend he took to dinner at Mrs. Bowen's the night she died."

"Steve Adams. I don't like him at all. I would say he's trouble, but for some reason, Ronnie Junior seems to worship him. Oh, my God," she said, her hand going to her mouth. "You don't think he—?"

"Right now I just have routine questions about everyone who was there that night," Dane quickly interjected.

"Oh," Robin said, visibly shaken. "Ronnie Junior is still sleeping. He was up all night playing video games. About Ronnie Junior. He is very confused. He has more of me in him than he does his father. He doesn't feel like he fits in. He struggles with what his father thinks of him, and what his peers think of him. He complicates his life by the choices he makes in friends. He's involved with things with Steve that he doesn't yet know how to handle. Steve is very sure of himself. He seems to be everything Ronnie Junior would like to be, muscular, a magnet for girls, and a guys' guy who doesn't care what people think about him. I think Steve does whatever feels good without having a case of guilt about what he's done the following morning. He takes total advantage of Ronnie Junior."

With tears in her eyes, Robin continued, "We are all devastated by Ethel's death. She is...was, a remarkable woman. She's always non-judgmental. She's never once scolded me to be a better wife, a better mother, or a better political partner for Ronnie. When the topic's been a dead elephant in the middle of the room that we all dance around, she's just said to me, 'Robin, you're stronger than you give yourself credit for, and when that strength is needed, you'll find it.' She never once, in all these years, treated me in any way but like a daughter, even though I don't have the upbringing that matches the circles Ronnie could attract. We didn't have money or advantages growing up. I never finished college. I don't really have any career aspirations or options at this point. But Ethel would tell me that someday I'd find myself and be surprised at what I can do."

"Had Mrs. Bowen been herself lately?"

"We haven't seen much of her this past year. Ronnie's been campaigning, I've been in my own world, and I believe she's been gone much of the time. I'm not sure, but I know Ronnie has complained that his mother has scheduled trips to avoid giving him any visible support in his bid for governor. He's been very disappointed in that."

"Do you know if she had any medical problems?" Dane asked.

"Not that I know of, but when we have seen her, she hasn't been like her old self," Robin said. "I can't understand why she had started wearing those ugly wigs. Oh, they're expensive and all but, I just thought for some reason she's trying to look younger. She was wearing tinted glasses last time we saw her and she said she was having trouble with her eyes. I'd probably ask Isabelle about Ethel's health. I know that unless there was something serious that was wrong, Ethel wouldn't tell us. She never wanted anyone to worry about her while we're all wrapped up in our petty problems."

"Did you know that if she changed her will, you would lose out on what I'm told would be a sizeable amount of money for yourself?"

"Ethel told me about that. She said a woman should always have something of her own, something separate from what her husband provides. I've never given it a thought. While I don't know the details, I know Ronnie's father left him money, and Ronnie always makes sure I know what is his is mine, and he means it. It's the thought of what Ethel wanted to do for me that's important, not the actual money. If she were to change her will, and I have to say that the story wasn't very believable to me, it wouldn't make a bit of difference to me. What was Ethel's was Ethel's to do with as she pleased."

"What do you mean that the story wasn't very believable to you?" Dane asked.

"Ethel has a deep sense of family, and her feet were so firmly rooted in Myrtle Hill that she could never bear for it not to be in the family. She'd no more give the land away while there was an ounce of Chapman blood left on this planet than she would chop off an arm."

"That leads into my next question. Do you think she could've taken her own life?"

"Never."

"You can't think of any reason that would cause her to do so?"

"She lived every minute of life. No, I can't think of a single reason for her to commit suicide."

"That's what everyone except your husband has said," Dane observed. "While he didn't say it couldn't have happened, he did allude to the fact that it could be a possibility, since Mr. Bowen had died."

"Ronnie doesn't really believe that. While it's obvious that the two loved each other, Ethel's too strong not to be able to survive without Harold. Ronnie knows that, too," Robin said.

"He even said something like Ms. Ricks was an old lioness who would protect his mother's way into heaven. What does that mean?"

"You don't have enough time for me to tell you my feelings about Isabelle. Let me just say I have a healthy respect for her the way I do friends' chow dogs. She's a one-family person, as loyal as the day is long. She'll do anything for any member of the family as long as it's in the best interest of the one she loves best, and that'd be Ethel. She's been there for Ronnie's whole life, normally in the background, unless someone did something to hurt Ethel. Then you'd feel Isabelle's wrath. I understand Harold tried to have her banished once when she took a broom to him for raising his hand to Ethel. Harold had to move to the house where Becky now lives until that storm blew over. I pity whoever did this if Isabelle finds out first. She won't need her magic to pull the flesh right off his bones."

"I've also heard a lot about special gifts, magic, and witches since moving here. Do you seriously believe in that?" Dane questioned.

"Of course, I believe it. We have daily examples of the powers people have here. I don't understand it, and I don't need to. I just know that certain people in town know things that there is no earthly way they should know, and there are those who can do things that science and medicine can't explain."

"What kinds of things do you think Isabelle can do?"

"I don't know that I can pin down examples. I just have a sense of a controlled power below the surface. With Mary Johnston, Audrey Baquet, or Lucy Aarons you know what they can do because they're out in the open. I've never seen Isabelle get involved with anything, but I know that she could if she wanted to," Robin explained.

Standing again, she said, "Let me go see if I can get Ronnie Junior out of bed," Robin said, leaving Dane alone in the living room to digest all that she had revealed, along with the change in the way she presented herself in comparison with his first impression of her.

Dane's interview with Ronnie Junior was much less confrontational than the interview he had observed with Steve Adams. Robin's insights gave him a better idea of how to interview her son, and the kinds of questions he needed to ask. Straight from bed, tousled, in a T-shirt and baggy shorts both much too big for him, the senator's son looked like a little boy. What sat in front of Dane was a respectful young man in contrast to the smart-aleck youth he'd seen during his first visit to the house.

"I'm going to ask you some questions that may upset or embarrass you and make you feel uncomfortable. I've asked your mother to leave us alone, because anything we discuss right now is between the two of us. Do you understand?"

"Yes, sir. Thank you, sir."

"I am going to start by talking with you about the night you went to dinner at your grandmother's house and took your friend, Steve."

"Yes, sir."

"Was it supposed to be a family dinner?"

"Yes, sir."

"Were your parents and grandmother expecting you to bring a friend?"

"No, sir."

"Why did you bring him?"

"I wanted to be with him, and if I didn't go by until after dinner, he'd probably be out partying, and I'd never find him."

"Did your grandmother mind?"

"Gram's pretty cool. Nothing much bothers her. She pretty much lets me get away with murder." As he said it, his eyes filled with tears. Wiping them away, he said, "Later she scolded me for making people uncomfortable. I bet Isabelle put her up to that one, but Gram just goes with the flow. She's always encouraged me to be spontaneous and said I worry too much about what I do and how I look to other people."

"Does that bother you?"

"Hey, I'm sixteen. My dad's a senator, my mom's usually drunk, my aunt is crazy, my grandmother owns half the world and thinks of a black woman as her mother and best friend. And look at me, I haven't grown as much as my classmates have. I'm supposed to be fucked up."

Dane could tell young Ronnie Junior was fully waking up. The coffee his mother had given him was kicking in. Smiling, Dane said, "I guess you are. How did you feel when your grandmother said she was changing her will?"

"Sad for my dad."

"Why?"

"I bet if you ask him, he'd give up everything to have Myrtle Hill. He loves that place. He'd make us all live there with Gram if she'd let us. Thank God she has more sense than that."

"Is that why you called her that night?"

"Yeah. I got pretty messed up after we left, so I called her and told her that I loved her, but that she was hurting Dad. I asked her to reconsider and told her the money didn't matter. She could give it all away, but Myrtle Hill should go to Dad. She didn't seem upset with me or anything. She said she loved me, too, and hoped I'd always know it, no matter what, and she told me not to worry about Dad; he'd be fine. She seemed a little sad and told me I needed to have more respect for myself and remember I'm one of a kind. She said nobody else would ever walk this earth with all the same qualities I have, and I needed to sort out who and what I was and go with it. She said if I didn't respect myself, no one else would. She ended the conversation saying, 'Always remember that no one loves you like your Gram loves you. Ciao, baby,' just like she has done every time we've talked since she took me to Italy last year. That was the last time I ever talked to her."

Dane felt bad for the young man who sat with tears rolling down his face, unembarrassed.

"I'm sorry. Listen. I haven't known anyone who's a junior who wanted to be called Junior after his twelfth birthday. What would you prefer I call you?" Dane asked to head the conversation in a different direction.

"I like Ronald. I hate Ronnie, Junior, or Ronnie Junior."

"Okay, Ronald it is. Ronald, what were you and Steve doing in your grandmother's bedroom?"

"I was afraid you'd know about that. Fingerprints, right?" he looked for and received confirmation from the shake of Dane's head. "I didn't have any cash, and Steve said if we wanted any more grass, I'd have to come up with something or he'd have to find someone else to party with. I figured Gram had so much stuff that she wouldn't miss something small if we took it. After the big scene, I took Steve into her room from the side terrace. There was nothing of any value in her jewelry box, just a bunch of junk. Mom'll kill me when she finds out, but I gave him my watch that night."

"Why?"

"I want to be around him."

"What did you do after you left there? Your mother tells me you didn't come in until after four in the morning," Dane asked.

"Mom knew? She didn't say anything."

"I think you might be surprised at what your mother knows. What did you do all night?"

"We ran into a friend of mine from school, Alice Garner. Her dad's a detective in Greenwood. We smoked some grass, and Steve wanted to have sex with Alice. At first she seemed okay, but didn't want anything to do with Steve, especially after he took off his clothes and she saw him naked. Steve wanted me to do stuff first, but I was too nervous. I've never been with a girl, and I don't think she'd ever gone all the way before. I think we were both scared. Alice finally said she had to go home. Steve was mad that he didn't get anything from Alice, but he took her home."

"Then what?"

"We went back to his place, and I stayed there until I came home."

"Did Steve ever leave?"

"I don't think so."

"But you don't know?"

"Not really. I was totally wasted, and fell asleep."

"What woke you up?"

"I don't know, but Steve was already dressed and told me I needed to get home before I was missed, so I got dressed, and he drove me home. You know the rest, because after you came over, the day was pretty much ruined."

"Have you seen or talked to Steve since?"

"No, I haven't. I wanted to, but things have been crazy around here."

"Ronald, I appreciate your honesty today. There may be other things we have to talk about later," Dane said.

"Do you have to tell my parents everything?"

"I've always found that if I do something I don't want anyone else to know about, it always comes out when I least want it to."

"Are you're telling me I should tell on myself?"

"I can't tell you what to do, but I think some of what you told me will come out naturally. Some may not. Remember, though, that you're not the only one who knows certain events. In fact, your friend, Steve, has already been interviewed in Greenwood and told pretty much the same story from his perspective. Are you entirely comfortable with that?"

"Point taken. Guess I have some thinking to do. Dad will shit a brick."

Smiling, Dane said, "Let me tell your mother goodbye for now. I'll catch you later, Ronald."

Showing Dane out the door, Robin asked if she should be worrying about Ronnie Junior.

"I'd say that you basically have a smart kid who may be running with the wrong crowd. He needs grounding, needs some family structure, and needs some areas where he feels it's okay to be himself. Talk to him. I bet you'll find out the same. Oh, by the way, he prefers to be called Ronald. It's part of the verging on manhood identity thing. He really doesn't like Ronnie Junior or just Junior."

"He's never said that."

"He has some fairly big shoes he thinks he has to fill as a junior."

"Thanks for everything today, Dane."

"All part of the job."

"Do you know any more today than you did yesterday?"

"Not much. Cases like these are like jigsaw puzzles. You just keep trying to fit all the pieces together until some kind of picture emerges. Until that happens, all the bits of information I gather are just pieces of the puzzle, some important, some just filler. But don't worry, we will figure it all out as quickly as possible."

"What's next?"

"Think I'll check in at the office and then head over to Myrtle Hill. I'd like to discuss a few things with Ms. Ricks. My wife and daughters are having afternoon tea with Mary Johnston and some of her friends, and I've no idea how long a tea might last. Might as well get as much done as I can!" Dane said with a smile. "Good talking with you, Robin. I'm sure we'll talk again."

Dane called Harvey as he drove off and discovered that the senator wanted to meet him at the office at five-thirty, Pat Lambe had made her entrance into town and was ensconced in his office, and the first press update had been scheduled for seven that evening. Looking at his watch, he saw it was already a quarter to three. He wouldn't have a lot of time at Myrtle Hill. He called to make sure Isabelle was home and available and then took off.

CHAPTER

EIGHT

The drive to Myrtle Hill seemed almost familiar to Dane, and he was able to take in more of the outside scenery while alone on the drive for the first time. Nearing the plantation driveway, he saw four television vans, one on each side of the driveway and two directly across the street, with the camera operators and reporters on the road to ensure they could catch anyone coming or going. He slowed the car, turned on the blinker, pulled into the driveway and stopped. Four reporters cautiously approached the car. They were all young, fresh-faced, and attractive and would probably all be replaced by more senior staff as soon as events began to unfold.

"Looks like y'all have drawn the guard duty," Dane said with a friendly smile as he got out of the car. He knew reporters could dog a case or give him the room to work, depending on the relationship he developed. "I'm Dane Hunter, chief of the Camden Grove Police," he said, sticking out his hand. The tall, dark-haired, blue-eyed reporter who would stand out in any crowd took his hand first.

"Kathryn Blanchard, WOLO, Channel Twenty-five in Columbia. ABC."

He went down the row of hands.

"John Peters, WHNS, Channel Twenty-one. FOX, out of Greenville."

"Stephanie Polk, WYFT, Channel Four, also out of Greenville. We're an NBC affiliate."

"Allison Andrews, WSPA, Channel Seven in Spartanburg. CBS."

"Will I see you all tonight at the press update?" he asked.

"You bet, but we're here and you're here. How about giving us a head start?" Stephanie said, flashing a winning smile.

"You know if I did that I'd have a pack of reporters on my heels every step I take. I assume you've already been up to the house?" he asked.

"A mistake none of us will make again," Kathryn said. "The lady wouldn't give us a name, just made sure we knew we were on private property and didn't want to make her mad. You know, she's right. I wouldn't want to make her mad."

Allison chimed in, "We've dubbed her The Dragon Lady."

Dane chuckled. "Well, I'm on my way up to talk with her, and I see cameras rolling back there getting some footage of our talk, so as I drive to the house, you can all do a little piece saying the good police chief is working overtime on this case and promises a full progress report tonight. Until then, I'll wave on my way out and look forward to seeing each of you later this evening."

Stephanie, with an overacted pout, said, "Is that the best you can do for us? We're out here in the middle of nowhere looking for our big break."

"I've no doubt you'll do fine," Dane said, "but I really have nothing to give you yet. I promise to keep you four in mind. I know what it's like to be working your way up."

Shaking hands again with all four, he got back into his car to head for the appointment with Isabelle. Myrtle Hill's front door opened before his car stopped and Isabelle was waiting at the top of the steps, arms folded across her chest and a sour look on her face. Even without the course in body language Dane had taken, he could see that he was in for an interesting talk.

"Can I assume you informed them to stay off private property, Chief Hunter?" Isabelle asked bluntly with no words of welcome.

"I don't believe I needed to do that. They know the rules and indicated that you'd put them in their place. I don't think you have to worry about this crew, but remember they may be replaced at some point by more experienced crews who may not be quite so intimidated. We'll be here to support you when needed," he answered in a friendly tone.

Isabelle said, "Hmmph. I hope you know how much trouble you've already caused me today."

"No, Ms. Ricks, I don't. What trouble have I caused?"

"I've had people all over the place all day long and have had to get Harold Baker down to make sure all the doors and windows will lock. Why didn't you put a muzzle on Harvey, telling the whole world we don't lock our doors here at Myrtle Hill?"

"I understand your concern, and while I can't take Harvey's words back, I can assure you that we'll all be more careful with what is said in the future. I didn't think that he would answer reporters' questions last night."

"Well, we don't need a police chief who just doesn't think, do we?" Isabelle snapped.

Dane bit his tongue and said evenly, "Can we carry on this discussion inside? I have a few questions to ask you, and I believe we'd both be more comfortable sitting."

Isabelle turned and walked into the house, expecting Dane to follow in her wake. He took his time, again getting his recorder and a notepad before walking up the steps and into the house. Isabelle was nowhere to be seen, so he looked first into the living room. She was sitting in one of two wing-back chairs flanking the fireplace. Her chair faced the door.

Dane looked in and she said, "Whenever you're ready." He walked into the room, took the seat facing Isabelle, and said, "Ms. Ricks, may I call you Isabelle? Ms. Ricks seems so formal."

"This isn't a social visit. I believe you're here on official business. Ms. Ricks suits me fine."

That almost brought a smile to Dane's lips, but he controlled it. "Okay, Ms. Ricks, like the last time we talked, I'm going to record our conversation for the record."

"Good Lord, just ask your questions."

"Ms. Ricks, do you know if Mrs. Bowen was receiving medical treatment in the months prior to her death?"

"You mean her murder?"

"We haven't established the cause of death, so I'm not referring to the cause. Do you know if Mrs. Bowen was receiving any kind of medical treatment in the months prior to her death?"

"Yes."

"Treatment for what?"

"Cancer."

"What was the diagnosis?"

"I'm not a doctor."

"Who is her doctor?"

"Here in Camden Grove, it's Dr. Jack Martin."

"Was Dr. Martin treating her?"

"No."

"Ms. Ricks, my interviews with you seem to be very difficult. I want to find out exactly what happened to Mrs. Bowen. I need your help to do that. I'm not the enemy."

"I know that you, like the senator, would like to say Ethel took her own life. That puts us in opposite positions. I'm telling you that she did not," Isabelle said.

"And I'm telling you that I'm going to investigate this fully until I'm one hundred percent certain I have all the facts to be able to report on what happened here," Dane said, leaning toward Isabelle to emphasize his point. "I want to find the truth. I don't want to say Mrs. Bowen committed suicide because it's easier, gets me out of work, or is politically expedient. I believe all human beings deserve to die in their beds peacefully when their time comes after a very long and full life. When one person in my area of responsibility doesn't get to do that, I take it personally. It makes me angry. I won't stop until we get to the truth. So, Ms. Ricks, we're not in opposite positions. I'm neutral until I know the facts, and I'm asking you to help me find the facts."

Visibly relaxing Isabelle said, "You can call me Isabelle. It'll make it friendlier if we are going to work together to get to the truth."

"I'd like that, Isabelle," Dane said, feeling almost jubilant at the small victory. "What exactly was wrong with Mrs. Bowen, and who was treating her?"

"In the past few weeks, no one. All the best and most expensive doctors we went to had given up on her. They'd exhausted their bag of tricks, sapped most of her strength with their poisonous drugs, and then sent her home with me to die."

"What was wrong with her?"

"Ethel had exocrine pancreatic cancer. I know more about it than you'd ever want to know. Her cancer was undetected until it spread. Men get this disease twice as frequently as women, but Ethel smoked like a fiend and loved fried foods. Smoking and high-fat diets are believed to be contributors to this cancer. I also believe, because it's often thought to be hereditary, that her mother probably died of the same disease, they just didn't know about it back then.

"We first got the diagnosis in Columbia. She stopped going to Dr. Martin about six months ago when she was sure she was sick. Her sickness was nothing he could have known about, because it's so hard to diagnosis, and the symptoms are often the same as other, more common problems. Once she heard the possibility of cancer, we immediately went to the Memorial Sloan-Kettering Cancer Center in New York for tests. After all the tests, Ethel was diagnosed with stage-four pancreatic cancer. We soon learned that meant a death sentence. Because the disease had already spread, Ethel was given six to nine months to live. She underwent both radiation and chemotherapy, not with the hope of cure, but more to relieve pain and reduce the tumors.

"Those treatments were terrible. They exhausted her, and she developed sores in her mouth. She was constantly nauseated and lost her hair.

She was diagnosed five months and ten days ago. She dropped out of sight, claiming travel and other events to cover the fact that she was staying in bed more and using more drugs to allow her the energy to attend the events she felt were necessary.

"So she didn't want anyone know she was so sick?"

"No, she didn't. She knew that they wouldn't really want to know, either, because it would make them refocus their activities. It was easier for everyone to think she'd gone off the deep end and wanted to look younger than to realize that she was dying, so she wore more makeup to cover how pale she was, and wigs to cover the loss of her hair. When she was around people, she was always bigger than life, so that they wouldn't see the changes in her, and then, when she was alone, she would stay in bed to store up enough strength for the next event she had to manage."

"You know, of course, that she was leaving you money in her will?" Dane asked.

"Yes, I knew that, but she also knew that I didn't need or want it. My whole life has been spent in this house. I've always received a salary. In the early years, I sent some of it home, but after a while, I stopped that and put it in the bank. I learned more about the world, and I began to invest and have done well over the years. I have a solid investment portfolio that will provide more money than I can spend for the rest of my life. I have no family to speak of, so I don't have a burning need to build up money for someone else to spend. Ethel was like a child to me. I didn't need any of her money."

"You think you know who killed Mrs. Bowen, don't you?"

"Yes, I do."

"You aren't going to tell me what you suspect, are you?"

"No, Chief Hunter, I'm not. Your investigation will have to reveal the truth step by step, or you won't be certain it is the truth. I told you before, I won't lead you down any path and won't share my opinion, but I will answer your questions as honestly as I can when you ask them."

"Fair enough," Dane said, turning off his recorder and standing to leave. "You know that Harvey believes you're a witch with special powers to read minds and know things."

His statement brought the first smile he had seen from her. Escorting him to the door, she said, "Harvey talks too much and thinks too little. I wouldn't waste my time trying to read his mind."

Dane smiled and stuck his hand out to shake hers. Isabelle smiled again and took his hand, and for a moment, she looked him straight in the eye and said, "But you know, Harvey is correct. I am a witch, and I can read minds. Be careful what you think. I'll know."

"You're really good at intimidation. When this is all over, I think I'll need some lessons from you," Dane remarked as he stepped out the door.

"I'll look forward to that," Isabelle said and promptly shut the door.

Driving out, Dane stopped and rolled down his window when he neared the reporters. John Peters said, "I see you survived the Dragon Lady's lair."

"She's not so bad once you get beyond the fire. I'll see you all in a little while." They waved, and Dane headed back to the office.

D ane walked into the police office to see a harried Harvey and said, "Looks like you've been busy."

"I've done just like you said. I haven't told nobody nothing except give them what Ms. Lambe told me to, directed them to the hotel, and told them where the meeting's gonna be. No matter what they asked me, my lips were sealed. Boss, I'm really sorry for the mess I made. Didn't mean to do things wrong," Harvey said with his head low.

"Harvey, you can't be blamed for what you don't know. We're going to take care of that when we have time. Now you know when you have questions or aren't sure what to do, you ask me. That's all I can ask of you," Dane said.

"I still feel real bad, and Ms. Lambe told me what a mess everything is. She said if I said one thing without her clearing it she would pull my lips over my head and shove my head up my butt."

The look on his face caused Dane to burst out laughing.

"It ain't funny, boss. I believe she'll do it."

Dane couldn't control his laughter.

"It really ain't funny."

"I know, Harvey. But I can just see Pat saying that to you, and I can see your face when she did. I should've warned you about Pat's sense of humor."

"Ain't funny. Ya don't see me laughing, do ya? Ha. Ha. Ha. It just ain't funny. And you don't know the half of it. She says she's taking me to get my hair cut and that she's gonna have them trim my eyebrows, pluck my ears, and shave my nose hairs. When I said no, she said, 'hush little man. We're going to make you presentable. That means a clean, white T-shirt underneath a freshly starched uniform to show off your new clean cut look." Harvey mimicked Pat's delivery. "And if you argue, I'm going to have them address the offensive things I cannot see.' I asked her what she meant, and she said, 'if your eyebrows are that bad, I'm sure you haven't done any manscaping. So if you fight me about the haircut and the eyebrow trim, I'm going to drop you off for a back waxing and have them trim any chest hairs you might have and work their way right on down your body.' She actually looked down from my face to my privates," Harvey said with a wail.

His face sent Dane into another round of laughter.

Finally, getting his mirth under control, Dane said, "Harvey, Senator Bowen should be here in about fifteen minutes. After that, I'm going straight into meetings with Pat, Forrest Sikes, and the mayor regarding the media briefing tonight. Is there anything I need to know before the senator comes?"

"Naw. I've been workin' on the crime board in the back room. Oh, and I put an envelope that was slipped under the door on your desk."

Dane went into his office and picked up the envelope by the edge. Typed on it were the words "For the Chief of Police Eyes Only." He went back out to the front office, holding it gingerly. "When did this come?"

"Guess sometime during the night."

"It was here this morning?"

"Yup."

"Why didn't you give it to me this morning?"

"Well, I put it on my desk while I was making coffee, then all sorts of things happened, and I didn't get back to it until a while ago, so I put it on your desk," Harvey said defensively.

"Bring me a letter opener, some gloves, and two evidence protectors," Dane instructed.

He went back into his office and laid the envelope on his desk while Harvey got him the things he asked for. When he brought them, Dane put on the gloves, slit the top of the envelope with the letter opener, reached in and took out the folded page inside. He put the envelope in the first evidence bag and sealed it. He gently laid the letter on the desk, carefully unfolded it, and slipped it into the second document protector before reading it. There was no salutation.

All things are not as they seem to be on the surface. You might want to do some background checks on a few people, some in town and some not. The pastor has quite a past and is tied to Becky Bowen in many ways. You might want to see where they were when the murder occurred or if their past might have come home to roost. Ms. Bowen's companion has a criminal record of her own, and a lot of people have a lot to lose, even the priest. There was a whole lot of traffic about town night before last, most unusual for our town.

—A concerned citizen

Dane asked, "Harvey, do you know how to run a background check?"

"Never had to, know'd everyone in town. But if you tell me how, I know I could do it."

Trying not to show his frustration, Dane said, "That's okay. I'll see if Forrest can get one of his staff members to help us do some research. This is another task I want you to put on your list of things you need to learn."

"I'll write it down right now. I sure have a lot to learn, don't I? Geez. We are lucky you were here; elsewise, who would have known all this stuff?"

They heard the front door open. "That will be the senator," Dane said. "Would you please show him in and call Pat Lambe and ask her to come over in about thirty minutes?"

"Sure, boss."

Harvey ushered the Senator into Dane's office.

"Senator, how are you," Dane greeted.

"Please, I'm Ronnie," he said. "I appreciate your taking the time to see me today. I'd like to talk about the media involved in mother's death, how we manage release of information, and a personal issue. If you don't mind, I'd like to get the personal out of the way first, so I can concentrate more on the media aspect."

"It's your time," Dane said.

"I asked to meet with you because I wasn't honest with you at the house when you told me about Mother's death. I'm normally as honest as the day is long. Mother always told me to think about everything I did. I haven't been honest with you, about where I was the night Mother died."

"Ronnie," Dane said setting a personal rather than formal tone, "let's go off record. Anything you say to me will stay right here unless it turns out to have an impact on the case. I have a lot of experience in dealing with politically sensitive cases, and you can count on my discretion in any matter you wish to discuss. With that said, please know that I do believe you're an honest man. I read the newspapers, listen to people talk, and I understand how you can sometimes find yourself in situations that get out of control. What I require from you, as both Ronnie and as Senator Bowen, is your complete honesty in dealings with me when it has to do with an investigation. Without that, you won't like me very much."

"I understand and assure you that you can trust what I tell you now. I don't want to sugarcoat things and don't know how to beat around the bush, so just out in the open, I had an affair with a pretty wonderful woman who knew my situation and didn't want anything more from me than I was willing to give. She had reasons of her own that made what happened work for her. That's over. Both she and I agreed that we were playing with fire, especially with the public eye on me, and neither of us wanted to jeopardize our personal and professional relationships for something that had nowhere to go. I was with her the night Mother died. We talked everything through to its conclusion and parted knowing that the next morning would find us working together with a complete comfort level of trusted friends. I love my wife, and I have no excuse for what happened. I'll end up telling her all I've told you. I know I'd better do it sooner, rather than later, because I hear Mother's voice in my head telling me the consequences. I've talked with my friend, and I'm going to give you her card with her personal number. She can verify that I was with her if you need to know my exact whereabouts." He took a card from his pocket and handed it to Dane.

Dane looked at it, took out his wallet and put it behind one of the credit card pockets. "I'll only use this if it becomes necessary. Otherwise, I'll destroy it when the case is closed," he reassured the senator.

"I appreciate that more than you know. Now, is there anything you can tell me about where you are, regarding Mother's death?"

"Not a whole lot yet. I have been gathering a lot of facts, and until we get the autopsy report, gathering facts is about all we can do. I'd like to go back on record with you now with a few questions. Did you know your mother was sick?"

"What do you mean by sick?"

"That she had a terminal disease?"

"No. Where did you hear that?"

"When we found your mother, she was wearing a wig. In transporting her from her home, it was discovered that she'd lost her hair, and the assumption was that she might have had radiation or chemotherapy. I've since conducted an interview that gave me information that your mother did have a terminal form of cancer and had been in treatment for several months, out of town and state."

"That certainly explains a lot. Mother has been unavailable for over six months. I assumed it was because she couldn't support my campaign, so she made excuses to be away more than she was home. I was so caught up in me that I didn't look beyond my own ego. It's all clear now, and I'm afraid it puts me to shame as a son. When Mother started wearing the wigs, she also started wearing a lot more makeup. We had words about accepting one's age and acting appropriately. She gave me a run for my money, telling me that how she aged was her business, and if she wanted to look like a painted hussy or install an Italian stud puppy at Myrtle Hill, that was her prerogative, as a widow over the age of eighteen. It's just like her to carry the whole burden herself. I can't imagine why Isabelle didn't let us know that Mother needed us, though."

"I'd think that's a conversation you need to have with Ms. Ricks, but from what information I have gathered so far, I'd say your mother probably had a reason for not telling anyone, and it was most likely something other than her vanity. Every person I've talked to has said only glowing words about your mother's spirit, generosity, and desire to help people," Dane said.

"I'm sure. One of Mother's best qualities was her ability to know just what people needed. She's going to be sorely missed. Where does the investigation go from here?" Ronnie asked.

"We should receive at least the preliminary autopsy report tomorrow, and that should give us a good idea of next steps. You indicated yesterday that you thought your mother might have committed suicide. You are the only one so far who believes that."

"You're pretty brutally honest, aren't you?" the senator said, his eyes visibly tearing. He paused, taking deep breaths, shoulders drooping before beginning again. "I'm going to have a hard enough time knowing that Mother died with anger between us, and the knowledge that she's been sick and didn't turn to us because we were so caught up in our own problems compounds the guilt. I spoke out of anger without thinking. I don't believe that Mother could've shot herself. Maybe she could have taken pills, if something was extreme, but I even doubt that, because it would be one of the big sins."

"I've had a difficult time trying to figure out how everyone else categorically stated that there was no way she could've committed suicide, while that was the first thing you said. I'm not sure I understand, yet, but I hear what you've just said," Dane said. "Do you mind telling me what you discussed with your Mother when you called her that night after you left?"

"I hate it when someone gets my goat. I called to tell her that, to tell her that I behaved badly, but also to remind her that Grandfather had always said she held the land and house in trust for me and generations to come. I don't care about the money. She can give it all to the church to buy some other piece of property, but I do care about Myrtle Hill and all it represents. I tried to tell her not to make any rash decisions. I'm afraid I ended up yelling again, and telling her I would fight for the land. She heard me out and then just said, 'It's mine to do with as I please. There is no law that requires me to give the land to you. You do have a sister, you know. I didn't hear you saying you and she would split the house and land.' Then she hung up."

"Why didn't you call back?"

"It wouldn't have done any good. I hoped she would come to her senses," Ronnie explained. "Do you have any more questions, or can we talk about the media?"

"Now it's my turn to apologize. I accept full responsibility for this morning's article. As a result, I've brought in the best public relations person I know. She'll be here in a few minutes for you to meet. Again, I recognize that this has the potential to become very political and that we're close to election day. You have my word that we'll manage all information releases to the best of our ability and that we'll keep you informed to the extent possible. I need you to hear the words 'to the best of our ability.' I want you to understand that there are many things in this community that I don't yet fully grasp, histories, backgrounds, things people have done or been involved in and the like. I can't manage people's knowledge of related and unrelated things, their desire to be part of an unfolding story, or their talking to friends, neighbors, or even the press. I also can't manage leaks that may come from other organizations or agencies that may be or may become involved in parts of this investigation. What I can manage is how my staff and I conduct ourselves. I'm working closely with Major Forrest Sikes at the Piedmont Region Investigation Services."

"Forrest is a good man," the senator interjected.

"I know he is. He, Pat Lambe, and I will be the only ones who know everything. I worked with Pat while I was in Washington. She is one of the best at managing information and public relations. I know we need the best right now. We'll be in constant communication. As you know, I have only Officer Turner to help me, and he hasn't had the experience he needs to be competent in this kind of investigation. I'll correct that in the future, but for now, it is my responsibility to manage what he does and how much he knows. Pat Lambe has put the fear of God in him, and you won't hear a peep out of him to the press again. I'm not sure how I'm going to pay Pat for her services, but I'll work that out."

"If she's good, don't worry about the money. The stakes are too high for me. I was going to offer my PR guy."

"I'd have had to decline. I think anything I do has to remain totally separate from you or your staff. Let them manage information from your perspective; I have to be on independent, neutral ground. Again, once you see Pat in action, I know you'll be comfortable that I have things covered from my end."

"For my part, I'm glad you're here," Ronnie said. "I don't know what in your life brought you from Washington to Camden Grove, but it's a miracle that you're here at this time when we need someone so desperately with your skills. You'll have my complete cooperation at all times, and I'll try not to meddle or push. But I'm used to action, and have a lot riding both personally and politically on this governor's race. There isn't a lot of time left, and Mother's death is bound to have an impact."

"I understand that, and I'll push hard to resolve questions surrounding your mother's death as quickly as I can. If you don't mind, I'd like to call Pat to join us for a few minutes. We're short on time and need to meet with Major Sikes to be fully prepared for tonight's first media update."

"Is it something I should attend?"

"Absolutely not," Dane said without hesitation. "Even without Pat's input, I'd say it would focus attention on you, make it look like you were controlling the investigation, and do us all a lot of damage. Just your coming in here today will likely generate questions tonight and possible assumptions we're going to have to deal with."

"I didn't even think about that."

"We'll have to. We don't know how many people are in town now looking for any kind of information they can get. From this point on, I'd prefer to make appointments with you, when necessary, and answer your questions and concerns by phone as much as possible." Dane took one of his new cards out of the holder on the desk, wrote his cell number on the back, and handed it to the senator. "Whenever you have any questions, just call my cell number. I'm the only one who ever answers it. It's only off when I am either recharging the battery or in an interview where I can't be disturbed. If I don't answer, I'm in a place where I cannot talk. But I will return the call as soon after as possible."

"I appreciate that," the senator said.

Dane picked up the phone and buzzed Harvey. "Is Pat out there?"

"Yes, boss, she is," Harvey answered nervously.

Dane stood to go to the door, saying, "Pat has Harvey about as scared as one human can make another, so I'd better bring her in here fast before he falls apart."

He opened the door and saw Pat for the first time since her arrival. She was in one of her trademark St. John's suits in pink with black trim. Her short hair, makeup artfully applied, and French-tipped nails were also her trademarks. Pink and black high heels, to make her appear taller than her five-foot-two-inch height, completed the outfit.

She kissed Dane's cheek, hugged his neck, and said, "Good to see you, Hunter," before turning to Senator Bowen, offering her hand. "Senator, I am so sorry for your loss. I lost my mother last year, and there is nothing anyone can say to make it easier."

"Thank you," he said, his eyes filling quickly with tears he struggled to hold back.

Dane could see Pat going into her professional mode as she took the chair next to the senator's and indicated he, too, should sit.

"Reporting has gotten off to a bad start," Pat said, "but that has changed. I can assure you that you won't be surprised by anything out of this office when you open a paper or turn on a TV. I assume that you have someone who will manage access to you?"

"Yes, I do. Jeff Price handles my PR."

"Make sure he lets people know he is available. He wasn't quoted in any of the papers; articles just say you weren't available. That looks bad. I took the liberty of preparing something he may want to consider, including in a short release thanking people for their support, stating that this is a tragic time for you and your family, and requesting that people respect your grief and solitude for the next few days until you are prepared to make a public statement. I'd suggest that you don't say anything else at the moment. Reporters are already probably camped out around your house."

"They weren't this morning, but I left early and haven't been available even to the office today."

"That's not good. It'll raise questions. I suggest you go straight home, call Mr. Price to come to your house, and stay put until we see how this story is spun on the networks and in the papers. It won't be a conflict of interest for Mr. Price to talk with me at any time." She handed the senator her card with her cell number. "I'm sure that I can get a signal, even out here in the country," she said with a smile.

The senator smiled and stood when Pat stood. They again shook hands before he turned and shook Dane's hand and said, "Thanks again. I look forward to talking with you."

After showing him out, Dane came back into the office.

Pat put her arms around his neck and said, "Now give me a real hug, Hunter, and then let's get down to business." As they hugged, she yelled out the door, "Harvey, see if Major Sikes is almost here." Releasing Dane, she said, "I took the liberty of asking Forrest to meet us here so that we can orchestrate tonight's meeting. I've drafted a script of the briefing we need to tweak. You both need to bring me up to date, and then I need to prep you both for questions. I know you're good at this, but I have no idea how Forrest will do."

"I think he'll be just fine."

"I'll be the judge of that," Pat said. "So what do you think of our good-looking senator? Is he a suspect?"

"Let's see if we have a murder or a suicide first."

"For the sake of the discussion, let's say we move to a murder investigation. Is he a suspect?" she persisted.

"He has as good a motive or better than most. There are some questions about his whereabouts when his mother died, and there are some anomalies in his story, so I would probably say he could be on a short list requiring a more intense scrutiny, should we move into a murder investigation."

Dane and Pat talked for the five minutes before Forrest joined them. Dane made the introductions, and Forrest said, "It's good to meet you. I hope you'll let me have my PR officer shadow you as a learning experience."

"Is it a he or a she?" Pat asked.

"He. Tom Atwell. He's been with us for about two years and is very good for what we normally do. I've never had to use him in a case with the potential stakes of this one, and he admitted that it made him nervous," Forrest said.

"I have just two rules. One, don't get in my way or try to take the lead, and two, don't think because I am small and a woman that I can be bossed around or need to be protected."

Dane laughed and said, "Forrest, you might want to have Tom talk to Harvey to set the stage. I bet poor Harvey starts shaking the minute he hears the click of high heels approach for the rest of his life. You've traumatized my officer, Pat, with your threat of bodily harm and potential grooming."

In mock horror, Forrest said, "You threatened an officer of the law?"

With a straight face, Pat said, "When I'm managing the information, I set the law and think it appropriate to establish the consequences for any violations. Officer Turner committed cardinal sins with the press. In the Department of Defense they have an information security saying that goes something like, 'Loose lips sink ships.' I merely explained to Officer Turner what would happen if there were to be a repeat of his earlier interview."

"Should I ask what the consequences are?" Forrest asked.

"Well," Dane said, "as relayed by Officer Turner, it includes something like taking his lips, pulling them over his head, and shoving his head up his butt. Do I have it correct, Ms. Lambe? In addition, she told him his hair, eyebrows, and ear and nose hairs were crimes of nature and that she was going to take him to get them fixed. To get that done, she threatened him with groomers to address whatever other nastiness lurks beneath his clothing."

Forrest burst out laughing; Pat smiled and said, "I may have been a tad extreme. I'll try to tame my tongue. Gentlemen, we don't have a lot of time. How about bringing me up to speed so I can finish preparing the statements and fact sheets for tonight and we can cover meeting preparations."

"Forrest, you want to tell her what you have?"

"In a nutshell, we responded to Dane's call with a team of crime scene analysts to gather any evidence available. Probable cause of death, gunshot wound to the head. The victim was in a sitting position propped against the headboard. There were wigs and costume jewelry spread on the bed. The room was scrupulously clean except for the items on the bed, a silk robe on the chair beside the bed, and blood and tissue on the wall that resulted from the force of the bullet entry. All the doors and windows, as Harvey reported, were unlocked. I have to editorialize and say that isn't odd in this area of the country. Only five different prints were found in the room, Mrs. Bowen's; her grandson's; a friend of his, Steve Adams; the plumber; and Isabelle Ricks. The grandson has been in minor trouble, nothing serious. Adams has a longer history of petty crimes, nothing violent to date. We questioned him and he is currently being held in Greenwood."

"On what charges?" Pat asked.

"We're working on charges unrelated to Mrs. Bowen's death. Seems he and the senator's son picked up a young girl who is most likely the daughter of one of my detectives, smoked pot provided by Steve Adams, and attempted to engage in some sexual activity. We're holding him on suspicion of contributing to the delinquency of minors."

"Just a thought," Pat interjected, "if you're holding him, he'll become the prime suspect in the press and cause more questions to be asked. If you do not think he is currently a threat, I'd read him the riot act, tell him to keep his mouth shut, and get him out of jail quickly, unless someone plans to press those unrelated charges against him."

"If this proves to be a suicide, we have nothing except that he was in the room earlier in the evening with the grandson," Forrest said. "While he admitted to smoking pot, there really isn't anything to hold him on. I'll phone over and tell them to let him go for now. He won't go anywhere."

"Anything else?" Pat asked.

"The autopsy should be underway or about to start. Until that's completed, we cannot rule out suicide and officially make this a murder investigation."

"Dane, what do you have?"

"Harvey answered a call from the housekeeper and companion, Isabelle Ricks, at ten-twelve yesterday morning. She said Mrs. Bowen had been murdered."

"She used the word 'murdered'?" Pat asked.

"Yes. We responded to the call, and found Mrs. Bowen as Forrest described. After a preliminary review of the scene, I interviewed Ms. Ricks while waiting for Major Sikes and his team to arrive. I then picked up the senator's pastor, Doug Reed, notified the senator, and then his sister, of the death. This morning I talked with Mrs. Bowen's lawyer, her aunt, observed the interview with Steve Adams, talked with the senator's wife, interviewed the senator's son, and clarified some information with Ms. Ricks that leads us to believe that Mrs. Bowen was terminally ill."

"You have both been gathering information but will not determine if a crime has been committed until after the autopsy results are available."

"Right," both Forrest and Dane said.

"So this is a potential suicide until proven otherwise?"

"The housekeeper and everyone I have talked to believe that suicide is not a possibility; however, with the knowledge of how sick she may have been, people's minds may change. The autopsy should give us the information we need to proceed," Dane said.

"That's all we say, then. We don't talk about what might have happened, we only talk about where we are right now," Pat summed.

"There is one other event that Forrest doesn't yet know, either," Dane said. "A letter was left under the door this morning. Harvey put it on his desk and forgot about it until this evening. The letter has been handled appropriately, and I would like to give it to you, Forrest, for testing and prints. The letter suggests that we need to do background checks on Doug Reed, his connections with Ms. Bowen, Charlotte Kirk, and the comings and goings of various people during the night."

Writing down the information, Forrest said, "I'll call and get background checks started when we finish here."

"Dane, I know how your mind works," Pat said. "If suicide is a probability, are there any obstacles?"

"Yes, Isabelle is adamant that Mrs. Bowen could never commit suicide because of her religion. Everyone else also believes she would've been unable to hurt herself."

"Religion is a powerful deterrent," Pat said. "If you rule out suicide as a probability, I'm sure you've already compiled a list of possible suspects, right?"

"The beginnings of a list."

"They are?" Pat asked.

"First let me explain that the evening of the murder, the family and the family lawyer had been invited to dinner where Mrs. Bowen initiated discussion about possibly changing her will to leave her estate to the Catholic Church and other charities. Six people were in the room in addition to Mrs. Bowen and her lawyer, Wayne Wenzel. Of the six, five of them stood to lose should the will be changed, Senator Bowen, his wife, his son, his sister, and Ms. Ricks. The sixth, Steve Adams, would have nothing to gain or lose from those discussions. During interviews yesterday and today I was able to put together some preliminary alibis for some of the folks, just in case we need them. Senator Bowen–and this information remains between the three of us in this room–was away from home that night and did not return until about four o'clock. The senator's son, Ronald, was at his friend, Steve Adams's apartment until somewhere around four in the morning when he returned home. The senator's wife, Robin, was home alone and knew the other two were out and when they returned. Becky Bowen's nurse discovered her outside this morning."

"Sorry to interrupt," Pat interjected, "but what do you mean 'discovered outside'?"

"Evidently she has psychiatric issues and has a nurse and companion who lives with her. The nurse, Charlotte Kirk, found Becky outside in the wee hours of the morning. She also already knew her mother was dead before I told her," Dane explained. "The last is Isabelle Ricks, who was in the house at the time of the murder."

"Did she know or hear anything?" Pat asked.

"No, she says their rooms aren't close, the house is big, and trust me, it is, and there was a bad thunderstorm during the night. The sixth person at the house that night was Steve Adams. As you heard, he has a record for petty crimes. Ronald Junior said Adams woke him up to get him home, and Adams was already dressed. Now let's move to the anonymous letter. Three individuals named in that letter–Doug Reed, the Senator's pastor and friend who previously dated the Senator's sister; Charlotte Kirk, the sister's nurse; and Father Rhett Leverette, Mrs. Bowen's priest. And as long as we are talking about suspects, it could be someone unknown who either committed a random crime or had some unknown reason to be at Myrtle Hill."

"So you're telling me the field, at this point, is wide open," Pat concluded.

"That about sums it up," Dane said.

Forrest whistled and said, "Wow, you have covered a lot of ground in a day. Now I understand your reputation."

Pat smiled. "He was the best Washington had. Well, down to business. I've heard nothing that would cause me to change the release information," she said as she handed them each a copy. "I will open the meeting, set the parameters, and then introduce you, Dane. You, in your own words that closely follow those I have crafted for you," she said handing him a typed statement, "will provide the information within your scope of responsibility."

Handing a similar sheet to Forrest, she said to Dane, "You will then introduce Forrest who will provide his information, and we will then take questions. I will moderate the questions. I'll leave you two to look over what I have given you while I see if I can motivate Harvey to get us all a snack before we go to the press conference."

CHAPTER
TEN

The media center was set up in the social hall of the First Baptist Church. Dane and Pat were surprised at the number of cars in the parking lot. Television crews were interviewing people outside the building.

"This is interesting," Pat said. "Guess we should have predicted that a lot of residents might be interested, too. Looks like we may have a full house."

Dane spied Kathryn Blanchard interviewing Mary Johnston. Mary and Doug Reed were the only local residents he saw that he could put a name to, but he also saw the other three fledgling reporters he had met earlier that day conducting interviews. Little clusters of people were standing around talking, and Dane heard snippets of their conversations as he and Pat made their way to the door. Mary smiled and waved at Dane, and a few stuck out their hands and introduced themselves to him as he, Pat, and Forrest walked by.

It was more of a madhouse inside than outside. Camera crews had already staked their ground and had their lights set up. Print media reporters were also getting interviews while waiting for the update to begin. With Dane and his team in the building, people quickly began finding seats. The church had set up a podium with a microphone and four seats behind it. At just a few minutes before seven-thirty, Pat indicated that Dane and Forrest should take seats in the front. Word quickly spread to those still lagging outside, and they rushed in to find seats.

"Good evening," Pat opened, "I'm Pat Lambe, and I'll be your contact person on behalf of the Camden Grove Police Department for all official media inquiries concerning the death of Ethel Chapman Bowen. This step has been taken to ensure that Chief of Police Dane Hunter has the time necessary for his investigation. In a moment, I'm going to turn the microphone over to Chief Hunter for an update. Major Forrest Sikes of the Piedmont Region Investigation Services will follow him. After their statements, we'll all be available for a question and answer session. For those of you with the media, I apologize for the lateness of this first update. We know you have deadlines. I'll be available after this meeting for your input on times and your preferences on daily meetings with me, or a call list that I can activate if there is any change from the previous day's update. I'm pleased, too, to see so many residents here. We know that traumatic events of this kind affect everyone in the community and make you wonder what actions you should be taking or how you can help. We have prepared a basic safety tips fact sheet that is being copied now and will be available in the back of the room when this meeting is over. We'll also have copies of the written update and short bios on Chief Hunter, Major Sikes, and me as background. Are there any questions before we begin?"

Kathryn raised her hand. "Ms. Lambe, Kathryn Blanchard, WOLO, ABC Channel Twenty-five in Columbia. Will the three of you be available after this session for follow-up, on-camera questions?"

"Because of the lateness of the hour already, and the number of people who are here, I'd say probably not during this first update, but we'll work with you for future individual time as needed," Pat answered.

"Thanks," Kathryn responded.

"Anyone else?" Looking around the room and seeing no other hands going up, Pat said, "Chief Hunter," and turned toward Dane, indicating he was up.

Dane walked to the lectern, leaned in and said, "I haven't met most of you yet, and I expected to have plenty of opportunity for us to get to know each other before there was the need for us to interact on a professional level. I'm a pretty straightforward guy, so what I'd like to do is give you a brief overview of events to date and what you can expect over the next few days. Major Sikes has graciously offered his service's forensics team and resources to aid in the investigation process. Thank you, Forrest," Dane said, acknowledging him.

"Let me begin with yesterday morning. Officer Harvey Turner transferred a call to me at ten-twelve a.m. It was our initial notification that something was wrong at Myrtle Hill Plantation. At Myrtle Hill, we found that Ethel Chapman Bowen had been shot, but the time and exact cause of the death hasn't yet been established. I immediately notified Major Sikes that we'd need his team to secure any potential evidence on site. Major Sikes?"

Forrest stood and replaced Dane at the lectern. "I don't have a whole lot to tell you yet. As Chief Hunter explained, we provided a forensics team to gather evidence from Myrtle Hill Plantation. All the information is being processed. The Greenwood County Coroner pronounced Mrs. Bowen dead at Myrtle Hill and arranged for her to be transported to Self Memorial Hospital, where an autopsy was scheduled for late today."

Pat stepped back up to the lectern. "Thank you both for that update. Both Chief Hunter and Major Sikes are available for questions."

Kathryn Blanchard's hand was the first up. "Chief Hunter, do you believe, as your office earlier released, that Mrs. Bowen was murdered?"

"Unfortunately that statement made by my deputy was a poor choice of words. We don't have enough facts yet to definitively state cause of death. If the evidence provided from autopsy results, combined with the other information we've been and are gathering, indicates that someone other than the victim was involved and further investigation is warranted, we will follow all leads to their logical conclusions."

Stephanie Polk asked, "The statement in the newspaper quotes Officer Turner reporting this as a murder."

"Again, a poor choice of words, but please remember this kind of event is unusual for Camden Grove, and Officer Turner has never had to deal with the media before. He's going to be a lot more careful in the future," Dane replied.

"Can you describe where Mrs. Bowen was shot?" Kathryn asked.

"Mrs. Bowen was shot in the head," Dane replied to gasps from the audience.

"John Peters, WHNS Fox Channel Twenty-one. Are the wounds and other things you saw consistent with a possible suicide?"

"Answering that question would be giving you my opinion. I'd prefer that we wait until after the autopsy report is completed to make those kinds of statements."

John pursued, "But in your experience, could this have been a suicide."

"My answer remains the same, Mr. Peters. It is important to first know the cause of the death. The county coroner will establish the direction of this investigation."

Another hand went up and a woman stood. "Sally Anderson, *The State* newspaper. I talked with Officer Turner last night, and he led me to believe that this was a particularly gruesome killing, and that there was a murderer loose in a community where people don't even lock their doors. Are you saying that the people of Camden Grove are safe?"

"No, Sally, I'm not." A murmur rippled through the residents. "What I'm saying is that we don't have the facts to recreate what happened at Myrtle Hill Plantation night before last. It is pretty obvious that Mrs. Bowen didn't die of natural causes. That leaves us four options, accident, suicide, homicide, or undetermined. It is now our responsibility to follow all facts to the conclusion of this investigation." Dane leaned forward and grabbed the lectern. "If I might comment on safety concerns, I've lived most of my life in large cities and have been able to feel relatively safe in locations where crime may be prevalent because I've always taken appropriate precautions. My door has always been locked at night, as well as during the day, normally, and certainly when I've been away from the house. I've never left my car unlocked or running and open while I ran an errand. As a responsible law enforcement officer, I'll always tell members in any community to take basic care to ensure their safety and the safety of others. As Pat Lambe stated earlier, safety information is available at the back of the room. You should all take a copy and make decisions about what you can implement. We can also provide seminars, if enough people are interested."

"Allison Andrews, WSPA, CBS Channel Seven. We understand that you have a suspect in custody. Can you respond to that?"

Forrest stepped forward. "We don't have a suspect in custody. While assisting Chief Hunter in interviewing individuals who may have important information, facts were revealed that were unrelated to the death of Mrs. Bowen, but caused my deputies some concerns about the activities of the individual questioned. He was held for a period of time, and then released."

Sally Anderson came back with another question. "Is the senator or any member of the family a suspect in this murder?"

"There are currently no suspects in this case and will not be any until the cause of death has been determined," Dane replied.

"A follow-up question, please," Sally said. "We have been given reason to believe that a change in Mrs. Bowen's will might have been in the works. Can you validate this information?"

"No," Dane replied.

"Are you saying our information is wrong, you don't know, or you just aren't going to comment?" Sally pursued.

"At this time, I can't comment. Matters of inheritance will be addressed through the appropriate legal channels," he said.

A timid-looking woman stood. "I'm Teri Ross-Web. I wonder if others feel that everything is changing and totally out of control here in Camden Grove. I've stayed here my whole life because it was safe. I never had trouble sleeping when Glenn Yarborough was in the apartment above our garage." There was a ripple of chuckles through the hall, but Teri continued. "I always joked that we had our very own policeman guarding us while we slept. Glenn is gone. I don't feel safe." She turned toward where Mary Johnston was sitting. "Ms. Mary, can't you do something? Can't you tell us what happened? You know everything. What happened?"

Mary answered, "Teri, none of us know what happened. That's what Chief Hunter will try to figure out for us."

"But you always know these things. You knew to be there for me after I found Glenn. Do your magic and make this all go away."

"Honey, there's no magic for this. We just have to have patience and wait. I don't feel anything sinister here."

"But did you know Ms. Ethel was going to die?"

"No, I didn't."

"Maybe Ned is right. Maybe it is time to leave Camden Grove like most people did when the mill closed. Maybe we stayed too long." Teri sat down, defeated.

Pat stepped forward again. "If members of the press will stay, let's decide on the best approach to release information. For residents, thank you for coming. As Chief Hunter said, we'll make sure we get you all the information we can as soon as we can. The pastor has agreed to let us post meeting times on the church directory board out front. That, plus the media, plus word of mouth will let you know when we have something for you. Again, please take the safety tips and any of the other information you would like from the tables by the door. Thank you, and good night."

One of Forrest's deputies was waiting in the back of the room and came walking up when Forrest and Dane were talking alone. "I have those background checks you asked for, sir. One of them is a real doozy."

Forrest took the two folders and briefly scanned them both before handing them to Dane. "Let's talk about these early tomorrow morning, along with strategizing about information releases. Pat, how are you planning to deal with psychic involvement?"

"I'll guarantee you that of all the things said here tonight, the magic comments will be the ones to appear on every station tomorrow and will be in every wire story. That can of worms has been opened, and every wannabe psychic will come riding into town."

Mary came over. "Ms. Lambe, I'm Mary Johnston."

"Nice to meet you, Ms. Johnston. You know that everyone in the press is going to want to speak to you now."

"Oh, they all know me. My friends and I work with police departments across the state occasionally when they have missing children or adults or other cases that they could use a little special help solving. They all know where to find me when they want to," Mary said.

"Pat, you're going to find that a few people here can do a lot of things you'll have trouble explaining," Forrest said with a smile, "but I honestly don't think you'll hear much about the magic." Forrest handed her the papers he had used that evening, and said, "It's been a long day, and it's time we all went home. Good job tonight." He shook hands with both Pat and Dane.

As Forrest left, Mary said, "Dane, the girls and I have left dinner at your house so you and Joan don't have to cook this late. Ms. Lambe, I know that our little hotel doesn't offer the comforts you're probably used to, nor the privacy. I have an old house that I don't use, but it is ready for someone to be in it. If you'd like, you're welcome to stay there while you're in town. I was told you have a smoking room at the inn, and it is perfectly okay to smoke in the house or on the terrace.

"By the way, I have read your book and hope you will write more. Logically, the next one could be, *What I Meant to Say Was*," Mary encouraged. "I left a key with Joan and turned on the lights before coming here. I think the ground floor suite is probably the best for you so you don't have to climb all the stairs. And you should probably lose those heels, or you're going to be flat on your back for days."

"Thanks for the offer and the advice. Vanity often comes at a high price," Pat replied.

"Now I know it's a big house, but it is safe, and you will have nothing to worry about staying there."

Turning to Dane, Pat said, "What do you think?"

"Well, let's see. The private Ms. Pat can stay in the Azalea Lodge room or a mansion all by herself. I'd say take Mary up on the mansion. Mary, this is awfully kind of you, and staying across the street will sure make it easier, since Pat doesn't drive. I would have had her stay with us, but we aren't unpacked yet."

"It's about time that old house got some use," Mary said. "The coffeemaker is prepared, all you have to do is turn it on. There is fruit and other snacks in the fridge, and even some Ben and Jerry's in the freezer," Mary said with a knowing smile. "Treat the house as if it were your own. Now, I have to run. We'll see each other tomorrow. Like I told Dane this morning, I think you and I are also going to be great friends."

Both Mary and Dane chuckled at Pat's discomfort as Mary turned to leave.

"Why do I feel as if I've been set up?" Pat asked. "Did you know about this?"

"No, but you will find that Mary will be able to keep you just a bit off balance, but also you can't help but love her. I already feel as if I've known her for years. How about we check you out of your room on the way. I know Joan will want to escort you over to settle in. We've been dying to see the inside of that mansion—and I do mean mansion—across the street from our house."

There was, of course, no trouble checking out of the Azalea Lodge. "Honey," Dorothy June said, "Mary Johnston called me earlier and told me that you'd be going to stay with her. This place is such a madhouse, I gotta say I don't blame you one little bit. Don't you worry about paying for tonight. As soon as you gather your things, I'm gonna send a girl right in to turn the room, and I already have someone in line to rent it. I love the business, but I'm real sorry about Ms. Ethel. She was a good woman. But as long as this circus is going on, I'm gonna ride the wave. I don't believe I've ever had one hundred percent occupancy before. I could've rented ten more rooms tonight if I had 'em."

As they gathered her things, Pat said, "Why do I feel I've lost control of my life in one short day?"

"It's Camden Grove. Since I've been here it's been a swirl of events that sweep me up and move me from place to place. This town is filled with characters who don't seem to march to our tunes, Pat. It's like they're in a different time and place, where anything and everything is possible. Something like a potential murder is alien to their concept of life. Interestingly, I already feel like I'm a part of this and kind of understand what's going on."

"You're scaring me, Dane. I know I'll dream of The Children of the Corn or some other scary tale of a town gone weird."

"Naw, it ain't like that, Ms. Pat," Dane drawled as they loaded the car. "It's more like the Hotel California; you can check in, but you can't check out."

It took just a few minutes to get to Dane's house. "See that place across the street?"

"Good God. Tell me that's my new home away from home."

"From your lips to God's ears. Welcome to the strange world of Camden Grove."

"You aren't doing badly yourself, Chief Hunter," Pat remarked as they pulled into his driveway. "A promotion from detective to chief of police and look at the house you live in now!"

"Didn't I tell you that this house belonged to Joan's great-grandparents, then her grandmother, and her mother since the late fifties? The house and the job here opened up at the same time."

"Quit talking. Now you're really spooking me. Let's go see Joan, and if she has turned into a Stepford wife, you're going to call me the limo and send me right back to the Greenville airport tonight, so I can go back to the insanity of Washington."

Joan was obviously thrilled to see Pat, hugging her neck as soon as she and Dane were in the door. She asked all the right questions while they ate the late dinner Mary had left and listened intently to all that'd happened since Dane had called Pat and set the trip in motion. Dane could tell, though, that Joan was preoccupied, and his feeling was confirmed when she declined to go across the street to help Pat get settled.

"We can't both go, dear. The girls are in bed, and if you expect either Pat or me to lug her stuff inside, you're mistaken. Besides, I would rather see the inside for the first time when it is daylight. Pat, I'll come over for coffee in the morning unless the taskmaster will have you in his office at six-thirty."

"Shoot, I planned on letting her sleep until seven, and have Harvey pick her up at eight and bring her to the office. I've found that Wayne Wenzel, the lawyer, is an early bird, and I have a few questions for him tomorrow. Thought I'd start my day there."

Pat replied, "Sounds like a plan, but if I'm expected to be up and ready by eight, you have to show me to my bed now. It's been one hell of a ride so far, Hunter. Can't wait to see what tomorrow brings."

As Dane carried her luggage across the street, he said, "I'll get you in, but I'm not looking at anything. I don't want to see it first, or I'll have to give graphic details tonight, and I still have some reports to read."

"Unless I'm mistaken, you aren't going to read any reports until you've had a talk with Joan. Something's on her mind."

"Don't tell me you're becoming a psychic already," Dane joked.

"Nothing psychic about it. Women's intuition. We're always a mystery to you blockheads. Get home, Hunter. See you tomorrow."

Back at his house, he sneaked up behind Joan at the kitchen sink and put his arms around her. She leaned her head back against his chest.

"Okay, my sweet wife. What gives? Something's on your mind, and you won't sleep until you get it out."

"You already have too much on your plate."

"There'll never be so much on my plate that I won't be there for you, Joan. Tell me all, or I'll start tickling," he said sliding his hands to her sides.

"Don't you dare. This is serious."

He stood still, waiting.

"We haven't had a chance to talk about what happened today. The hard part is once we left Mary's, Rose and Julia didn't say another word and seemed to go back into their own world."

"What do you want to do?"

"I don't know what to think. What if Mary is right? What if the girls do need some kind of help that we can't give them?"

"I don't believe or disbelieve in psychic abilities. Things can't always be explained logically, but normally there are enough facts there that allow us to use intuition to come to the right answer. In this case, I don't know what we should do. It's clear that doctors can't give us the help we need. If the girls are responsive only in situations where Mary is there, then we have some questions to ask.

"I'll talk with Mary tomorrow, and we'll take this real slow. I know that Mary will want us to be comfortable with any decisions we make. It is obvious that people in this town trust her and accept that she has special abilities. I'm willing to go down just about any path to help Rose and Julia lead a normal life."

"I was hoping you would say that, but I didn't know how you would react."

"Nothing we've been doing so far has worked. What father wouldn't pursue any avenue?"

"Maybe this is why we ended up here in Camden Grove," Joan said.

"There seems to be many reasons we have ended up here. Two of them need a story read before we go to bed, so let me get going. Are you going to be long finishing up down here?"

"No, just a few minutes," Joan answered.

"I'll read fast and be waiting between the sheets, buck naked."

"Well, Randy Andy, read real fast, because I just might leave the rest of the dishes right here in the sink," Joan said with a smile.

The two folders Forrest gave him didn't get read until much later.

After just falling asleep, Dane received a phone call from Harvey, who was on call for emergencies. "There have been shots fired at Teri Ross-Web's house. All the neighbors are out and I think you might want to come over, boss."

Harvey gave Dane quick directions, Dane got dressed, and arrived some ten minutes later.

Harvey met him at the car. "Here's the lowdown. John Ackerman, the chubby guy over there holding the dog," Harvey said gesturing with his head, "was walking Everette without a leash. He's been told before not to do that, but John don't listen to anyone. Well, Everette's just a pup and ran into the bushes by Teri's bedroom window and wouldn't come out. At least that's John's story. Rumor has it that Teri don't close her blinds too well when she changes clothes," Harvey said in a whisper. "So John's over under the window trying to get Everette when the shooting began. Six shots, but only one came out the window. Lucky for John he dropped soon as the shooting started. The neighbors called me."

"I'll talk with Teri. You send everyone home. Tell them this was a reaction because Teri was scared, and we'll talk more about safety at the next press conference." Dane knocked on Teri's door and entered when she opened it.

"I'm so sorry," Teri began. "My husband works the night shift, and since Officer Yarborough died, I'm here by myself most nights. Glenn gave me the gun in case I ever needed it, and told me I needed to take shooting lessons; but he died before he could teach me."

"I'm not going to lecture you about the responsibility that goes with owning a gun, but you do realize that tonight could have had a very bad outcome. I understand you may be afraid, but shooting six times, and I see holes in the walls and ceiling in addition to the broken glass, could have gotten you and others hurt. Officer Yarborough gave you good advice. You need to take lessons before you think about shooting again. In the meantime, do you have any friends who might stay with you at night?"

"Well, if it is only for a little while. But not for long."

"Can they come tonight? Harvey is calling someone to board up the broken window until you can get it fixed."

"I think I will just go to Mamma and Daddy's house tonight," Teri said. "I won't get a wink of sleep here."

Dane took her full statement, and by that time, Harvey had a young man in tow with a sheet of plywood he tacked up on the window.

B ack at his house, Dane sat at the kitchen table, and opened the first folder. It was the background material on Charlotte Kirk that included a murder conviction and prison time. He read it, whistled, and got himself a cup of coffee. He opened the folder on Doug Reed. In the beginning it was about his pranks as a youth, but when Dane got to the event in college that others alluded to, he felt almost sneaky for reading the details of Doug's beating and Becky's rape.

With this new information, his next day was already beginning to fill up with people with whom he needed to talk. He reviewed his list. "Wayne Wenzel, heads up about inheritance questions; Mary Johnston, girls; Forest Sikes, thoughts; Charlotte Kirk, background; Doug Reed, background; and Father Leverette." Dane added "autopsy report and media update" with question marks. He knew the list would grow as the day went on.

Putting the list on top of the two folders, he went back upstairs to shower, shave, and get dressed. He was out of the house by five forty-five to find a note under his windshield wiper that said, "I'm up and have breakfast ready if you want to talk for a minute. Mary."

He smiled, got into his car, drove the few houses down, and pulled into Mary's driveway. She met him at the door saying, "I know you have a lot to do, but you shouldn't start a busy day with just a cup of coffee. I've made some eggs, bacon, cheese grits, and biscuits. And you're going to have a glass of orange juice, too. I don't think you've been eating so good since you began your move, and from the looks of you, you ate a lot of fast food in Washington."

Dane laughed and replied, "Guilty on all accounts."

Mary ushered him into the kitchen and started making him a plate.

"Joan and I talked about the tea party," Dane said.

"And what did you think?"

"Well, I'm still in shock from hearing how well they can talk. Joan said they had not talked again after leaving here, and they didn't say a word when I read to them last night. We've tried everything and seen every kind of doctor, with no results. In two meetings with you the girls have spoken twice. We're willing to pursue any avenue that may benefit Rose and Julia."

"You surprise me, Dane Hunter. Here I was ready to assure you that all we'd be doing is helping them get in touch with themselves, understand what is going on in their minds, and how they can deal with it all. We would not do anything, especially with your children, without your consent. Yesterday demonstrated that they are like sponges. All they had to do is see one of us do something, and they mimicked it. What I was going to propose is that we do some exercises with you to heighten your awareness of energy fields. I can tell you already use a lot of intuition in your work. That's why you're so good. The ability to see energy and colors would help you. You could tell when someone is being evasive, when they are afraid, or when they have bursts of anger that they are suppressing."

"Again, I'm open, and would gladly engage with you when I have a little time. Until then, you have our agreement to spend time with Joan and the girls, or just the girls alone, and see where it goes. You'll be working with the three people who are most dear to me though, and I ask that you always remember that in all you do with them," Dane said with conviction.

"You have my word," Mary said solemnly.

Dane shifted the conversation as he absentmindedly took a bite of cheese grits.

"I have a lot of interviews this morning. Care to tell me what I will learn?"

"I could do that, but it wouldn't help you with the puzzle pieces you're sorting out in your head, if I did," Mary said with a wicked smile.

"Am I that transparent?"

"Anyone who knew you for a day could read you, Dane Hunter. You take your life and your work seriously. You're an honest, honorable man who wants to do the right thing, and you're extremely compulsive and want every detail wrapped up nicely so that the overall package is perfect."

Dane laughed. "I guess I resemble that remark, Ms. Mary. It would be a far more pleasant day if I could just sit here and have you tell me all I need to know, but I guess you're right. I have a mind that has to gather all the data and sort it in my head before I can begin to solve the puzzle. Do you know the outcome already?"

She shook her head sadly. "Unfortunately, no. None of my senses are helping here. It's most uncomfortable."

"So good old detective work is still needed occasionally in Camden Grove?"

"Of course. Wouldn't life be boring if we always knew exactly what was coming?"

"Well then, let me get on to the job of collecting all the pieces of information. Thanks for breakfast. And thanks for caring so much. Whether or not anything comes of the time you spend with my girls, I appreciate your wanting to do so." Impulsively, Dane leaned over and kissed her forehead before heading for the door.

As Dane suspected, Harvey was already in and had prepared the coffee.

"What's today's brew, Harvey," he asked.

"We have Tarrazu from Costa Rica. It's made from young beans from the highest mountains of Costa Rica. It's light with little acidity and a distinctive fruity taste."

Dane laughed. "You sound like a walking coffee ad." In an offhanded manner he said, "Something's different about you. What is it? Did you get a haircut?"

Harvey turned red from the neck right up past his trimmed brows to his close-cropped haircut.

"Tell you what; we'll make you a friend for life. Pick Pat up at Mary Johnston's big house at eight with a thermos of hot coffee, black, and a cup, and you will have her eating out of your hand."

"Please don't make me be alone in a car with her. She scares me," Harvey said, screwing his face into look of abject misery.

"Hell, Harvey, she scares us all, but she's the best at what she does and a great friend. Eight, sharp. I have to go over and talk with Wayne Wenzel." Taking a sip of the coffee, he said, "You're right, Harvey, light and fruity without the acid bite."

He walked across the street smiling.

"Seen the paper yet?" Wayne asked when Dane walked in the door.

"Don't tell me; it isn't a positive story, is it?"

"Well, it isn't bad if you like reading about murder, money, and fear in a small town."

"Great. I can't wait to read it. But I actually came for something other than a daily newspaper update," Dane joked.

"How can I help you?"

"First, I need to warn you that *The State* reporter asked questions about a changing of the will and said she had inside information."

"Don't know where it could have come from except from one of us who was there. Legally, any talk is just that—talk. Until the change is made, signed, and filed, talk isn't worth anything."

"Just wanted you to know that I skirted the question but think it will continue to surface until information is more readily available."

"I'll meet with the family whenever Ronnie and Becky want to do it. There are no secrets in this will for the family."

"I know that Harvey got too busy to pick up a listing of those who stand to inherit something. If you don't mind, I'd like to take it with me," Dane said.

Handing Dane a brown envelope, Wayne said, "The list is long."

"You mean that a lot of people are getting something?"

"Yes. Ethel left most of the estate to Ronnie and Becky equally, with money to Robin, Ronnie Junior, Isabelle, and Charlotte Kirk, as we discussed yesterday. Others are designated for particular items."

Dane opened the envelope and glanced at the list inside. There was a full page dedicated to individual jewelry pieces going to a number of women. "I guess there is real jewelry."

"Of course. Ethel had a lot of old pieces, and she wanted to give them to women in town to remember her by. She was a funny one. She put in a stipulation that they each had to say a prayer for her. Don't know why she'd think she needed prayers to help her get into heaven. She was such a good and giving person here, I'm sure she'll go straight on up."

"Mary started to explain purgatory, but instead told me to ask Father Leverette."

"That should be an interesting discussion," Wayne said and laughed. "The good Father can't tell a short story. He'll give you a complete history of purgatory, why one would go there, and how one would get out."

"Do you know how she selected those who will receive a piece of jewelry?" Dane asked.

"Sure. Each of them at some point gave her a piece of homemade jewelry. She loved the pins and such that people made and gave to her."

"Mary told me about the pins. She said Mrs. Bowen treasured each one."

"She did. It touched her that people would take the time to make her something. She really didn't realize how much she did for others. She just saw it as her responsibility."

Dane's phone rang. Looking down at the number, he said, "Excuse me, Wayne, I have to take this call." He pressed the talk button.

"Forrest, good morning."

"No, not particularly. The coroner has released the autopsy report. I've got a copy of it and will fax it right over to you. He's determined that there's absolutely no way it could be a suicide. We officially have a murder on our hands."

"Well, guess that means we have our work cut out for us. I'll give the senator a courtesy call so that he's not blindsided. Harvey's picking Pat up at eight. We need to put together a press conference to release the information. I'll ask Pat to arrange it at the same place as last night. Can we talk to the coroner prior to the press conference?"

"I'll try to arrange it for nine."

"See you then."

"I'll call you back if there is a problem."

Hanging up, Dane said, "I'm going to have to run,"

"Sorry, but I could hear it all. I wish I hadn't expected to hear that it was a murder instead of a suicide. I knew Ethel couldn't have done it herself. This is a sad time for the Bowens and Camden Grove," Wayne said.

"It surely is. Thanks for the list. I'll be back in touch. Two days in a row does a pattern make," Dane said of their early morning meetings. Across the street at his office, Dane found Harvey standing by the fax machine.

"Boss, before you say anything, I didn't tell anyone the stuff that reporter printed in the paper. I didn't even know most of that stuff. It wasn't me. I promise, I haven't said a word to nobody. Nobody," Harvey said, hardly taking a breath.

"Harvey, slow down. I haven't even read the article yet, but I know that you wouldn't say anything. Hell, if Pat talked to me the way she did to you, my lips would be sealed, too. Don't worry. Where is it? I'll read it now," Dane said, accepting the paper from Harvey. He headed toward his office. "Don't forget the coffee when you pick up Pat. It'll help you get in her good graces."

"Can't believe you're gonna make me go get her," Harvey mumbled.

Laughing, Dane spread the paper on his desk. The laughter stopped quickly when he began reading.

Mystery Surrounds Bowen Death
By Sally Anderson

COLUMBIA, S.C. More questions than answers were raised at Tuesday evening's press update regarding the shooting death of Ethel Chapman Bowen of Myrtle Hill Plantation in Camden Grove. Bowen is the mother of South Carolina District 10 State Senator Ronald D. Bowen (D).

Facts provided in an update by Camden Grove Police Chief Dane Hunter and Major Forrest Sikes, director of the Piedmont Region Investigation Services, were sketchy at best; however, they did confirm that Bowen was shot in the head. They wouldn't confirm if murder was suspected, stating that they had to wait for the results of an autopsy being performed yesterday.

When questioned about information from a reliable source that a suspect was in custody, Sikes stated that an individual had been questioned and then held for a period of time on concerns unrelated to Bowen's death. Sources say those concerns included inappropriate sexual activities with minors.

Sources also relay that Bowen was in the process of changing her will, cutting out her children and giving her property and money to the Catholic Church and various charities. Hunter refused to comment on the accuracy of this information, as well as on questions about suspects, including family members.

Preliminary autopsy reports are expected today and may shed light on the mystery surrounding Bowen's death.

Dane knew immediately that information had to come from Forrest's office. Harvey didn't know most of the information attributed to a reliable source. He called Forrest at work, catching him before he left, headed to Camden Grove.

"Dane, I already know what you're going to say, the leak has to be somewhere in my operation, and I know you are partially right. There aren't that many people who know a lot of this information. I'll take care of my hot-head detective who had to be the one to make the comments about inappropriate sexual activities, but you have to remember his daughter was involved, and he has a burr up his butt over it. The part about the will, however, came from somewhere else. Sally Anderson brought it up last night and isn't backing off. Sometimes she's like a dog with a bone. You won't get anywhere trying to get her to tell you her source, so just write it off and move on. If Harvey didn't tell her, we may never know who did."

"We need to get a handle on who knows what and how information is fed to the press. I know we can never stop everything, but remarks like sexual activities with minors can certainly cause long-term embarrassment and potentially other problems for the kids involved."

"I'll talk to my detective."

"I'll see you when you get here. I'm sure Pat will have some comments, but overall, the article was pretty accurate. I was going to call the senator to let him know what's going on, but I think I'll wait for you and Pat to be here. Oh, by the way, we also had an incident last night. People are a bit jumpy and one of our residents heard something outside her bedroom window and opened fire. Luckily, no one was hurt, but we'll need to address safety again at tonight's meeting."

"Sounds like a plan. I'll be there by a quarter of nine, and we'll have a few minutes before Jimmy Johnson arrives. He's normally late everywhere," Forrest said.

Pat and Harvey came in shortly after Dane hung up, joking with each other. When Pat walked into his office, Dane raised an eyebrow in question.

Pat reacted immediately saying, "I can forgive anything when a man picks me up bearing coffee as good as the coffee Harvey brought me this morning. Anything else he needs to know, I can teach him."

With a chuckle Dane asked, "So, how's the house?"

"Oh, my God! I could get used to living like that. I wandered around this morning, and it's unbelievable. You have to take me home this evening before dark, and you and Joan have to explore with me. If it weren't in the middle of nowhere South Carolina, I'd probably be begging to stay here, but alas, I'm a city girl through and through."

Dane laughed and said, "Okay, down to business. We're going to have a press conference at ten regarding the autopsy report. Suicide is out. The coroner, Dr. Jimmy Johnson, will be joining us. I have a copy of the entire preliminary report, and you have a few minutes to get settled. You may also want to read *The State* article. Once Forrest gets here, we're going to have to call the senator so that he isn't blindsided by any information released today. Oh, Harvey didn't leak any of the information Sally Anderson put in that article. He didn't know parts of it, and you have him totally afraid to speak out of school."

"Afraid of little me?" Pat asked innocently, getting another chuckle out of Dane.

"Not buying it, Lambe," Dane said. "And also get Harvey to tell you about last night's shoot-out. We'll need to include that in our remarks."

"I've already heard the whole story. I'm on it." Pat went to the outer office and began reading and drafting up a press release, along with orchestrating questions to make sure all were prepared.

When Forrest arrived, the three talked briefly before placing a call to the senator.

Ronnie answered his cell phone immediately. "Bowen."

"Senator, Dane Hunter here. I have Major Sikes and Pat Lambe with me, and you're on speaker phone."

"Good morning, Forrest and Pat. How are y'all doing?"

"Fine, Ronnie. I'm really sorry about Ethel," Forrest said.

"I appreciate that. Still can't believe she's gone."

"Senator," Dane began, "we have the preliminary autopsy report, and we wanted to talk with you before it is released at ten a.m. today. Dr. Johnson will be with us at the press update. Bottom line, the report indicates that it couldn't have been a suicide, so we officially begin a murder investigation today."

"I appreciate the call. Pat, have you spoken with Jeff Price?"

"No, I haven't, but I think it might be wise to talk with him about a statement from you for release today. I'll prepare a general press release about the autopsy report, but I think your office should also release a prepared statement."

"Any advice you can give him is much appreciated. Seems like picking up the paper has me learning something new each time. Any idea how Sally Anderson got hold of the information she wrote today?"

Forrest answered, "I believe one of my detectives probably made the statement about Steve Adams and sexual misconduct. It appears his daughter may have been involved, along with your son, senator."

"What?" Ronnie asked.

Dane replied, "Senator, you may want to ask your son before you hear it anywhere else."

Forrest guiltily raised his hands into the air.

"Great," Ronnie said. "Something else to hit the news, I presume."

"I can assure you that no more information will come out of my office," Forrest said.

"Forrest, I'm not asking for any special privileges. If information is pertinent to this case and would normally be given out, do it. If it's something that would not normally be given out, I certainly hope it's treated the same way, despite my position or candidacy. I'm not sure exactly what the sexual comments are, but Ronnie Junior is sixteen. I don't believe he should be subjected to anything in the press just because of me."

"I agree, Senator," Forrest said.

Dane added, "Senator, we don't know where the other information is coming from. No one here has spoken about a possible change in your mother's will. Sally Anderson brought it up last night, and as you read, I didn't comment."

"Well, Sally certainly has sources of her own," Ronnie mused, "so there's no telling where she got her information, and she is known to be very pro-Republican in everything she does. I'll just have to weather this storm."

"Senator, we have to prepare for the press update. If you have any questions, please feel free to call us," Dane said.

"I will actually want to discuss this in detail, along with what it all means," Ronnie replied.

"I'll talk with Dr. Johnson and set up a time when we can all meet. I have a few interviews to fit in today. Would late afternoon work for you?" Dane asked.

"I'll make it work. Text me the time. Thanks, all."

Harvey stuck his head in the door and said, "Boss, I got the first part of the crime board up in the back room, if ya want to see it."

Dane, Forrest, and Pat all followed Harvey and found the wall covered by a pull-down screen. "I thought we needed to have a way to keep it covered from prying eyes, so I put up an old screen we had in storage," Harvey said. Harvey raised the screen and then a flap covering the center of the board.

Both Dane and Forrest whistled, and Pat said, "Harvey, if the photos weren't so gruesome, this would be a work of art."

Photos from the crime scene were in the center of the board. Below it was a box labeled, in beautifully executed block letters, "Dinner Guests." Within that box were individual cards for each guest that had a photo of the individual in the case of Wayne, Senator and Mrs. Bowen, and a mug shot for Steve Adams. Each of the others had a place for a photo. On the card it had the name, and below it, separate lines labeled and filled out to the best of Harvey's knowledge, Name, Motive, Alibi, Alibi Confirmation. Harvey had filled in each box as far as he could with Dane's notes. Off to the left side, was another box labeled Crime Scene Fingerprints, with three labeled cards labeled Ronnie Jr., Steve Adams, and Nathan Web. Under the name were blocks labeled, Where Prints Found, Alibi, Alibi Confirmation. There were three other boxes, one to the left and two to the right, ready to be labeled. On the top there were blocks for the Coroner's Report, Significant Events/Timeline, and Important Observations.

Forrest said, "Harvey, I can honestly say that I've never seen a crime board executed this well. When we finish with this investigation, I hope you and Dane will let me take photos of the finished product to show my team how to do it right. In fact, if you take a daily snapshot we can show it as the case develops."

Harvey beamed.

"Good work, Harvey. Two things, how about you make me a duplicate of each of the suspect cards that I can carry with me and put together a file with all the reports, pictures, and anything else we collect on this case. I like to keep a complete file I can take with me if I need to—or can carry home. I would also like you, Pat, and me to start each day with discussing the updates that need to be made," Dane said as they heard the front door open and knew Dr. Johnson had arrived.

Back in Dane's office, the group began discussing the update and what would be said. While they hadn't had much time to prepare, Pat drafted a press release that included generic autopsy results. Jim Johnson approved the content. Pat worked on it up until it was time for them to leave, leaving Harvey to make copies and deliver them before the end of the session. When they arrived at the church, even more people filled the social hall than had been present the previous evening. Word spreads fast in a small town.

Promptly at ten, Pat opened the update session. "Good morning. For those of you who were not here last night, I'm Pat Lambe, and I am serving as the point of contact for the Camden Grove Police Department for all media inquiries concerning the death of Ethel Bowen. I apologize for the shortness of the notice for this update, however, we were informed this morning that preliminary autopsy results were available that will influence the course of this investigation and wanted to get you the information as quickly as possible. Dr. Jim Johnson, Greenwood County coroner, has joined us this morning to provide an overview of the autopsy report. We'll have a prepared press release available on the back table by the end of this session.

"This session will be conducted in the same fashion as the one last night. Dr. Johnson, Police Chief Dane Hunter, and Major Forrest Sikes, the director of the Piedmont Region Investigative Services, will speak and then we'll open the floor for questions. Dr. Johnson," Pat stepped away from the lectern to allow room for the doctor to step up.

"Good morning. An autopsy was performed yesterday on Ethel Chapman Bowen of Myrtle Hill Plantation to determine the time and cause of death. This medical examination proved to be especially challenging because there were three competing traumas, each of which could have been the cause of death: a gunshot wound to the head, terminal pancreatic cancer, and an apparent overdose of morphine. Let me begin with the cancer.

"Mrs. Bowen was in what is best described as phase IV pancreatic cancer. This is the most advanced stage and means that cancer has spread from a tumor in the pancreas to nearby organs, including the small intestine, surrounding lymph nodes, the stomach, spleen, colon, and also to distant sites, including the liver and lungs. There is evidence that Mrs.

Bowen had undergone a number of therapies in relation to her cancer, including surgery, radiation, and chemotherapy. We are in the process of confirming all our information. It is normal to employ a combination of therapies to relieve patients' symptoms and enhance their quality of life in the final stages of the disease. When used this way, these therapies are palliative, meaning that they are not expected to cure the cancer, but are used to relieve pain.

"Pain relief is provided in a ladder that starts with aspirin and other nonsteroidal anti-inflammatory drugs and elevates to continuous doses of narcotics, normally morphine and or Hydromorphone, to control the pain when it intensifies in the final stages of the disease. I estimate that Mrs. Bowen would have most likely died from cancer-related causes within a matter of weeks.

"With all the issues, it was, however, the trauma to the head from a bullet that caused Mrs. Bowen to die between twelve and twelve-thirty Monday morning."

Dr. Johnson looked out at a room of faces that were registering the shock of all the facts they had been given. He completed his prepared statement. "Suicide has been categorically ruled out because the amount of morphine in her system would have made it impossible for Mrs. Bowen to commit an act of violence herself."

Dane followed Jim at the lectern. "The facts outlined by Dr. Johnson have an immediate and direct impact on the course of our investigation into what has now been determined to be a murder case. I've nothing to add to my statements from last night at this time. We'll continue gathering information and conducting interviews that will help us discover what happened Sunday night at Myrtle Hill Plantation. You have my assurance that we'll pursue every lead in our attempt to complete this investigation and apprehend the perpetrator as swiftly as possible. Major Sikes, do you have anything to add?"

Standing, Forrest said, "Not at this time, Chief Hunter, except that my office stands ready to assist you in any way possible to solve this crime."

Pat came to the microphone and said, "Questions?"

"Do you have the murder weapon?" John Porter asked.

Forrest took the question. "Yes, we do. It was a thirty-eight caliber special with wooden handles and a two-inch barrel found at the scene of the crime. It was a gun owned by Mrs. Bowen."

"Where was it found?"

"It was in the victim's hand," Forrest answered.

Stephanie Polk asked, "Were there any fingerprints on the gun?"

"Only those of the victim," Forrest responded.

"Is there a leading suspect?" Kathryn Blanchard asked.

"No," Dane responded. "As discussed last evening, we are still in the preliminary information-gathering phase. Now that we know it wasn't a suicide, we'll approach the investigation appropriately."

Sally Anderson asked, "Does Senator Bowen know it is now being considered a murder?"

"We talked with the senator prior to coming here," Dane answered.

"Is it likely that a total stranger was responsible?" Sally asked.

"In my experience, and according to national statistics, random homicides are rare. In most cases you'll find some kind of connection between the victim and the perpetrator," Dane replied.

Sally pushed, "Is the senator a suspect?"

"I will be having discussions with Senator Bowen just as I will with any- and everyone else who may have any information that will help us resolve this case."

Mary stood. "Could Ethel have known what was happening to her when she was shot?"

Dr. Johnson replied, "With the amount of medication she had in her system, there is no way she'd have been aware of what was going on in the room around her."

"Could she have felt the pain of the gunshot?" another voice asked.

"No," Dr. Johnson said.

Sally Anderson again stood and said, "Last night I asked about a potential change in the will, and you avoided the question. Now that murder is a certainty, will you answer the following questions? One, do you have any knowledge of a change in the will? Two, if so, does a potential change make any members of the family likely suspects?"

"Ms. Anderson," Dane began, "this is a very sensitive case and it's not appropriate to answer your questions at this time."

"In refusing to answer questions like that, would you say that you are giving Senator Bowen special consideration because of his position and because he is running for governor?" Sally asked.

"Absolutely not," Dane fired back. "What I'm saying is that we have what looks to be a murder of a very prominent and influential woman. She happens to have a politically prominent son, as well. I will not rush to a solution or divulge any information that may unduly influence a fair, honest, and complete investigation. If, while in pursuit of the truth, the senator or any member of the family, or any friend, or any acquaintance, is needed to provide information to resolve this case, they will all be treated fairly and equally. If I obtain evidence that indicates any individual might have been involved in this act of violence, I'll pursue his or her testimony to the extent that the laws and my authority will allow, so I can provide all facts to the appropriate authorities to prosecute this case. I cut no special deals. Let me challenge you, Ms. Anderson, to deal with the issues of this case as fairly, honestly, and in as unbiased a manner in your writing as I'm going to do in my investigation."

Dane saw Sally start to turn red and knew that he had probably made his first enemy in South Carolina.

"Let me also address the facts about last night's shooting in town. There were, luckily, no injuries, but a resident was frightened by noises outside her window and fired her gun," Dane began.

John Ackerman, sitting in the middle of the room, interrupted Dane. "Teri 'bout near killed me and Everette. Don't know what he found under her bushes, but he didn't want to come when I called. Bullets flying scared the both of us to death, Teri."

Teri turned red and put her head down.

"Good thing you can't shoot for crap. But I want you to know I had to go home and change my knickers, and Everette hasn't done his business yet today," John said as the room erupted in laughter.

"The point is," Dane said as the mirth subsided, "that many people may be on edge. So think about that when you take late night walks. If you hear or see anything out of the ordinary, call us. We will respond. Don't take the law into your own hands."

Pat brought the meeting to a close, reminding people that additional copies of information regarding safety and security that provided the previous evening were available on the back table, along with the most current press releases.

Sally was the first one to corner Dane. "Chief Hunter, I resent your remarks and your implication that my reporting is biased, and I take these allegations very personally."

"Ms. Anderson, I'm an officer of the law and a believer in freedom of the press, however, in reading your article this morning, I was surprised to see that you wrote and your paper published unconfirmed allegations, alluded to inappropriate behavior with minors, made vague insinuations about a political candidate, and attributed your facts to a 'reliable witness.' In my humble opinion, in an effort to make a political statement, you came dangerously close to crossing the line and compromising my investigation. And, Ms. Anderson, I take that very personally. I've pledged to give all the information I can give without jeopardizing any portion of my investigation. You can count on my doing that, and I hope that you'll work with me to get to the truth without further confusing an already difficult case with rumor, innuendo, and political intrigue."

"Well, I never," Sally said and turned and stormed off. In her wake, Pat said, "And it shows, honey."

B ack at the office, Dane looked at the list of people he needed to talk with before his late afternoon meeting with the senator and decided to speak with Father Leverette first, if possible, Charlotte Kirk second, and Doug Reed last. He knew he would probably need to talk with Becky Bowen, also, but left that decision for later. He called and set up the appointments. Father Leverette agreed to a meeting within the half hour at the rectory. He made plans with Pat and Harvey to have lunch together at Lucy's Café to discuss next steps.

When Father Leverette answered the Rectory door, he was exactly what Dane expected from his voice. In his early fifties, the father was dressed in black pants, black shoes, and a black shirt with the white clerical collar. His white hair was thin on top, his complexion ruddy, his eyes a piercing blue, and his welcoming smile genuine.

"So good to finally meet you, Chief Hunter. I knew that events would eventually bring you to my door, since Ethel was such a big part of the church here in Camden Grove. I'm going to miss her sorely," Father Leverette said as he walked with Dane into his library and indicated chairs that faced each other for their conversation. "She made my job much easier by the example she set every day. On the personal front, a priest couldn't find someone more ready to help, no matter what the chore, or more of a friend. To boot, I'm definitely going to miss her regular Sunday dinner invitations. As you can probably tell, I love good food," the father said deprecatingly, "and Sunday dinner at Ethel's was the best. Isabelle is one great cook. Ethel and I had the most wonderful debates over dinner. Would you like some coffee or tea? I'm afraid that's about the extent of my culinary capabilities, but I do have a cake to offer. One of my parishioners made it for me."

Dane smiled. "Thanks, but nothing for me."

Father Leverette said, "I know, constant flow of dialogue. Living alone does that to you. When I have a captive audience, I love to talk."

"That's going to make this a lot easier, because I want to know more about Mrs. Bowen, her state of mind, and what she'd been thinking about. The best way to get that information is from people who knew her, cared about her, and spent time with her."

"I read in this morning's paper about people thinking she was changing her will to leave her property to the Catholic Church and much of her money to charities. While I can assure you she loves the church and would do anything to help, Myrtle Hill is not something she'd have given away. She considered the plantation a sacred trust of which she was the temporary trustee, responsible for passing it to the next generation of Chapman/Bowen offspring in the shape as good as or better than when she had inherited it. As long as there is Chapman blood flowing in someone's veins, that property will be in the family. And I can tell you, too, that the topic never even came up in any discussion we ever had. Contrary to what many people think, the church does not give us a quota of property to gather. I'm not Richard Chamberlain's character from *Thornbirds*, about to be elevated in the church hierarchy if I can bring in a big land holding," the father joked.

"More what I'd like to understand from you is her thoughts about her religion. From all accounts, she was strong in her beliefs. From the beginning, everyone has told me that she would have never have committed suicide, no matter what."

"Technically, you're correct, and Ethel and I actually had that very debate some months ago. On the surface, as a Catholic, a person would not take his or her own life because scriptures teach us that suicide is unlawful. Ethel had done her homework and pointed out, rightfully, that the church does have some loopholes."

"Loopholes?" Dane asked.

"Ethel debated that there are times when taking one's own life could be considered permissible and even an act of virtue."

"I don't think I understand."

"Most people, even those raised Catholic, wouldn't. Basically, we're taught that people are not bound to preserve their lives by employing remedies that would be considered extraordinary. For example, if someone is very sick, he or she does not have to accept a painful treatment, surgery, or a treatment that's untested. As an old-school Catholic, Ethel also argued that there were circumstances where exposing yourself to death, when it will not necessarily shorten your life but will help others, is a good thing. In that case, the death could be considered permissible and even an act of virtue if it helps others. In these instances, the act becomes a venial rather than a mortal sin."

"Well, thankfully at this point we know that Mrs. Bowen couldn't have taken her own life, so I probably don't really need to understand this. But what do you make of her desire to debate it?"

"We debated many things over the years, but this one seemed to be really on her mind. Ethel had been traveling a lot of late and told me she was just tired. I believed she was more than tired. I've had a lot of experience with people who are sick and feared the course of their disease. They struggle with many thoughts during that time. I believed that when she was ready to discuss it with me, she would. I didn't press her. Ethel liked to come to things in her own time. I'm most bothered that she didn't come to me of late, that she didn't confess her sins as she always had in the past."

"Your intuition is good. We've found that Mrs. Bowen had terminal pancreatic cancer and would have probably died within a few weeks, had she not been shot. What makes it more difficult is that she also had enough morphine in her system to cause her death, but the gunshot is what actually killed her. According to the coroner, there's no way she could've shot herself. From others I have already talked with it appears that her afterlife was a real concern for her. Enough so that she took steps in her will to make sure people will pray for her to shorten her time in purgatory," Dane said.

"That would be our Ethel. She'd had the sins drilled into her as a youth. She had no doubt that when she died, she'd depart life in God's grace, but also knew that she wouldn't be entirely free from venial sins or have not fully paid the satisfaction due for her transgressions here on earth."

"You're over my head again, Father. In terms I will understand?" Dane said, smiling.

"The church teaches that a punishment is due for sin, even after the sin itself has been pardoned by God. Throughout the Bible, there are cases where God forgave men for their disobedience, but still punished them. A good example is that while God forgave Moses for not believing, he punished him by preventing him from going into the land of promise. The church has always taught that where people work off their punishment is purgatory. Basically, purgatory is the place where the soul is purified before going into the presence of God. Catholics believe that souls in purgatory are not separated from the church, and that the love of those in the church should also be given to those who have died in God's grace and that our prayers and our sacrifices can help those who are still waiting in purgatory. If they are to die conscious of an imperfection that they have no time to correct, they know that there are others who are able to make intercessions on their behalf."

"Can you think of anyone who might want to end Mrs. Bowen's life?"

"Absolutely not. In all the years I have known her, as a member of my parish and as a friend, she's been one of the kindest, most giving people I've ever encountered. She had a tremendously agile mind and wit, strong convictions, and a desire to do good. She was one who had a lot to give and didn't stint in the giving. And I'm not just talking about material gifts. She did much behind the scenes to help people realize their dreams, to ease suffering, and to improve their quality of life. I can't imagine that there is anyone who knew her who could've ever caused her harm."

"Father, I don't have any other questions right now," Dane said. "I appreciate your time this morning. While I don't think I'm any closer to a solution, you've given me information that helps me put into perspective some of the thoughts and statements made in other interviews. I haven't talked with her family about the funeral arrangements yet, but I assume that you'll be performing the services."

"Ronnie contacted me this morning, and we'll be having the service on Friday. Ethel will, of course, be buried at Myrtle Hill next to her husband and parents. All Chapmans have been buried on the land since they've owned it."

"That's good to know. Thanks again for taking time to see me on such short notice. Any words of wisdom for me as I work this case?"

"I wouldn't know where to begin except that in a town this size, someone knows just about everything that goes on. That person may not know what they know, but I'm sure you'll sort it all out. I wouldn't want to be in your shoes right now, though. Talk about the proverbial hot seat! If I can help in any way, you know how to reach me."

"I appreciate that and will take you up on it," Dane said, standing and walking with the father to the front door. The two shook hands and Father Leverette opened the door and let Dane out.

Pat and Harvey were both ready for lunch by the time Dane returned to the office. Harvey locked the office door and they walked the three doors down to Lucy's Café. Dane opened the door for Pat and Harvey to go in, and as he stepped in Lucy came rushing toward them, reaching a chubby hand to grab Dane's hand saying, "Sweetie, it's about time you walked those famous dimples into Lucy's!"

Every head in the café swiveled and showed amused, welcoming smiles. Pat laughed as Dane turned red. "And you, Ms. Lambe, every bit as chic and metropolitan as Mary said you were. And you looked great on TV, the camera really loves you. The local boys wouldn't know how to handle you, especially since you are already a legend after the tales of the makeover you have done on our Harvey spread," Lucy said with a smile across her broad face, winking lasciviously at the quickly reddening officer. "You do look delicious," she cooed at Harvey.

Everyone within hearing laughed at Harvey's discomfort, and Pat put her arm protectively through his as Lucy led them to an empty table.

"Here at Lucy's you'll get the best home cooking in town. Oh wait, you'll get the only cooking outside the home unless you want Dairy Queen. We're the only dining establishments within a five-mile radius of downtown," Lucy grinned. "Let me tell you your options," she drawled. "Today is Wednesday, so your meat choices are either fried chicken, and darlin's, its real fried chicken, not fast food," Lucy said winking at Dane, or meatloaf in tomato gravy. It's yummy. You get your choice of one meat and two sides for six ninety-nine. The sides are on the board over there," Lucy said pointing toward the cash register. And save room for my deluxe pecan pie. It's got brandy and cream in it and is to die for, if I say so myself.

"Now if you're one of those vegetarians, Lord love ya, you can pick any four veggies for four ninety-nine. If you don't want a full meal, you have four sandwich choices, chicken, tuna, or egg salad, or Lucy's Big BLT. All come with fries. If you can only handle a salad, we have the chicken popper salad today, full or half. Harvey, I know what you want. Pat, Dane, what'll it be?

"It all sounds lovely," Pat observed, "but I can assure that the collard greens, okra, and beets will never pass my lips. I think I'll go with the BLT, without the lettuce, and just a hint of bacon. No fries."

"Darlin', I don't see a ring on your finger, and if you don't put some meat on those bones, pretty as you are, you aren't going to attract a real man. Men like a little cush for the push, not pickin' bones, right Dane?" Lucy said, winking.

Throwing up his hands in mock horror, laughing, Dane said, "I'm staying out of this conversation.

"Smart man!" Pat replied, adding without missing a beat, "and Lucy, where I'm from, the men prefer 'pickin' bones,' though I'm not revealing if mine are being picked or not."

"I think she looks mighty fine just the way she is," Harvey injected before embarrassment caught up.

"Thank you," Pat said, reaching across and patting his hand.

Everyone in the small café laughed. They were all hanging on every word.

Dane ordered the popper salad, much to Lucy's horror, claiming the few extra pounds he was carrying and the promise of a big dinner called for caution.

Still chuckling, Lucy walked off to get their orders going.

Waiting for their food, the three talked quietly about what they would do during the afternoon. Dane was setting interviews with Charlotte and Doug, and potentially would try to meet up with the senator. Pat was going to review all the files and any press coverage and see if they had anything for an updated, late afternoon press release.

"Harvey, while I'm running around on this case, I'm counting on you to keep all normal activities running smoothly and assisting Pat if she needs anything." Dane said.

"You can count on me, boss!"

Lunch came, and Dane eyed Harvey's massive lunch, jealous that Harvey could stay rail thin, while he would gain three pounds if he were eating that lunch. With a sigh, he stuck his fork into his salad.

Finishing up, Dane paid, they said their goodbyes to Lucy, and assured her she would see them again soon. Walking back to the office, Dane asked, "Are we on for dinner tonight? We want to see the house."

"We're on as long as you're bringing it. Don't expect me to cook in that house. I'd have to shop for everything. I don't know where anything is, and it would be a disaster."

Laughing, Dane said, "We'll cover dinner. I'll talk with you later today. I have my last appointment at five. Let's the three of us meet up at 5:45. That means six-thirty for dinner. It will still be light."

Back in his car, Dane called Charlotte Kirk and told her he was on his out to see her. When he pulled up to the house, she was sitting on the porch swing and got up, walking to meet him near the car.

"Becky is napping, so let's talk over in the garden chairs. I don't want to disturb her; she had a bad night."

After sitting, Dane began, "Ms. Kirk, yesterday I received an anonymous letter that said you had a criminal record. Last night, I received a copy of a report that basically outlined your prison time for killing your husband."

She sat looking at Dane, not saying a word.

"I'm wondering why you didn't think to tell me about this."

"You're talking about someone else's life. Things happened to someone I used to be. I took matters into my own hands, paid the price for my actions, did my time, and when I walked out of that prison, it was behind me. I don't think about it, and certainly didn't realize that anytime anything happened in a place where I live, I'd have to step forward and tell everyone about a woman who I no longer know."

"You don't have to tell everyone; however, I need you to tell me. You were tried and convicted of killing your husband. You shot him in the head while he slept in the bedroom you shared. I read your file, but I don't have the court records, so I don't know the circumstances. I assume that some sort of fight was involved."

"I'm sorry, Chief Hunter, but you don't know anything. If you're assuming that because I killed once I would kill again, I again say you don't know anything. Did I kill my husband? Absolutely, yes, I did. We were married for five years. During that time I was regularly beaten to within an inch of my life because the house wasn't clean enough, the meal wasn't tasty enough, I wasn't smart enough or pretty enough or sexy enough. I was never enough. If you review my medical records, during that five years, I fell a lot, breaking arms too many times to remember, breaking my nose, my jaw, my foot, my ribs, getting numerous black eyes and burns from scalding water, and although people said, 'I know your husband must have done this to you,' no one ever stepped in to help me. I was isolated from friends and family. They knew my husband couldn't stand them, so after a while, they just stayed away.

"On the night I shot him, I was five months pregnant. Don't ask me why, but I wanted that child. Not because of him, but because I needed something that I could love and protect. Part of me knew even then that I couldn't protect myself, so how could I ever protect a child? But I wanted that child just the same.

"I was particularly ugly that day, and he was drunk, so the beating was bad. He hit me on the right side of my face with a bat. I think he didn't really mean to, because he had scared me many times before, by swinging at me and stopping just before he made contact. He had been drinking so much that his space perception was off and he connected, breaking my jaw. I covered my face and fell to the ground, and that so incensed him that he began hitting me on the back and shoulders. When he got tired of that, he kicked me. He killed my baby that night and made sure I would never be able to conceive another. When he was finished beating me and kicking me, he was so tired that he went to bed, leaving me lying on that floor.

"I finally got up, and I knew my baby was dead. I knew. So I got his gun. The same one he had often threatened me with by holding it to my head and pulling the trigger. I never knew if he'd put a bullet in it or not. Can you imagine what it felt like to hear that click, not knowing if it was the last sound you would ever hear?"

Dane watched Charlotte intently as she told her story matter-of-factly, detached from the horror of it.

"Well, I made sure the gun was loaded, and I sat by the bed while he slept. Just before dawn I decided it was time. I got a glass of cold water and threw it in his face. While he sputtered, I shot him in the groin for giving me my baby and then his foot for taking it away. Then I shot his hand that hit me and then took my sweet time with the gun pointed at his head. I shot him in the chest to finish the pain he had caused me. I shot every part of him that offended me. After all of that, I sat and looked at him for a while. He wasn't nearly as scary as he had been.

"I called the police and sat at the kitchen table waiting for them to come. I was arrested and tried, and though everyone felt sorry for all I had been through, they said the violence of the crime required that I serve some time. I went to prison. After four years, I was released. I had a nursing degree, but try to get hired at a hospital with a record. Even though I'd served my time, people don't want to let you forget it.

Sitting up straighter and looking Dane in the eyes, Charlotte reengaged with the present. "Then an extraordinary woman came to see me. She had a daughter, she said, who had been a victim one horrible night and was not able to recover from it. She couldn't keep the demons away, and she needed constant supervision. She offered me the job because, she said, she knew that I would understand what it was like to feel helpless, but that I also had overcome that helplessness to reclaim my life. She thought what I'd learned could be used to help her daughter take the journey she needed to take without violence to others.

"Since that day, I've spent every precious moment here in Camden Grove, living in this house, and thanking my lucky stars that an angel named Ethel Chapman Bowen gave me a new life, allowing me to put the past behind me. Mrs. Bowen was shot, but nothing in my thought process connected her shooting with the person I once was. Now, here we sit, and I assume you're saying to yourself, she shot her husband in the head, perhaps she shot Mrs. Bowen in the head. If she could do it once, could she do it again?"

"No," Dane said, "that's not what's going through my head. Like I said, I don't have the details of what happened to you, only that you'd shot your husband. Your story is a horrible one. I can never understand how a man could do what your husband did to you, but I can understand how you could finally reach the point where you fought back. Why I'm here has nothing to do with that, but everything to do with not knowing about it before getting an anonymous tip," he said with conviction

Charlotte's and Dane's conversation was so intense that neither heard Becky approach, but she stood before them, hands on her hips. "If you think she would shoot Mother for me, you're sadly mistaken, Chief

Hunter," Becky said. "She has always said that you have to face those things that haunt you and are out of your control, always without violence. She's told me all she should have done, but didn't have the courage to do. I have no courage. On the night Mother died, I came home very upset. Not about Myrtle Hill or the money, but because I didn't know if my house would be taken away from me. I felt helpless again. Something bad could happen, and I didn't know what to do to prevent it. I told Charlotte everything that had happened. She fixed me dinner and then told me to sleep on it; everything would look different in the morning, and we would see where we were. She gave me my pill to make me sleep. I take pills for everything, you know. Pills to go to sleep, pills to wake up. Pills to give me energy, pills to make me forget. Pills to lift my spirits, pills to stop the voices. Pills, pills, pills. So Charlotte gave me pills to go to sleep, and I pretended to take them.

"When she went to sleep, I called Doug to come and talk to me. It got stormy while he was here, and he told me not to worry, everything would be okay. When he left, I danced in my garden in the rain, and then Charlotte came out of the darkness and found me, and we went into the house together. When I woke up, I knew Mother was gone, and then you and Doug came over."

"I have to ask you both, did either of you have anything to do with Mrs. Bowen's death?"

Both women shook their heads. Dane didn't know what else to say at that time. He thanked them, left them in the garden, went to his car, turned the key and just sat for a minute. He turned on the radio to the classical station for some quiet background. No matter what people said, he could never become hardened to the tales of horrible events. He could remember the details of everyone he had ever investigated. The music helped him process so he wouldn't take the sadness to the next appointment. He backed around and drove down the driveway, and headed into town for his next interview wondering what new revelation his talk with Doug Reed would produce.

"Reverend Reed," Dane said, when Doug opened the door.

"Reverend sounds awfully formal, Dane."

"Well, I'm here in my official capacity to talk with Reverend Doug Reed, who evidently withheld information from me when I talked with him previously," Dane said.

Doug looked down, not making eye contact. "When we first talked, Dane, I had no idea what events would unfold. I didn't even think to tell you I'd talked with Becky the night before. Then there was no easy way to bring it up," Doug explained.

"Right now, that doesn't matter. What does is that we need to be straight. I have an anonymous letter that merely states, 'The pastor has quite a past and is tied to Becky Bowen. You might want to see where the two of them were when the murder occurred.'"

"You've got to be kidding," Doug exclaimed.

"No, not kidding. When talking with Charlotte Kirk, Ms. Bowen let the bomb drop that you were with her when Charlotte thought she was sleeping, and after you left, she danced in the storm. That puts you around Myrtle Hill near the time of Mrs. Bowen's death. That definitely gets my attention. I didn't say anything when you accompanied me to inform Ms. Bowen of her mother's death, but I sensed then that there was more to your relationship than met the eye. Is there something you need to tell me about?" Dane asked.

"Please come in. Let's not have this conversation on the porch." Doug led Dane into his living room, where they sat. "I told you briefly that day that Becky has not been herself since she was twenty-one. What I didn't tell you was that she and I had been dating while she was attending Columbia College for Women. We were in the wrong place at the wrong time on a Friday night in her senior year. We went to an isolated location to make out. There was a group of young men who pulled in and backed their car up behind mine, blocking me in before they began harassing us.

"Tough guy that I was, I didn't want to back down, even though there were five of them. I ended up getting overpowered, beaten up, and forced to watch as some awful things happened to Becky. I was hurt and had a couple of broken bones, but that was minor, compared to the emotional trauma of watching what they did, knowing I was powerless to help her. She never recovered from that night, but she said that the only way she got through it was by looking in my eyes. I never wavered then, trying to tell her that we would survive. Well, we did survive, each in our own way. Believe it or not, she still counts on me when she's in trouble, and I drop whatever I'm doing when she needs me."

"Why did she call you that night?" Dane asked.

"She was afraid that she would lose her house and not have money to live. She said the same things to us the next day when we went out there."

"What did you tell her?"

"I told her that everything would be okay, not to worry about anything, nothing would happen to take her little house away from her."

"Why would you say that?"

"How could I let her worry? I knew Ethel would always make sure Becky was looked after and safe. I'd planned to talk with Ethel the next day," Doug said.

"What time did you leave Miss Bowen?"

"I guess about a quarter to twelve."

"Where did you go?"

"I just rode around for a while and then came home and went to bed."

"Your ride didn't take you past Myrtle Hill, did it?"

"If you're asking if I went to confront Ethel that night, the answer is no. I didn't."

"Did you have anything to do with Mrs. Bowen's death?"

"Are you seriously asking me this question?"

"You said you are always there to protect Becky. How far does your protection go?"

Doug clenched his jaw. "Well, certainly not to murder, if that's what you're implying."

"I'm not implying anything. I'm just gathering information. I don't know everyone's history. That's a disadvantage, because I don't know how to react to information when it is parsed out to me. You've put things into a different perspective. All I can do is follow every lead right now and try to gather every piece of this puzzle."

"I understand that, but am I also to understand that I'm now a suspect?"

"I'm not ready to say that I have any suspects, but I will say that your connections and your visit that night put another puzzle piece on the table. Whether it fits or doesn't, I don't know yet."

"It was never my intent to mislead you," Doug said. "Some things are just very difficult to share with people."

"What happened to the five men?" Dane asked.

"Someone else evidently witnessed it and made an anonymous call to the police. Police came too late to save us from the nightmares, but in time to catch the men in the act. Harold and Ethel pulled every connection to make sure the case didn't become public and that the five plead guilty and ended up with twenty-year sentences in prison."

"That would be about eighteen years ago, right?" Dane observed.

"You don't think..."

"I think I'll have to find out. I appreciate your telling me today," Dane said, sticking out his hand to shake Doug's, not wanting to leave with the awkwardness between them that might later be insurmountable.

As he left, his cell phone rang. It was Mary. "Would you mind terribly stopping by my house on your way home?" she asked.

"Of course not. What's up?"

"Just a feeling I have that I'd like to discuss with you."

"How about I come now? I've got a little time before I have to be back at the office."

"That would be great."

When he arrived, he could tell she sensed that he was not himself.

"Tough day?" she asked.

"I'm just surprised that residents of a town this small could have experienced so much pain. I am having trouble shaking off what I heard today."

"There are five types of people in Camden Grove," Mary responded. "Those who live here because they can't imagine living anywhere else; those who live their whole life here because they're afraid to try anything else; those who can't wait to leave, and once they do, will never look back; those who leave and come back when they fail or need to heal, and there's a whole lot of healing that goes on in Camden Grove; and finally, those who come here for reasons that aren't always clear, even to themselves at the time. I fall into the first category of people. I can't imagine life anywhere but here. You, my friend, fall into the last. Many reasons brought you here; you have a long way to go to know why you'll stay. That brings me back to the reason for my call. I told you before that I often have feelings but don't know the details. My mother always said, 'Trouble comes in threes.' I sense more trouble is coming, and for some reason I sense that part of that trouble revolves around you. I don't know what it is, but it's serious. I just want to make sure you take some common precautions."

"That just makes the hair on the back of my neck stand up. Is that the best you can do? What precautions should I be taking?"

"I'm sorry, but that's all I have right now. If I get a better sense, you know I'll call you."

"I do, and I'm not trying to be flippant, but I'm in the middle of a murder investigation, and the last thing I need to be doing is looking over my shoulder."

"I know, but I just felt I had to say something. You'll know if you need to do anything with the information."

"Okay. Well, for now, I'm heading back to the office to set up another round of interviews for tomorrow, then there's a funeral on Friday, and the pressure continues to mount." Dane could tell Mary felt awkward about what she told him, but didn't know how to ease the feelings.

Back at the office, Dane postponed the meeting with the senator and called Forrest to get him or his team to help run down the five men who should still be in prison for what they had done to Becky and Doug.

Dane, Harvey, and Pat talked in the back room about the two interviews. Dane suggested that Harvey add Charlotte Kirk and Doug Reed, along with the five prisoners Forrest was checking on to one of the empty boxes on the crime board.

"On the facts column, I think we need to highlight the three potential causes of death instead of just focusing on the gunshot," Dane said. "The cancer we can just let ride, but I want to make sure there is no connection between the shooting and the morphine overdose."

"You mean like a robber came in through the door, was going through the jewelry when Ethel woke up," Harvey speculated. "But she was real groggy from the morphine. She went for the gun in her bedside table and the robber threw the pins from the jewelry box at her, went to grab for the gun. They struggled, but he was stronger. The gun went off, Ethel was dead, and the robber hightailed it right on out the door."

Both Dane and Pat smiled, and Dane said, "Well that's one theory, but let's not get too far in the weeds yet. We need to remember to collect facts and not eliminate any potential clues too soon. Harvey, why don't you take Pat back to the big house. I'll quickly type up today's notes and leave them on your desk."

Not fifteen minutes after Harvey and Pat left, Dane's typing was done, he locked the office and headed home to clean up and put the day behind him. Lucy arrived at his house just as he was pulling in the driveway.

"Surprise," she said. "Two times in one day. I'm your babysitter while y'all have your dinner party."

"I had no idea. Come on in."

A short time later, Dane and Joan crossed the street leaving Lucy ensconced in Rose and Julia's room with books and toys at hand.

Pat and Mary greeted them at the door. "Audrey is finishing up the dinner, so let me give you a quick tour of the house," Mary offered. "At least this floor. Above us are four suites with bedroom, bathroom, and sitting room, and a large gathering room."

"How big is this place," Dane asked, looking at the massive foyer and the staircase curving to the second floor.

"It's about fourteen thousand square feet, and much too big for me," Mary exclaimed.

The entrance foyer was dominated by the great stone staircase that went up half a floor to a landing lit by a sixteen-foot leaded glass window, the stair continuing on to the second floor. The staircase was six feet wide with wrought-iron balustrade. Murals covered the wall where the staircase met it, broken in the middle by a niche with Italian Renaissance statuary in it. There was about fourteen feet from the inside of the staircase to the wall with another niche, also occupied by a stone statue. The rest of the walls were covered in old oil paintings, mostly large landscapes.

Mary took them through to the one-story grand salon painted in a pistachio color with neoclassical paneling. Fluted pilasters framed the six fourteen-foot French doors topped by and semicircular window that made up the outside wall of the forty foot room, and faced the terrace and gardens sloping to the Saluda River. The pilasters and all the molding in the room was gold washed. Filled with comfortable-looking antique sitting areas, oriental carpets on the stone floor, the room was both overpowering yet cozy. "I never liked this room much and left it the way it was when I came into the home," Mary explained. "I spent more time in the next room," she said, leading the way, "called the Chinese Salon because of the classical paneling borders and eighteenth-century painted canvases that depict Chinese life."

The tour went through a formal dining room that matched the grand salon except that it was dominated by nineteenth-century English mahogany table flanked by twenty-two chairs. "This room always gives me the creeps with generations of the Bowen lineage looking down from the walls as you eat," Mary said, leading them through one set of the double doors with the fireplace and ten-foot arched mirror in between to the smaller dining room with a circular English mahogany table with eight places set for their dinner. "This was my preferred place to dine," Mary said. "The tapestry is a seventeenth-century Aubusson, and the paintings are landscapes that don't stare you down.

"Through those doors," Mary said pointing to the opposite side of the room, "is the kitchen, but we'll go out the side door here to the office, and library. The master suite is on the other side of the entry foyer and has the sitting room, bedroom and bath. Unfortunately, it is a long way from the kitchen, as I am sure you discovered, Pat," Mary said.

"Once I took my shoes off and saw the bathtub, I didn't want or need to go any further," Pat said. "But I could, and will, spend hours walking from room to room admiring all the treasures. Aren't you afraid leaving all this with no one living here?"

"Oh, I have a great security system, and there is a caretaker's cottage where the gardener, Robert, and his wife Martha live. Martha keeps the house like you see it today, as if a family lived here and used every room daily."

"Well, everything is lovely and I so appreciate your letting me stay here," Pat said. "This is a once in a lifetime opportunity, for sure."

Back to their starting point, Mary said, "Now you can see why I don't live here. It's just too big for me. The girls and I have been thinking about making it into a research center to learn more about our gifts. We went to the Edgar Cayce Hospital of Research and Enlightenment in Virginia Beach some time ago and thought that we had just as much reason to establish such a center here in Camden Grove. Now that Rose and Julia are here, it would be a good endeavor to help us all."

With that, Audrey announced that dinner was ready, and Mary said, "We all have to agree to make dinner upbeat, avoiding any talk of the murder."

Linking her arm with Mary's as they went back to the small dining room, Pat said, "You know, I've always been curious about psychic powers. Tell me more about your plans." The two walked off chatting happily.

Dane took Joan's hand, and they followed behind, both lost in their own thoughts.

A thought suddenly occurred to Dane, "Mary, you said you and your friends sometimes help in local investigations. What does that mean?"

"It really depends on the type of investigation."

"Let's say this one," Dane said.

After a thoughtful pause, she said, "I think the best thing would be for Katherine and Audrey to go to Myrtle Hill. Katherine to read the energies, and Audrey to recreate what happened in the room. I don't know why I didn't think of it earlier. Audrey, are you available? I'll check to see if Katherine can go after the funeral tomorrow."

"I can try it," Audrey responded.

"I think I should check with the senator and make sure it's all right with him. Because it's a little out of the norm, I'd like to have his go ahead. And I would like him to let Ms. Ricks know we'll be coming," Dane said.

"Both are excellent ideas," Mary said.

As agreed, they talked about everything but the murder while they ate lettuce wedge salad, chicken cordon bleu, pan-fried potatoes, and a squash, asparagus, tomato medley with a creamy béarnaise sauce.

"Audrey, this was all delicious," Mary said to everyone's agreement. "Audrey and I will clear the table and put on some coffee to have with my spackle cheesecake."

"I probably should not ask, but I've never heard of spackle cheesecake," Pat said, intrigued.

Mary laughed, "My cream cheese cheesecake always cracks as it rises, so I put on a topping of sour cream, sugar, and vanilla and bake it for ten more minutes and you cannot see the cracks. Everyone calls my topping spackle," she explained. "When we come back, it will be time for your first foray to the dark side, Dane. Audrey has abilities to see things that most of us do not. I think it's time to give you a little demonstration. While we're gone, you three can decide who will get the first reading."

"I'm really, really interested," Pat said, "but I don't want anyone knowing my secrets or repeating them in civil company."

Joan declined in favor of hearing Dane's reading.

"Well, I guess I'm the guinea pig," he conceded.

Fifteen minutes later, Mary and Audrey were seated at the table Audrey said, "If you would be so kind, write your name and birth date on this piece of paper."

She slid Dane the pen and paper across the table.

Audrey said, "Before I start, I say a little prayer. I surround myself in the white light of Christ. Nothing but good will come into me; nothing but good will go from me, in the name of Jesus Christ. This means I must tell you the truth. I surround you in the same white light, and then I surround the room and ask that if you have any angels, they identify themselves if they want to come in to work with us." Audrey passed her left hand over the paper on which she had asked Dane to write his name and birth date.

"It looks like you have six to seven guides and guardian angels who would like to talk with you. I will give you names until they stop. Is that okay?"

Dane felt a little silly, but replied, "Yes."

"The first is an angel named Mida. M–I–D–A, Mida. She's the guardian angel of your temper. She says she's very happy with you. You have good temper, good control, and she says you don't sulk or pout when you're angry. She says that when you have something to say in your professional capacity, you just say it and get it out and take any repercussions later. Again, her name is Mida, and she gives you the thumbs-up sign, but says you need to better incorporate this ability to speak your mind into your personal life.

"The second is a guardian angel named Millie. M–I–L–L I–E, Millie. Millie says she is seven, and she's just for fun. She says you have already seen her out of the corner of your eye on the hardwood floor between the dining and living room carpets. She says both your dogs can see her, even though they are blind, and says to tell you to chop the food into smaller pieces for the little three-legged dog. Without teeth he has more trouble eating and wishes you would mush the food more."

Dane looked at Joan, raising an eyebrow. Joan shook her head and shrugged her shoulders to let him know she had no idea how Audrey could know this.

Audrey continued, "The third is a Guardian Angel named Little Crow. L–I–T–T–L–E C–R–O–W, Little Crow. He says he thinks he died in the 1860s or 1870s; he isn't sure, but says he's very handsome, and that you can find his picture if you look in a book on Native American Indians and Wounded Knee. Your ability to compartmentalize and multi-task is a result of his influence. You are one of the rare people who can start ten things simultaneously and get them all done, unlike most people who must start a task and finish it before beginning another. You can do many things at once and not get flustered. He said it's going to be important for you to concentrate on compartmentalizing over the next few months, because you have some very important things that need to be accomplished. He also says you have everything you need to solve your current case, just trust your instincts; they'll never let you down.

"The fourth angel is Daniel. D–A–N–I–E–L, Daniel. Daniel says he's proud of you because although you're outspoken like he was, you'll never get yourself into the same predicaments he got into because you know when to stop pushing. You push and push until you see change or get the results you want, but you don't go too far. If you will read Chapter 2 and 3 in the book of Daniel in the Bible, you'll see what you are here for. He says you have an important mission to accomplish.

"The fifth angel is Saint Paul. I don't know what the saints were for, but I know they walked the earth in the times of Jesus. Paul says you have an easy time learning. Once you see something done, you retain ninety percent of what you see, but only about twenty percent of what you just read. There's nothing that you can't learn or do, and you're not to worry about leaving the earth any time soon. You'll never be in a wheelchair, and you will always have your full mental abilities until the day you die. No Alzheimer's or Parkinson's. He says you'll see your eighty-ninth birthday, but not your ninety-second, and it'll be your kidneys that take you home.

"Next we have Archangel Gabriel who talks to God regularly to let him know how you're doing. The angels frequently go over to God just to keep him aware of what's going on with all of us. Gabriel does that for you. Gabriel is the one who will blow the trumpet at the end of time. Any time he is around you should be able to smell cinnamon or vanilla. He uses those scents to get your attention. Gabriel says to tell you that he loves you and you don't always feel like anyone does. You need to accept the fact that the Father loves you and has a purpose for you. Whenever you need to talk to him, just do it. Although he has arms like you do, he wants you to know that he also has one-hundred and forty wings that can shield you when you feel sorrow. He says when they come out they're a magnificent sight, and you'll—"

Audrey stopped in mid-sentence and turned deathly white. "I'm sorry. I'm suddenly feeling very sick. I really need to go," she said jumping up, grabbing her purse as she headed for the front door.

"Audrey, what's wrong?" Mary asked, rising from her seat.

"Nothing. Nothing. I'll be fine, and I'll talk to you tomorrow. I'm sorry, Dane. We'll finish this another time, I promise," she said without looking back as she rushed out the door, leaving everyone else looking at each other in an uncomfortable way, not knowing what to think about the abrupt departure.

"I swear I have never, in all the years I've known her, seen Audrey act so strangely," Mary said. "I need to go see if there is anything I can do," Mary said and quickly followed her friend out.

"I always knew really understanding you might cause someone's head to spin," Pat joked to ease the tension. "But I'm not going to let this keep me from trying that spackle cheese cake. Who is with me?"

Even though they were all off-balance from the strange ending to the reading, the three enjoyed a cup of coffee and piece of cake, which was scrumptious, before Joan and Dane left for the short walk home.

CHAPTER

FOURTEEN

It was Thursday morning. In the office, Harvey had coffee brewing. Dane was already looking forward to Harvey's coffee of the day when he entered the building. "What do we have this morning, Harvey?"

"Today we're taking one of our European coffeehouse tours. Café Sperl in Vienna."

"Joan and I used to eat a lot in Vienna. We'd drive over, have dinner, then go home," Dane joked.

"Don't think so. Can't drive to Austria."

"Oh, you meant Austria. I thought you were talking about Vienna, Virginia."

"Very funny, boss. This one is a little stronger than some we've had this week."

"I'm going to need it to jumpstart me today. After a cup, I'm going over to talk with Wayne while you get Pat. After I talk with her, I'm going to be out most of the day with interviews. If you can make sure she gets wherever she needs, and cover the office here, I'll be available on my cell."

As Dane sipped the coffee, he thought what good habits he was developing, a cup of great coffee and a morning talk with a new friend before getting down to business, possibly lunch at home, and early evenings with the family. Take away the murder investigation, and it was just what he had envisioned. He made a quick note of the people with whom he needed to talk: Steve Adams, Senator Bowen, Robin Bowen, Ronald Bowen, and Claire Davis. He took the card from his wallet and decided to set up a meeting with Claire Davis first, because she lived north of town in Laurens. Dane set the meeting for ten o'clock and got good directions.

He then made arrangements to see the Senator and his family starting about three o'clock, and would meet with Steve Adams at five o'clock when Steve got off work.

Dane decided to read *The State* article before visiting Wayne, so he wouldn't be surprised, for a change. Sally Anderson, however, did surprise him.

Residents Shocked by Camden Grove Murder
By Sally Anderson

CAMDEN GROVE, S.C. Residents of the former mill town were shocked yesterday when the Greenwood County coroner announced that suicide was ruled out in the gruesome killing Monday of Ethel Chapman Bowen at her Camden Grove mansion. Bowen is the mother of South Carolina District 10 State Senator Ronald D. Bowen (D).

According to Dr. Jim Johnson, his medical examination of Bowen proved challenging because there were three potential causes of death, which included the gunshot wound to the head, terminal pancreatic cancer, and a suspected morphine overdose, indicated by levels showing in the results of urinalysis and the count of prescription pills assumed taken. In his opinion, it was the presence of morphine in the victim's blood that proved that she could not have committed suicide. In his statement, the county coroner said, "Suicide has been categorically ruled out. With the amount of morphine in her system, it was impossible for Mrs. Bowen to do this herself."

Dr. Johnson said that in his professional opinion, Bowen would have most likely died from cancer-related causes within a matter of weeks. He added that the amount of morphine in her bloodstream was enough to cause her to die from an overdose, but he stated emphatically that the trauma to the head from a bullet was what killed the senator's mother on Monday.

According to Camden Grove Police Chief Dane Hunter, the weapon found at the scene was a thirty-eight caliber special with wooden handle and a two-inch barrel that was owned by the victim. Major Forrest Sikes, director of the Piedmont Area Investigative Services, reported that the gun was found in Bowen's hand and that no other prints were on the weapon.

Hunter has only been in the job for a week and was last a detective on the Washington, D.C., police force. Hunter couldn't provide residents much information, responding to questions by saying only that his investigation was in the fact-finding phase. He added that now that it is known that suicide is ruled out, he'll approach his investigation as a murder.

Senator Bowen was not available for comment, but a spokes-man for the family said the senator and entire Bowen family were shocked by the murder and could not believe anyone would want to harm the senator's Mother. The spokesman added that the family wanted to thank everyone for the support and under-standing of their need for privacy during this difficult time.

Mrs. Bowen has long been a vocal force behind various political events and local and national charities. Funeral ser-vices will be held Saturday, eleven a.m., at St. Mary's Catholic Church in Camden Grove. A private graveside ceremony at the family cemetery at Myrtle Hill Plantation will follow.

Dane thought the article fairly represented the press update, and he made a mental note to tell Sally Anderson the next time he saw her.

He refilled his cup and poured an extra to take to Wayne. Across the street, Wayne thanked Dane but refused the coffee, saying, "Harvey didn't speak to me for weeks a while back when he offered me a cup and I told him I can only drink decaf. He said something like it was a crying shame to ruin good coffee with antifreeze to take out the caffeine. Anyway, you don't want to see me on caffeine. I'm hyper enough without it."

Changing the subject, he said, "Heard you took on Sally Anderson yesterday. Must have worked. Her article this morning has less opinion and innuendo than she usually includes."

"I'm often too sensitive about the press when I don't believe they're unbiased or when they release information that may an impact on my investigation. I was a little hard on Ms. Anderson."

"I'd say don't back down. You've raised her game." Wayne laughed. "So you now have a murder investigation going?"

"Yes, I kind of expected it. Women don't normally shoot themselves in the head, but it would have been a lot easier had the results pointed to suicide. Because it is now a formal murder investigation, I have to revisit everyone who was involved in her last hours to see if there is anything they may not have remembered before or may have thought of since I talked with them. Have you had any additional thoughts since we talked?"

"Not a one. I still don't understand the whole will routine and don't know if it is important or not. I do know that I can't think of a single per-son in this town who could have been involved."

"Does that include all family members?"

"Absolutely."

"There aren't many lawyers in town. You aren't by chance Steve Adams's lawyer, are you?"

"I guess you could say that I am. I've represented him in a few of his brushes with the law."

"Then I guess I shouldn't ask you to tell me about him."

"There's no conflict there. I would say that he's a young man who hasn't had many breaks in life. A lot of people have exploited him because he's good looking and wild. I believe he wants to be something better than he is, but it's like the saying, 'Your reputation precedes you.' People expect only the worst from him. I've seen the vulnerable, wrong-side-of-the-tracks kid in him when he's been in trouble."

"Do you think he could have done it?" Dane asked.

"Now that, my friend, would be stepping over the line. If he were to be accused, I might find myself on his defense team, so you'll get no opinion from me," Wayne said.

"Question withdrawn, counselor. I'll form my own opinion."

"A change of subject. Are y'all about settled in, or has all of this kept you too busy?"

"Thank goodness Joan is able to do all the move stuff and setting up our home with little help from me. She saves a few moves of furniture for me, but that's about it. I think almost everything is unpacked, and I put most of the pictures up on the walls late night before last. We'll have to have you over for dinner as soon as we have an evening to entertain," Dane said.

"I'd love that. Just know that my thinness hides a huge appetite, and though I cook myself, I never pass up an invitation to eat at someone else's house. I even reciprocate on occasion."

"I promise you'll get an invitation to our first dinner party. Joan is a great cook and loves to share that talent with someone who enjoys eating. As much as he would like to stay and chat," Dane said, "I guess I better head back. I have to talk with Pat before I begin my work for the day. I'm sure I'll see you at the funeral tomorrow."

"It will be a sad day for Camden Grove," Wayne said. "Tell Harvey that when he's prepared to drink some good stuff, I'd love for him to make me a cup of decaf. On second thought, don't. I hate it when he sulks."

Across the street, Harvey returned from his assigned chore of picking up Pat.

Joining them in the front office, Dane stated, "I have a full day. Do you need anything from me, Pat, before I get started?"

"Until you have more information, you're no good to me. I want answers. Go forth and find them. Bring me answers, and I'll make you a hero."

Dane took his directions and headed northwest out of town. In Laurens, he found the house easily, and it showed him she either came from money or had married into it.

When Claire Davis answered the door, Dane was taken by surprise. He was looking at an easy double for Robin Bowen, but with a hard edge and without the look of vulnerability. He quickly said, "Ms. Davis, I'm Dane Hunter. Thank you for seeing me on such short notice."

"Senator Bowen said you might call," she said with a South Carolina accent with lazy vowels that turned one syllable words into two. "Please come in."

She escorted him into the living room and indicated a seat opposite the sofa where she sat, a table between them.

"I know this is awkward, and I apologize for needing to see you. The coroner has said that the senator's mother was killed, so I need to verify where people were the night of the murder."

"I appreciate your discretion. The senator and I have known each other much of our lives. Right now we're both serving in the state Congress. Ronnie in the Senate, and I've replaced my deceased husband for the remainder of his term in the House. You're right, this could be most awkward."

"I understand."

"On Sunday evening, Ronnie called me late after he had left his mother's, and his wife had, shall we say, gone to bed? After my husband's death, Ronnie helped me adjust to my work in Columbia. He was gracious with his time. We were both lonely, and I thought, why not? I think I took him quite by surprise and didn't really give him a chance to think things through before he was involved with me. I'm used to getting what I want. However, sometimes when you get what you want, it isn't exactly what you'd had in mind. I found that he'd never really be mine, and I'm not a woman who likes to share. Thankfully, we've had a long history together and were able to work through the fact that neither he nor I were really invested in a relationship that had nowhere to go. We really value and want to maintain our friendship. We worked through that Sunday evening into Monday morning. I think Ronnie probably arrived around eleven fifteen and left around three-fifteen."

"If I need you to make a formal statement, are you willing to do so?"

"I suppose if I must, but will it come to that? I just can't bear to think how my friends and acquaintances will react."

"I don't know yet if it will be necessary, but it might," Dane answered.

"That will certainly put a crimp in both our careers, but he was here, so we must accept the responsibility that goes with our stupidity. If you need me, I'll make an official statement."

"I appreciate that and will let you know," Dane said allowing her to shepherd him to and out the front door, thanking her for her time and thanking his lucky stars that he had a woman with a heart at home.

Dane's drive home left him enough time to have lunch with Joan before his next appointments. He picked up Pat to join them and found that Mary was already at the house chatting with Joan while the girls played in their room.

After lunch, Dane dropped Pat back at the office, composed his thoughts, and developed questions before heading over to the senator's house for interviews with him and his family. At their house, Dane asked that they each meet with him individually, beginning with the senator. They decided the library would be the most private place to conduct the interviews.

"I met with Ms. Davis this morning and assured her that nothing need be formalized or said at this point, and, I hope, never. She did confirm the times you were there," Dane said.

"Again, I appreciate your personally handling this. Surely I'm not a suspect," the senator stated.

"There are no suspects at this time, but you may have key information that you haven't yet thought of. I already have your comments from earlier meetings. Is there anything you can think of that may have an impact on my investigation?"

"Nothing that I've been able to come up with, and I've tried," he replied.

"For the record, did you know that your mother was terminally ill?"

"Sadly, no."

"Did you have any knowledge of or play any role in the death of your mother?"

"Absolutely not."

"Thank you, senator. That is all I have for now. Please use my personal number should you think of anything that may have any bearing on solving this case."

"I will."

Robin came in shortly after his departure.

"That didn't take very long," Robin said as she closed the door.

"These meetings are mere formalities at this time. Now that it has been confirmed that your mother-in-law was murdered, I have to ask you a few questions, for the record. Can you think of anything at all that we haven't previously discussed that could have a bearing on this case?"

"I just can't believe anyone would want to kill Ethel."

"For the record, did you have any knowledge that your mother-in-law was terminally ill?"

"I should have seen it, but no, I didn't. I was so wrapped up in my problems that I didn't see it."

"Do you have any knowledge of or did you have any part in the death of your mother-in-law?"

"Oh, my God, no. You don't suspect any of us, do you?"

"There are no suspects yet, I'm just formalizing our other discussions and establishing who was where and when," Dane answered.

"This has to look bad for us all, then. And of us all, I'm probably the only one without an alibi, since I was home here alone," Robin said. "I never left the house after we came back from Myrtle Hill."

"Okay, thank you," Dane said, handing her another of his cards with both office and cell phone listed. "If you think of anything that you think may help us solve this case, please call me."

"I'll keep thinking, but I can't imagine what it could be. There's no one I know who would have a motive or the ability to do such a terrible thing."

"We'll figure this out," Dane said, standing and ending the interview. "Would you send Ronald in, please?"

"Surely you don't think he could be involved. He's only sixteen, and he loved his grandmother more than anything."

"Robin, I have to talk to everyone who was there on Sunday night to try to have every possible piece of information."

"This is all so upsetting," she said as she turned to go.

Ronald appeared shortly after his mother had left.

"I've read the articles in the paper. Can you tell me that Grams didn't suffer?" he asked.

"Yes, I can. Dr. Johnson said that there was no way she could have known what happened."

"Well, at least that's something."

"Ronald, when we talked before, you told me where you were, what you were doing, and when you came home. Do you have anything to add or change to what you told me?"

"No, sir. And you were right. I should've told Dad earlier. Like you said, bad things always have a way of coming out. It would've been better if I'd told him."

"I know. When the individual made the statement, he was unaware that your father didn't know where you were or what you were doing that night."

"Well, he knows everything now, and it wasn't a fun afternoon when he found out."

"I imagine it wasn't. Ronald, for the record, did you know that your grandmother was terminally ill?"

"No sir, but I guess I should have, huh?"

"No one else did. It seems that she wanted it that way. For the record, did you have any knowledge of or play any part in the events that ended in your grandmother's death?"

Tears welled up in his eyes. "No sir, I didn't, I didn't. No sir."

"If you think of anything that might help us solve this case, I want you to call me. I don't care what time it is, use one of the numbers on this card."

"Yes, sir, I will," Ronald said.

Both the senator and Robin were waiting in the living room and met Dane in the foyer when he and Ronald walked out of the library.

"So what's the next step?" the senator asked.

"I keep gathering information and will keep you up to date on anything that I can tell you, so that you'll never be surprised by what you see in the press. At least as far as I can control it," Dane promised.

"I can't ask for more than that. Thank you."

Leaving, Dane saw he had time to go back to his office and type up some notes before his five o'clock meeting with Steve Adams. Pat and Harvey were both out when he arrived, so he was able to shut himself off and type up his thoughts before time to leave for his last scheduled interview of the day.

At Steve's house, he was greeted by a young man with a distinct attitude.

"I suppose you're here to accuse me of murder," Steve said.

"No, I'm not, but I would like to ask you a few questions."

"I ain't got nothin' to hide. You can ask what you want. I've already told the cops everything I know."

"I've read the reports."

"Well, there ain't no more to tell. I was here all night until I took Junior home around four in the morning. You can ask him."

"Mr. Adams, I have asked him. He confirmed that you were here, but also that when you woke him up, you were already dressed. Had you been somewhere before you woke him?"

"Did he say I was gone?"

"I'll ask the questions, please. You provide the answers."

"Well, I did go out for some cigarettes about one. You can check at the Seven Eleven. Shellie was on duty. She'll remember that I came in."

"I'll check that out."

"I didn't have nothing to do with bumping off the old lady. Y'all can't pin this on me."

"I'm not looking to pin anything on anyone. I just want to find out what happened to Mrs. Bowen. For the record, did you have any knowledge of or play any part in the death of Mrs. Ethel Chapman Bowen?" Dane asked.

"Hell no. I shoulda never have gone over there with Ronnie. They say I'm trouble, but look at what hanging out with a rich kid got me into."

"As long as you're straight with me, you have nothing to worry about."

"Yeah, that's what I'm always told, but it seems I always end up the one in trouble. But no one is gonna pin that old lady's death on me. I was there earlier, but never went back."

Taking a card from his wallet, Dane handed it to Steve and said, "If you think of anything that might help me solve this case, I want you to call me on one of these numbers."

Leaving, Dane saw he still had enough time to stop by the Seven Eleven store. Fortunately, Shellie Turner was already working and confirmed that Steve had come in around one Monday morning for cigarettes, just as he had said. She said there were security tapes that could verify the time. It didn't clear him, because the time of death was earlier, so Dane would have to get a better chronology from both Steve and Ronald regarding their evening.

He drove back to the office to add the latest notes to his files. Pat updated him on the press queries and Dane reported the facts to be added to the crime board, with Harvey making notes of what he had to change.

"I'll have all the cards and the file ready for ya tomorrow, Boss," Harvey said. "If you don't mind, I thought I would take Pat over to Alicia's Mexican Food in Greenwood. It is number one of the Greenwood restaurants rated on TripAdvisor, and really, really good."

Dane shot Pat a questioning look, before she said, "Mexican has always been one of my comfort foods. And I may as well see a little more than just Camden Grove while I am down here," coyly adding, "Harvey is such a dear to offer to take me."

After they noisily left, Dane did his typing and left for home.

CHAPTER
FIFTEEN

The night before the funeral, Father Leverette held a Rosary Service, giving family a friends the opportunity to gather and pray together. That service contrasted with the arrivals of political and business leaders, and the rich friends and acquaintances who arrived in their limos and fancy cars, wearing tastefully understated but expensive clothing. It was a veritable Who's Who in South Carolina and the nation, a true tribute to how wide the Chapman and Bowen wealth and involvement in business and politics had been felt.

Intermingled in the arrivals and in the pews were those who were a part of the daily life in Camden Grove and the surrounding area. Many arrived on foot, others in their practical cars, all proud and attending to pay their respects to the woman who had so generously improved their lives in so many ways.

Dane arrived with Joan, Mary, and Pat, and they made their way into an already crowded church and found seats about halfway down the rows of pews. The church was being renovated, but had been quickly put into a semblance of order for the service. There were, however, bare studs in places where walls were either being removed or added. It was not a lavish cathedral, but rather a unique local church with some beautiful windows and paintings that had most likely been gifts from parishioners over the years.

Not long after Dane sat down, there was a rush for seats, and some were left to line the outside aisles near the windows to allow the center isle to remain free. Altar boys were scurrying around the front of the church setting up the communion table while the organist played softly, looking to the back of the church. Glancing back, Dane saw the casket being placed on the table. Father Leverette swung an incense burner over the casket and handed the censer to the altar boy. He took the holy water, and sprinkled it on the casket before placing the decorated white funeral pall cloth on the casket. On cue, the music changed. A boy carrying a cross, another, the holy water, and Father Leverette with the incense began their march down the center aisle followed by the casket and then the family.

When the casket and all family members were in place, Father Leverette signaled for all to sit.

"A reading from the book of Wisdom, Isaiah forty, verses one to eleven," Father Leverette said.

He read, "Comfort ye, comfort ye my people, saith your God." He continued to read down to "behold, his reward is with him, and his work before him.'

"The word of the Lord."

The congregation said, "Thanks be to God."

"A reading from Romans, Chapter eight, verses twenty-six to thirty," Father Leverette said, and continued to read the verses, finishing with, "The word of the Lord."

Again the congregation said, "Thanks be to God."

Finishing the selected scriptures, the Father said, "A reading from the Gospels, Mark, Chapter thirteen, verses thirty to thirty-seven," and later said, "The word of the Lord."

"Thanks be to God," the congregation responded.

The organ began and was soon joined by the choir singing. At the end of the song, Father Leverette said, "We gather today as a congregation not only to mourn the passing of our sister, Ethel Chapman Bowen, but also to give thanks to God for Christ's victory over sin and death and to commit Ethel Chapman Bowen to God's tender mercy and compassion. It is always difficult to say goodbye to someone we love and respect. Ethel touched all our lives. She felt she had a mission here on earth, and as with everything she took on, she gave it her all. Ethel was passionate about her God, her family, her community, and her politics. I'm sure most of you in this sanctuary have at one time or another had a fiery debate over some topic that was on her mind at that particular moment. I can see her now debating with Saint Peter regarding his interpretation of her actions here on earth, and swaying him to her way of thinking," he said to a chuckle from the congregation.

"Born into wealth and privilege, she didn't keep her blessings to herself, but willingly shared them with anyone who was in need. And in the sharing, she didn't seek recognition, but truly gave from her heart. That she has been taken from us in this way is a mystery to us, but not to God. There is a reason and a purpose in all things.

"So what can we learn from Ethel's approach to life and the life she led? Each of you will take something different away from each of the moments your lives walked side-by-side. I know that my life, my beliefs, and my actions were touched immeasurably by my friendship with the woman named Ethel Chapman Bowen. She was a wife, a mother, a grandmother, and a friend, always challenging us to do the right thing, to support a cause in which we believe, to reach our full potential. And she did it in such a way that we wanted to do it for ourselves, never dictating, never forcing, but leading us to our own desire for the action.

"We especially must tune out the noise from those who would capitalize on this horrible event. Tune out the noise of those who would create scandal where there is none, or create controversy where there are no answers. Remember that Ethel Chapman Bowen lived her life fully, every day, and thought first of others, every day.

"My grandfather once told me that success is not measured in the positions we hold, the possessions we gather, or the money we have, but rather is measured in the lives of those we touch. I know that by this measure, Ethel was the most successful person I have had the privilege of knowing. Scriptures encourage us to pray for our deceased members. These prayers reflect our Christian belief that death is not the end, it's a transition from one realm to another and prayer to our merciful God on behalf of our sister, Ethel Chapman Bowen, will benefit both her and us. Our relationship does not dissolve with her death. We honor her by giving her body this Christian burial, and we help her on her journey to heaven by our prayers so that once she enters into the presence of our mighty God, our prayers, and hers, will bear great power. Please join me in silent prayer for our sister."

More music, the celebration of Holy Communion, followed by a call to prayer before the service ended with Father Leverette leading the recessional, followed by the casket and the family. The service over, Dane, Joan, Mary, and Pat saw all those who did not find a place in the church lined the walk in respect. They knew the burial would be private at Myrtle Hill Plantation. The casket was being put into a hearse for the short trip.

Dane watched as Alice Garner sought out Ronald Junior, who was near enough that Dane overheard Alice saying, "My dad has forbidden me to see you, but I had to come to make sure you know how sorry I am about your grandmother. I know how bad I felt when my Granny died, and she died in her sleep. Nothing like this."

"It's been horribly hard to imagine Grams in the last minutes, but Dad told me he has seen the autopsy report and there is no way she suffered at all. She was real sick, and this ended her pain."

"I guess that's a good thing."

"Yeah, I guess so, but it sure doesn't feel very good," Ronald answered.

"I know this isn't a good time, but I also want you to know that I hope we can be friends without too much weirdness between us over the other night."

"Me, too. I'm sorry about what happened. It wasn't fair to you, and it was weird. I've never done that before and don't think I'm ready for it."

"Me neither. Even though I thought I was ready, I'm not. I think I still want to be a kid a while longer before I jump into all the adult stuff. It sure has made my dad crazy, though."

"Yeah, my dad's kinda crazy too. I don't know what I expected or what I want, exactly, but I do know that I want us to be friends. That's if your dad will let us."

"Dad doesn't pick my friends, but I know it is going to be a while before he trusts me again. I'm pretty much grounded right now."

"Me, too."

"I guess I'll see you at school, then," Alice said.

"Great," Ronald answered. Impulsively he kissed her quickly on the lips and walked away.

Alice smiled and left for her car so she could get home before her father returned.

As the family made final farewells to those who came to the funeral and got into the limos for Ethel's last trip through Camden Grove, Dane was struck with the vision of the street lined with people holding flowers that they threw on the road in front of the hearse when it drove by. Ethel Chapman Bowen had been a well-loved hometown girl.

The senator had told Dane it would be best for him to bring Mary, Katherine, and Audrey to Myrtle Hill in the late afternoon, after the burial and visitation of family and close friends.

On the way, Audrey apologized for her quick departure during his psychic reading the night before. "When Gabriel was speaking of sorrow, I felt a wave of such intense grief surrounding you that it broke my concentration and made me sick. I've never had that kind of reaction before."

Dane looked at her with an incredulous look on his face, then looked at Mary and said, "That's the second warning now of impending personal doom. You're making me paranoid."

Further discussion was halted by their arrival at Myrtle Hill, and although Dane wanted to pursue with them the impact of their predictions, by the end of the visit, it was totally out of his mind.

The senator greeted them at the door. "The rest of the family has gone home," he said, "and Isabelle is upstairs fuming. She doesn't approve of this visit." He kissed Mary on the cheek. "I thought you would come to the burial, Aunt Mary."

"Ronnie, you know I can't stand to go to the gravesite. It was hard enough going to the service, and I feel bad that I never had the chance to say goodbye."

"Well if anyone has more of an opportunity to do that than the rest of us, it would be you, Aunt Mary. What do we need to do here now?"

"You and Dane go into the library and leave us girls on our own for a while? I know the way to the bedroom."

"Of course, you do. Dane, want to come with me?"

The three women headed toward the master bedroom.

It wasn't even five minutes before Mary came to the library door and said, "Would you two mind coming back here with us?"

The senator and Dane followed.

"We won't be getting anything from here," Mary said. "The whole room has been cleansed, as has the outside."

"Isabelle didn't clean until after the forensics team told her it was okay," Ronnie said.

"I didn't say cleaned, that would have been fine, but these rooms have been cleansed. None of us got anything when we came in: no lingering energies, no feelings, no colors, no thoughts, and that just doesn't happen on its own. We discovered that there has been a ritual cleansing done."

"How would you know that?" Dane asked.

"First, whenever something tragic happens, there is a lot of energy that remains behind, especially when an occupant has been sick or died. The room should feel heavy or dark. Pools of negative energy should be able to be felt by some, seen by others. Katherine should be able to see them and Audrey feel them. Nothing. So we looked around and found signs of the ritual cleansing.

"There are a number of ways to cleanse a room. Most common would be to sprinkle the room with salt while turning clockwise to bring the grounding elements of earth into the room, after which you either vacuum it up or use a new broom and sweep it out. Before you finish, you put some salt in each corner of the room. Come look, there are small mounds of salt in each corner and sprinkled along each doorway and window. The small water spots tell me that water was used after the salt, and I believe candles were used in each of the four corners of the room after the water, followed by fresh herbs that are strewn and smudge sticks that are wrapped herbs, cedar, and sweet grasses. You can see pieces of rosemary, basil, and lavender still in the cracks of the flooring and on carpets."

"What would these things have to do with your abilities to feel anything?" Dane asked.

"Everything that has happened has been cleansed from the room, so we can tell nothing. There isn't any negative energy, and even positive energy isn't strong in here right now. That means we cannot help you at all," Mary said. "Interestingly, we also found four protection talismans, one in each corner of the room, in little satin bags," she said as she produced what looked like an eight-sided copper charm with a design engraved on it. At first glance, the design looked like a snowflake, but on closer look, each end of the four lines set in a star pattern was capped with what looked like a pitchfork with arrow tips. Each one centered on one of the corners of the eight sides. At the twelve, three, six, and nine positions there were three dots, one each above each of the three arrows. Finally, just below the arrows, on the straight part of the line was another line with a dot on each end.

"While I've never seen this particular charm, I would say it is for protection of some sort," Mary said. "Very interesting. Can we talk to Isabelle?"

"I'll ask her to join us in the library," Ronnie said, leaving the room in search of Isabelle.

When Isabelle joined the group, it was clear that she was not in the mood for questioning, but Mary began anyway.

"Isabelle, did you cleanse the rooms?"

"Of course I did. I was told it was okay to do it."

"But why did you do it?"

"You, of all people, should know the answer to that. We can't have bad energy hanging around here. It takes a lot to keep a house this size clean and protected."

"How did you know what to do?"

"Oh, please. I've been doing this since the day I came into this house. There was so much negative energy here then, and there's been a lot made while I've lived here. I had to keep everything in balance. Ethel counted on me to do that."

"What other gifts do you have?"

"Gifts? I don't have any gifts. I just know how to make the energy clean and get protection charms. I've always done that. You can check all around the house and property."

Dane chuckled as he saw Ronnie's eyes widen with surprise.

Mary was incredulous as she said, "But you blocked our abilities by what you've done."

Isabelle merely shrugged and turned to leave the room.

Dane interrupted her departure, saying, "Isabelle, could I have a private moment? I have a couple of questions you might be able to help me with."

She led him to the kitchen where they took seats at the table.

"I want to ask about Mrs. Bowen's pain management. Did she use injections or pills?"

"Mostly pills here at home, although we do have a prescription for injectable morphine when needed," she responded.

"Did you inject her or did she do it herself."

"I would be the one to do it, but we had not done so at home before her death. The pills were working, and she managed them herself."

"As you know, the coroner said she had so much in her system it would have killed her."

"I read that, and don't know how to answer. She knew how many to take, and knew the consequences of taking too many."

"Do you think she took a large dose on purpose, or accidentally?" Dane asked.

Isabelle did not answer immediately. Measuring her response, she said, "I can only presume, not knowing how many she may have taken. I did not manage her pills, she did that herself."

Did she keep them by the bedside? I don't remember seeing them."

"There was six days of medicine sorted by day in a plastic case in the drawer of her bedside stand. She typically kept additional Dilaudid tablets in the Saturday bin. We were warned that among the serious side effects was confusion. That would be my guess."

"That makes sense. Do you know how many she could have taken?"

"I really don't, as she did not take them all the time. If she did, we could figure the amount from the last refill."

"I'll see what I can do," Dane said. "If you think of anything else, please call."

Isabelle stood and busied herself at the sink as Dane walked to join the others.

The senator walked Dane, Mary, Katherine, and Audrey to Dane's car. The ride home was silent, and after dropping the ladies off, Dane headed home and turned on the television. He was just in time to catch the tail end of a piece by Kathryn Blanchard about the funeral. He was impressed by her on-camera presence and the balanced approach her stories took. What followed, though, took him by surprise. The regular newscaster said, "In a strange political twist, South Carolina Governor Adam Baxter made comments about the senator's mother's death that were caught on camera." The television screen filled with Baxter at a function talking to friends while waiting to make a speech. "I heard old Ethel was going to change her will to leave everything to her church. I bet that really frosted Bowen's ass. I think we'll see some real differences without her guiding hand. People say I'd sell my mother for a vote, and I probably would." He laughed. "I think Ethel's death might have snagged my second term. Ain't that a kick?" The picture ended with someone yelling, "Governor, your mic's on."

The newscaster wrapped up the piece with a smile. "When speaking in public, always check your mic. You never know who might hear what you say. Governor Baxter and Senator Ronald Bowen are battling for the state's highest office in a bitter campaign that has seen more than one personal attack from the governor. When we come back, we'll have a look at tomorrow's weather."

Dane looked at the screen with his mouth hanging open, neither believing what he had just seen nor believing that the station had run it. The stakes of this case just went up. While realistically he knew that he was doing everything within his power to figure out who had shot Ethel, every lead was coming up empty, and he felt like he was missing something really important.

It had been disappointing to find that of the five men in prison over the attack on Doug and Becky, only one was still alive, and he was still in prison. Three of the others were killed by other inmates in prison fights, and the fourth was hit by a car the day after he was released on parole. A dead end there.

Talking to himself, he said, "Focus, Hunter. Take the information one piece at a time, examine it, see how it fits with the other pieces, and put what doesn't seem to fit aside." He went into his home office with all his papers, reading the first report he'd prepared, and then all other information in the order he had received it. He read and reread all documents.

He spent most of the rest of Friday locked in his office at home. Knowing his crazy focus, Joan made sure he wasn't disturbed for anything except food, which she quietly left for him until she went to bed. He took the index cards with information on potential suspects that Harvey had provided, discarding those that no longer made sense. He picked up the first card, Ethel written across the top. Under it he read: victim of violent crime, terminally ill, manipulating family, and taped her card in the center of the large wall.

At random he picked up another card. Steve Adams. Under his name was written: petty crimes, angry, needed money for drugs, knew about possible jewelry, no substantiated alibi at the time of the murder. He taped it on the wall near Ethel's card.

He grabbed another card. Doug Reed. Emotionally tied to and protective of Becky Bowen, no substantiated alibi was written on the card. He taped it opposite Steve Adams' card and picked up the next.

The senator: angry/hurt over lack of political support, angry over potential loss of childhood home, substantiated alibi. Robin Bowen: protective of husband, no substantiated alibi. Ronald Bowen: high on pot, needed money, sad for Dad's possible loss of plantation, no substantiated alibi. Becky Bowen: mentally unstable, potential loss of home, knew mother was dead before told, no substantiated alibi. Charlotte Kirk: killed someone else before, protective of Becky, grateful for second chance, no substantiated alibi. Isabelle Ricks: knew of terminal illness, thought of Ethel as a daughter, knew Ethel self-administered morphine—could have ended pain with drugs, no previous violence, no substantiated alibi. Father Leverette: no knowledge of potential will change, no firsthand knowledge of illness, no known motive, no substantiated alibi.

He figured he had to put Wayne Wenzel back up, because he had been at the house that evening, too. Under his name Dane wrote: no known motive, no substantiated alibi.

Dane had all the cards in a circle around Ethel's card on the wall. He picked up one more card and wrote on it, "Unknown Suspect" and taped it outside the circle.

He reread the autopsy report. So much morphine that Ethel could not have shot herself. Who would've or could've done it and why? He read each of his reports again. He looked at the photos from the scene, even though he could close his eyes and see every detail of the room. He listened to the tapes he had made.

Dane hit the desk. The answers had to be there, but they were out of his reach. He was missing it. He had a nagging feeling that he was staring at the missing piece, but couldn't see it.

It was one thirty-two in the morning when he finally decided it was time to go to bed. He was getting nowhere, and an hour and five days had passed since Ethel had been killed.

He trudged up the stairs, quietly took off his clothes and crawled into the bed next to Joan. He used the mind-emptying techniques he had always used to go to sleep, no matter what was going on. He wouldn't be any good to anyone if he didn't get some down time.

He dozed off, but his mind kept sorting the pieces, trying to fit them together.

It was after four when the final piece fell into place, and he woke knowing that the wigs on the bed and all the button jewelry were a key in what happened at Myrtle Hill Plantation on that stormy night. Even so, there were still unanswered questions regarding the violence of the crime, things that didn't quite fit.

He slept right through his five-thirty alarm and woke at six-thirty.

D ane once again drove up the driveway to the front of Myrtle Hill Plantation where the door opened as soon as his car came to a full stop, as if Isabelle had been standing inside the door waiting for his arrival.

"What brings you out so early this morning?" she asked.

"You said to come back when I had questions, so I'm here."

She showed him into the library and took a seat in the wing-back chair facing into the room, in front of the window. Dane took the seat opposite and smiled because she had chosen the seating so that he would be looking into the light from the window, which at this time of day was pretty bright.

"So what do you want to discuss?" she asked.

"How about I talk, and when I come to a specific question, I'll ask it. Do you mind if I record this?"

"No, I don't mind, but this conversation will have a purpose, won't it?"

"I believe so and appreciate your indulging me. It sometimes helps to think out loud and have some validation for the thought process."

She nodded her head.

"Even before we got the coroner's report, there was almost unanimous agreement that Mrs. Bowen would never take her own life, but in hindsight, I'm surprised that you didn't tell me immediately that she was critically ill. Why is that?"

"You didn't ask about her health; you asked about her state of mind. If you remember, you had told me initially to keep my answers simple. Then, when you wanted more, you were just fishing. I knew that if I had said then that Ethel was terminally ill, you would've been ready to write her death off as a suicide. I couldn't have that."

"Didn't you know that an autopsy would have been required anyway?"

"I think many people are basically lazy, and pressure to rush to a conclusion encourages people to do sloppy work. I knew there had to be a reason for people to perform their jobs correctly, or Ethel's death would have been listed as a suicide for convenience's sake. She would've hated that."

"I understand your perceptions, but I would never have closed a case that carelessly."

"And I was to know that how? I didn't know you. I saw Harvey and his new hotshot boss from Washington. Neither of you inspired my utmost faith and trust."

Dane smiled. "You have to admit that you didn't make our first meetings easy. I would characterize them as fairly adversarial."

"That was my intention. When you were angry, you wanted to do the most professional job you could."

"Isabelle, haven't you ever heard about catching flies?"

"I doubt anyone in this town would describe me as sweet. I say what I mean."

Dane laughed, and Isabelle smiled with him.

"I spent the entire evening going over every minute of this case since I first pulled up to the door out there," Dane said.

He could tell Isabelle sensed the shift in the tone of the conversation.

"I actually made up an index card on every potential suspect. But in my mind, nothing rang true. When I compared potential motives to the actual violence of the crime, the closest I could come was that someone was either caught in a robbery or angry because there wasn't any good jewelry in the room to be had. One of my potential suspects could fit into that category, and I keep going back to him. I tried to picture his getting angry and putting a gun near Mrs. Bowen's face to scare her into telling him where the good stuff was. I could actually see that person doing that, but I couldn't see him pulling the trigger and killing Mrs. Bowen. So I tried it out as an accident. While threatening her, he threw the cheap jewelry on the bed, put the gun to her face, shoved it into her mouth and accidentally squeezed the trigger. It could've happened that way, but the individual in question, in my opinion, wouldn't have been able to think logically about wiping away all his fingerprints and making it look as though Mrs. Bowen had killed herself."

Isabelle waited patiently as he continued talking.

"None of that felt right. Something kept nagging at me that I couldn't grasp. Reading and remembering each of my interviews didn't seem to help, either. Things just didn't fit as a violent crime.

"My mind often continues sorting information after I go to sleep. It did so last night, and I woke realizing that I was looking at everything from the wrong perspective. I was looking for the reason for violence, but the information and the scene didn't support that theory. I'd like to test my new theory on you."

"It appears that I'm a captive audience. What is your theory?" she asked.

"Actually it was something you said from the very beginning. You said you didn't need to go all the way into the room to know that Mrs. Bowen had been murdered. After seeing the configuration of the room, you would've had to have gone in more than just to the door to see anything, and I believe a more natural reaction would have been to rush to the bed and check to see if she was alive or dead. That, and the things on the bed, made me think the room was the scene of a terribly nostalgic, loving evening."

"Excuse me?" she said tightly.

"What has been nagging at me were the wigs and button jewelry on the bed. I thought about evenings when my mother brushed my sister's hair and talked all the while, so brushing the wigs would probably be a calming activity. I can see the two of you sitting like mother and daughter, brushing the hair of the wigs and talking. And then the light went off in my head about what Mary Johnston and Wayne Wenzel both told me about the button jewelry, how each piece represented a good deed done for someone, and how Mrs. Bowen had often said that they each represented a person who would say a prayer and shorten her time in purgatory. I realized that the evening was geared toward bringing closure to Mrs. Bowen's life and preparing her for her death."

Dane saw tears start to slide down Isabelle's cheeks.

"When I added to this the understanding that you had raised this incredible woman and were confronted with her in the final stages of her cancer, I realized how difficult it must have been for you to watch her slipping away, and how hard it must have been for you to know that she was afraid of the pain she couldn't bear. So you gave her morphine to dull her pain and anxiety. Now comes my big question, Mrs. Ricks. But before I ask it, law requires me to inform you of your Miranda rights. You have the right to remain silent. Anything you say can and will be used against you in a court of law. You have the right to have an attorney present now and during any future questioning. If you can't afford an attorney, one will be appointed to you free of charge. Do you understand these rights?"

"Yes," Isabelle said quietly.

"Do you wish to have an attorney present or to confer with an attorney before we go any further?"

"No," she answered.

"If at any time you change your mind, you only have to say so, and this conversation will cease at that point. Ms. Ricks, I believe you didn't have to go back into the room because you already knew Mrs. Bowen was dead. My question is this: according to the autopsy report, the amount of morphine Mrs. Bowen had been given would have, in all likelihood, caused her death that night. Why did you shoot her?"

Isabelle sat bone straight, hands folded in her lap, reminding Dane of their first interview when she had given him reasons why Mrs. Bowen wouldn't have shot herself and planted the seed that there were many others who may have had reasons to commit murder.

Tears streaming down her face, Isabelle said, "I'll answer your questions, but first, I need to speak with Senator Bowen. I'd also like you to contact Mr. Wenzel and ask him to come to witness my confession, I'd prefer it if we could do it here, but I'd understand, if you decide that you need to take me to the police station."

Dane considered her requests, reached over, and cut off the tape recorder. He pulled out his cell phone and called the senator's private number. It was answered on the second ring.

"Senator, Dane Hunter. I'm at Myrtle Hill and need you to join me here as quickly as possible."

"What's going on, Dane?"

"Ms. Ricks needs to talk to you in person. I'm also going to be calling Mr. Wenzel to join us. How quickly can you be here?"

"Give me twenty minutes."

"See you then," Dane said. Pressing the end button, he dialed Wayne's cell phone and arranged for him to come, also. When Dane hung up, Isabelle said, "Thank you. If you will excuse me for a moment, I have a couple of things I need to get for my meeting with Ronnie. You needn't worry about my running. I'm seventy-eight and wouldn't get far. I'll be back down in a few minutes."

"I'm not worried, Isabelle," Dane said and watched her leave the room, back straight, head high.

When both Ronnie and Wayne had arrived, Isabelle produced an envelope for each of them. Dane stopped her from handing them over.

"You don't need to worry," she said. "You'll find that these were written by Ethel, in her own hand. The letters should contain only her fingerprints, as she wrote each one, folded it, and sealed it in the appropriate envelope. The envelopes should have only her prints, mine, and now yours," she said.

"Gentlemen, to keep this as pure as possible, let me open these and place them in protective covers before you handle them. I have everything

I need in my car," Dane said, excusing himself to retrieve gloves, a letter opener, and document protectors. Returning, he quickly prepared each letter so that it could be read without disturbing any prints, just in case.

While he worked, the senator asked, "Isabelle, what's this all about?"

"I never liked this whole ordeal, Ronnie. You know how your mother was when she wanted something. This was something she believed was necessary for her to leave this world, accomplishing as much as she could on her way out. I've struggled with the part I was required to play, but in the end, I knew I'd do whatever was needed to give my baby peace. I didn't know if I'd have the ability to do what she asked of me, but I gave her my word, and in the end, I honored my word as I have my whole life. I basically know what is in your letter, Ronnie. I can only guess what is in yours, Wayne. In the hall closet, there is also a small box that was mailed last Saturday so that the letters inside would not be here Monday. In that box you'll find a number of letters, including, I believe, one for you, Dane. Ethel wrote a letter to all the people she thought needed explanations or final messages."

Dane, the senator, and Wayne were intent on what Isabelle was saying as she delivered what was apparently a rehearsed presentation.

"Dane, after Ronnie reads his letter, I'm prepared to answer any questions you have," she concluded, sitting back in her chair and waiting for the senator to read.

He picked up his letter and said, "There's no doubt this is mother's handwriting. She was always extremely proud of her penmanship." Out loud he read, "My dearest and favorite son." He let out what Dane wasn't sure was a laugh or a sob. He looked up and said, "From the time I was seven, Mother always told me I was her favorite son. I would reply, 'thanks, but I'm your only son,' and she would say, 'Then aren't we lucky, because mothers should not have favorites. I fortunately can have a favorite son and a favorite daughter. Life is good.'"

He began reading again. "I know you will say that I'm using a sledgehammer to kill a gnat, but I want you to know why I've done what I've done. Had I told you I had only a short time to live, you would've ended your candidacy to spend that time with me. Selfishly, I almost did that. I realized what it would mean to the people of South Carolina who, I believe, need you right now as their governor. I know you don't believe that I support you in your bid for this high office, and it has pained me to further your belief and drive a wedge between us. I know if given enough rope, that ass-bite Adam Baxter will show his true, small-minded, bigoted, greedy personality. He has ridden so long on other's coattails that he truly has no mind of his own, but is the puppet of special interest groups who support him while he mortgages the future of our state for his and their personal gain. Good investigators can document all of my allegations of waste, bad decisions, kickbacks, and cronyism I outline in a letter Isabelle can give you. Son, you also know where many of these skeletons lie but have been too fair-minded to use them in the campaign. I know your ethics, my son, and know that you won't stoop to his level to win this race. My plan created an opportunity for him to reveal his true colors. The choice will be his. I know you'll say this is too drastic. Please know that I have only a matter of weeks to live, and the pain increases each day, making it harder to hold everything together. I hate using the drugs to mask the pain, but I find more and more that I need the sweet release they give me. Make my last feeble attempt to stop this hurtling Republican freight train worth something. Know that I love you, believe in you, and am certain that you're destined for great things. Sometimes the end does justify the means. Never forget the one who loves you more than life itself. Follow your destiny, my favorite son. I'll be watching and loving you always.' It's signed, 'Your devoted mother'"

With tears flowing unashamedly, he said, "That's Mother. To the point, powerful, challenging me to be all I can be by making a huge sacrifice to set the example. From the first I can remember, she drilled into me our responsibility for the incredible privileges our ancestors secured for us."

After a few moments of silence, Isabelle said, "Wayne, I don't know what is in your letter, but Ethel insisted you be here when her scheme began to unravel."

He picked up his letter and read: "My dear friend. I can still see that earnest boy standing uncomfortably in front of me telling me he hoped to become a lawyer. I'm proud to have been a small part of your incredible journey. Unfortunately, I must ask you to return a favor, because I've knowingly placed my dear Isabelle in harm's way. I ask you to devote your considerable knowledge, skills, and talents to ensuring that she does not suffer for my willfulness. I know she'll do what I ask of her, even though it breaks her heart, because she can't bear to see me suffer. She knows I haven't the strength or courage to accomplish my last wishes on my own. I entrust her safety to you. Keep her free,'" he read. "It's signed, 'Your biggest supporter, Ethel.'"

Isabelle immediately said, "I don't much care what happens to me. Chief Hunter, all your assumptions about what happened last Sunday night were correct. Thank goodness Governor Baxter is as arrogant as he is stupid, or this would have all been for naught. Ethel's plan did not take into account your skills. It's been difficult to know where your mind was going and how soon you'd put it all together. You asked me earlier why I shot Ethel rather than let her slip away from an overdose. According to Ethel, there were two reasons. First, an overdose would not have given her the media attention she felt necessary for her plan to work. Second, in her mind it gave her passing the greater purpose and sacrifice she felt she needed to leave this earth and face her maker, having followed the absolute letter of the laws of her faith as she understood and believed them."

"After talking with Father Leverette, I believe I understand," Dane said.

"Explain it to me," Ronnie interjected. "I still can't wrap my mind around this whole cockamamie plan that left mother dead. And quite honestly Isabelle, I cannot believe she would ask you to do such a thing knowing you would support her any way you could. You should have known it was the pain or drugs talking."

"The last part, I can't explain," Dane said, "but in conversations with Father Leverette, he told me about debates he and your mother have had about suicide, among many other topics. According to him, the Catholic faith views on suicide have changed, but your mother still believed God would look at it as, I believe the father said, 'a most atrocious crime,' and deny Christian burial to someone who takes his or her own life. He said he and your mother had debated this issue and that your mother had pointed out that there are some loopholes in the scriptures that allow for taking one's own life under certain circumstances. One is by not accepting treatments to extend life when you are terminally ill, and the other is when your act will help others. In this case, your sin is downgraded and can even be considered an act of virtue."

"I can see Mother having the debate, entertaining the thought, and even concocting this plan," Ronnie said, "but what I can't understand is your going along with it, Isabelle. What were you thinking? Do you know how much pain you have caused?"

Isabelle teared up again. "It's easy for you to sit there and say that, Ronnie. You haven't lived through what I lived through. You didn't have to hold her hand as she dealt with fears about her death. You didn't have to watch her struggle with pain so bad that she couldn't catch her breath. You didn't have to watch as everyone she loved ignored all the signs that she was sick and attacked her because she was dressing or behaving badly. Yes, I know how much pain's been caused. Yes, I took that gun and shot your mother just as I promised her I would. And yes, I've played this stupid game that she created to show you how much she really loved you, in an attempt to force you to help yourself into an office that she wanted for you. What did you do but believe some silly story that she was going to leave Myrtle Hill to the Catholic church. Please. If you knew your mother at all, you wouldn't have fallen for that one. Your little huff set the stage for this whole drama. Had you reacted differently, the plan probably would have never been set in motion. So don't you lecture me, young man. Your mother counted on me to do something totally alien to my nature, but I loved her so much that I did it," she said indignantly.

Dane interjected, "There are a couple of issues that still puzzle me. First, Sally Anderson seemed to have information that only those here would have had regarding Sunday's discussions about changing the will."

"I sent an anonymous letter to her," Isabelle said.

"Why?" Ronnie asked.

"She's been in Baxter's pocket, and it was part of the plan to create the opportunity for him to launch a personal attack on you," Isabelle replied.

"So did you also send the anonymous letter about Charlotte Kirk, Becky, and Reverend Reed?" Dane asked.

"Yes. I know in my heart she wasn't thinking right, but it was what she wanted. Ethel thought there had to be multiple angles to make the plan work. Getting Ronnie Junior involved was never part of the plan. Had we known he had been in the bedroom with his friend, I would have made sure every print had been cleared away."

"How did you know Doug would go to Becky's house that evening?" Dane asked.

"He is always her first call when something goes wrong," Isabelle responded.

"Seeing how events have unfolded, I would say that Ethel's plan was brilliant," Wayne observed.

Turning her gaze back to Dane, Isabelle asked," So where do we go from here?"

"I'll need to talk with Judge Ladner and Major Sikes. Let me try to get them on the phone. Wayne, would you stay with me?"

Wayne nodded. "Senator, I'll need you to leave us alone."

Isabelle stood. "I think I'll fix some coffee for myself while y'all debate my fate. Would any of you care for a cup?"

All agreed, and both Isabelle and the senator left the room.

Picking up the phone, Dane called Forrest Sikes and gave him a quick overview before asking him to set up a conference call with Judge Ladner and asked that he call Dane back on the number at Myrtle Hill so he could use the speaker phone and include Wayne in the conversation.

In less than five minutes, the four of them were discussing what to do next. Dane went through the entire scenario with Judge Ladner and Forrest. At the end, Judge Ladner said, "Jesus Christ. Ethel has pulled some interesting stunts in her day, but this one is unbelievable. We're going to have to convene a grand jury. But for the violence of the act, we would have only had to deal with an assisted suicide. Assisted suicide creates enough turmoil in polarizing beliefs, but by shooting Ethel, Isabelle forced our hand. Chief Hunter, take Isabelle in, get her written statement, and process her arrest. Mr. Wenzel, get me a written request to release her into the senator's custody pending the grand jury. She's seventy-eight, and I won't leave her sitting in jail because she followed this foolish drama. Major Sikes, put together all the evidence. We'll have to give a detailed package of information to the state prosecutor. What a debacle."

After the call, Dane explained the next steps to Isabelle and the senator. The senator agreed, and along with Isabelle, accompanied Dane to the station. Everyone left at the same time to prepare their portions of the work Judge Ladner had directed.

Dane had already finalized Isabelle's statement and gotten Judge Ladner's signature on the document to release Isabelle to the senator, who took her back to Myrtle Hill on house arrest until after the grand jury was convened. He was in his office going over events with Pat and Forrest in preparation for the afternoon press conference when he heard the phone ring in the outer office.

"Boss, Bill Carroll, Greenwood police chief, is on line one."

"Can you take a message and tell him I call back later this afternoon," Dane asked.

"No, boss, you have to take this call."

Punching line one, Dane said, "Hunter here."

"Chief, Bill Carroll. I'm sorry to have to interrupt you, but your wife has been in an accident and has been transported to Self Memorial here in Greenwood."

"Is she okay?"

"I understand it's pretty serious."

"My daughters?"

"They're uninjured at the hospital. I'll meet you there at the emergency room."

On hearing the news, both Pat and Forrest immediately ended the session. Pat said, "Honey, do you need me to go with you?"

In a daze, Dane said no. "You and Forrest need to be prepared to handle the press conference alone. I don't know how serious this is or whether or not I'll be able to come back in time."

Forrest said, "Dane, don't you worry about a thing. You just focus on what you need to do for your family. If any of us can help, just let us know."

Dane took off immediately.

At the hospital, Bill Carroll, true to his word, was waiting for Dane inside the emergency room door, and they were shown into a private office. Bill stayed with Dane while the attending doctor gave him an update.

"Your wife is in critical condition, and we had to put her on life support. She sustained severe trauma to the head and hasn't been conscious since emergency technicians arrived at the accident site. Witnesses say she didn't move from the time they got there. We're doing everything we can."

"My daughters?" he asked.

"They're fine. A town resident brought them in behind the ambulance. They've been checked out and have no problems whatsoever. I'll have one of the nurses take you to them."

Dane suddenly thought, in that blink of an eye, Mary's uneasy feelings and Audrey's intense sense of sorrow and grief surrounding him became reality.

While they waited, Bill filled Dane in on what he knew. "Tom Griffin turned his truck from of a side road, right into your wife's path. Your wife's car hit the back of the truck sideways, driver side impacting. Looks like her head hit and cracked the driver's side window. At the same time, a fence post flew from the truck and struck the window on the other side. She was knocked unconscious.

"Tom was thrown into his windshield. He wasn't wearing a seat belt and hadn't even seen a car coming. The sun had been in his eyes when he pulled onto the street, but he could have sworn the road was empty. The blow to his head disoriented him, but he quickly got out of the truck to see if everyone was okay. He told us that his chest hurt from the impact on the steering wheel. As he got to your wife's car, he said he saw your two girls in the back seat unbuckling their seat belts. He said they looked unhurt, concerned, but not afraid. He opened the door and let them out before trying to open the front door.

"About that time another car pulled to a stop. Gary and Susan Buckley were on their way to Columbus, Georgia, to visit their daughter. They jumped out of the car to see if they could help. Gary opened the passenger side front door. He said, he didn't think they should move your wife and turned off the key. There didn't seem to be any danger in leaving her where she was. He said he checked your wife's pulse, which seemed weak. His wife, Susan, said your daughters were holding hands and she tried to get them back to their car, but when she touched them, both girls shrieked. She said the three of them remained standing beside the door of the car, both girls humming and rocking, their eyes closed.

"Gary used his cell phone and dialed the emergency number and gave them the location. He said he felt odd that he never thought to try again to get the two girls from the side of the car.

"When the ambulance driver and emergency technician arrived, the girls let Susan take their hands. They walked to her car, where they waited in the back seat, quiet, holding hands, until Officer Jerry Blackwell arrived on the scene.

"When Jerry checked in the car, he found your wife's wallet and driver's license. We had put out your name earlier in the week as a new member of our law enforcement family. When he radioed the dispatcher, he asked that I be told so I could notify you."

"Thank you for all you have done," Dane said as the nurse arrived to take him to his daughters. Just down the hall, he saw them through the window sitting on a sofa, side-by-side. As he walked in, they separated so he could sit between them. The nurse closed the door after herself. A few minutes later, she looked in and saw Dane sitting, looking straight ahead, tears streaming down his face.

Sitting between them, both girls rocking and humming, Dane's emotions broke when he heard the girls saying, "It's going to be okay, Daddy. We went with Mommy to the river. A nice lady was there to meet her and walk with her into the light. She told us not to worry because Mommy was with family and friends. She told us we are going to have to take care of you for a while." It was the first time they had ever spoken directly to him. He'd never known if anything he said to them had registered. Rose looked up at him, touched a tear, and said, "Daddy, tell us the story you used to tell us about the zoo kingdom."

Harvey arrived with Mary not long after. Mary took over with the girls, telling Dane she would take them with her until Joan's parents arrived. Dane hadn't even thought about making that call.

CHAPTER
EIGHTEEN

At two p.m., Pat and Forrest stepped to the front of the First Baptist Church social hall serving as the media center. There seemed to be even more press members than had previously attended, with some of the bigger names from the news stations there along with the young reporters who had been on site throughout the week. Pat wasn't surprised that the local stars were ready to step on the younger reporters for the final story. It was a cutthroat business.

Pat opened the update saying, "Unfortunately, Camden Grove Police Chief Dane Hunter won't be with us this afternoon as we bring closure to events preceding and following the death of Mrs. Ethel Chapman Bowen at Myrtle Hill Plantation seven days ago. Chief Hunter's wife has been in a serious car accident, and he is with her at Self Memorial Hospital in Greenwood as we speak. We ask that you remember Chief Hunter and his family in your thoughts and prayers.

"As has been the case with each press update, we were preparing the fact sheet up to the time to leave for this gathering. It's being copied now and will be available at the back of the room before we finish today. This fact sheet will provide a complete chronological summary of all events to date.

"We previously reported that Mrs. Bowen was in the final stages of terminal pancreatic cancer, a disease that often results in excruciating pain in its final stage. Morphine was being administered to help manage the pain; however, it was the gunshot wound to the head that caused the death. It has been determined that the victim dictated how she was to die and persuaded Isabelle Ricks, who had been with her since Mrs. Bowen was born, to promise that she would follow her wishes."

The room burst into a series of questions.

Kathryn Blanchard was the first to be heard. "I've met Ms. Ricks, and while she's formidable, it's hard to imagine her in the role of murderer. How was this conclusion reached?

"Good question," Pat responded. "Certain things about the crime scene have not been released. Among those were the facts that there were a number of wigs spread on the bed, along with a large number of pieces of homemade jewelry made of buttons. In the course of the investigation, Chief Hunter found from a number of sources how much Mrs. Bowen treasured each of the button pins that had been made for her over the years by various residents of Camden Grove. As he went over all the facts of the case, something about the wigs and the pins bothered him. He finally realized that they represented a closure. What Chief Hunter couldn't get to fit the picture was the violent nature of the death. It was in discussions with Ms. Ricks that she revealed that she was fulfilling a promise she had made to the woman she had spent her life serving."

Exasperated, Sally Anderson said, "This is all just a little too convenient and trite. Can't you do better than 'the maid did it?' Is she a scapegoat for someone, or is this stunt aimed at getting the story out of the news during the election?"

Forrest stepped in. "We not only have a signed confession from Ms. Ricks, but we also have, in Ethel Bowen's own handwriting, a letter detailing why she chose the method of death she did."

"Are you going to release the letter?" Sally asked.

"It was a personal letter to Senator Bowen and is not a public document. Only he can release it, should he so choose."

"I'm sorry, but this all stinks," Sally said.

"Be that as it may, only the senator can release the letter. We have confirmed that it was, indeed, written by Mrs. Bowen and was one of several letters that she left behind. The others have not yet been delivered to the intended recipients pending the confirmation of their authenticity."

"Who else will get letters?" Sally asked.

"That's not information that I can release," Forrest answered.

"You're asking us to swallow this whole tale without any evidence other than a feeling that Chief Hunter had, and a signed confession he extracted? Surely you can't expect us to just walk away taking your word for it," Sally rebutted.

"No, we're not asking you to take our word. Judge William Ladner has directed that we provide a complete case documentation to be used by the state attorney general and a grand jury that will be convened to determine what will happen next in the legal proceedings," Forrest said.

Allison Andrews broke in. "I agree with Ms. Anderson. This has all been wrapped up too quickly, and no real evidence is being released to us to support the conclusions that you have reached. How do we report to our viewers that they should accept on blind faith that there is no dangerous murderer still lurking out there?"

Pat stepped back to the lectern. "While I appreciate your concerns, let's focus on what we do have. We have a signed confession from Isabelle Ricks stating that she, at the request of her employer and friend, ended Mrs. Bowen's life. We have an authenticated letter to the victim's son, along with authenticated letters to others that detail Mrs. Bowen's frame of mind and her involvement in the planning of her death. The documents will be reviewed by the appropriate legal authorities, who will determine what actions will be taken next. This is all part of the legal process that must be followed. When there is more information to be released, it will be," Pat concluded.

"Where is Ms. Ricks now?" John Peters asked.

Forrest stepped back, and answered, "She has been released into the custody of Senator Bowen for the time being."

"So we have a confessed murderess walking around?" Sally mumbled.

"Ms. Ricks is a seventy-eight-year-old woman, with no prior record, who has committed what would commonly be thought of as an assisted suicide. The violence of the crime is troubling to us, and, I might add, equally as troubling to Ms. Ricks. Judge Ladner agreed with a proposal by Ms. Ricks' lawyer that she posed no threat to the community."

"Who is her lawyer?" Sally asked.

"Wayne Wenzel, a local attorney who was also Mrs. Bowen's attorney," Forrest answered, adding, "and retained by Mrs. Bowen, after the fact, for Ms. Ricks' defense."

Pat stepped to the microphone, "I see we have the complete chronology available now. This should provide you all the information we have. Thank you for attending today. We believe this will be the final update meeting and future information will be provided by a press release through normal channels," she concluded.

At the hospital thirty miles away, Dane caught the portion that made it onto the six o'clock news, and wasn't surprised to see the reporter asking for Governor Baxter's opinion. The governor's response was true to the off-the-cuff remarks he had made previously. "I guess it's a good thing that this tragedy has come to an end. We'll probably never really know what Mom said to her son, since she hadn't come out in support of him.

As far as the campaign goes, now maybe we can focus on the issues. I sure would like to see the senator make this a real race for the office."

Dane called Pat to thank her for managing the last press conference and to update her on Joan's condition. She said she would stay as long as he needed her, but thought her "official" usefulness in Camden Grove was probably at an end.

"Not exactly," he said. "I think a certain senator could use some advice about how to respond to a sitting governor who can't control his mouth."

"I was thinking the same thing. I'll give him a call tonight with some thoughts."

Late that evening, as Dane sat in the room, just watching Joan, he remembered that he had all the other letters that Isabelle had given him before they left the house. He went to his car, got his case, and took it back into the room. Putting on gloves, he opened each and put both the envelopes and the letters into separate document protectors. It was busy work, but it kept him occupied. He'd get them to Forrest for processing in the morning.

He picked up the first, addressed to him, and read it.

> *Chief Hunter, I know I'll be presenting you with a strange case to solve when you first come into our community. You come to us with an excellent reputation and I only hope that when you read this, enough time has passed to allow my feeble plan to unfold. Please treat my dear Isabelle with the respect she deserves. What she's done, she's done out of her bottomless love for me, and at my request. She's never wavered in her support of me, and while I know it's unfair of me to ask her help with this plan, I have no other option. I hope that the rest of your time in Camden Grove will be more peaceful than its beginnings and pray you will forgive me for the challenge I placed in your lap. Ethel.*

The next letter he picked up was to Becky.

> *My dearest daughter, of all the letters I have to write, yours is the most difficult, yet I know of all who will mourn my passing, you'll be the most understanding of my need to leave the pain behind. I wish I could take with me the pain you suffer every day, and I feel a bit cowardly for seeking relief a few moments earlier than God intends to grant it, while you have faced your demons over the years in your own way. I still hope for you to be able to someday move beyond your horrible experience. Remember, the best revenge is going on with*

your life. You continue to make progress, and I want you to know that I will be watching over you, an angel in your corner. I'd like you to think about taking a roll in the Chapman Farms operations. You were studying to be an accountant, and it's never too late. Isabelle needs to slow down on her work, and I would love for you to transition in as she goes out. Think about it. I know you can do it. Continue to heal in Camden Grove. Hold me close in your heart, my precious child. Know I love you always. Mother

To Doug she wrote:

Douglas, it's well past time that you quit blaming yourself for what happened so many years ago. Move on with your life. I've long thought that you and Becky have been crippling each other, even though you both only want the best for the other. Sometimes crappy things just happen in this world. It doesn't mean you deserved it and you certainly don't have to let it ruin the rest of your life. Move on, Douglas, move on, and in so doing, I bet you will see Becky move on with you. Just an old woman's musing, one who cares about you and appreciates your continued devotion to her daughter. Ethel

To Charlotte Kirk Ethel wrote:

Dear Charlotte, I begin with an apology, as I know my actions will result in surfacing old memories for you. By the time you read this it will be over, but I know your past will have undergone scrutiny. Remember it is your past and has nothing to do with the woman you are today. Please know that if I could have prevented this pain for you, I would have. You've been a godsend to my family, and I only hope you will continue in your role with my daughter. You've done so much for her already, and I know there are better days for you both in the future. Ethel

To Robin she wrote:

Daughter-in-law, it's time to step up to the plate. My son needs you now more than ever. I know his choice of public life is a difficult one for you, but find a way to make it tolerable. As a team, the two of you can accomplish so much. I won't be there to pick up the pieces that my actions will leave scattered behind. You need to do that for our family. You need to become the glue that binds the Bowens together. I know you see so much more than anyone believes you do. Use your good common sense to be a full partner in my son's and grandson's lives. I also ask that you consider taking over Chapman Farms management. Ronnie will never want to be part of the Farm, but I believe Ronald will. Make Chapman Farms even stronger for the next generation! I have asked Becky to step into the accounting operations. Time will tell. You are loved and needed, and I know you're up to the task. Believe in yourself. Much love, always. Ethel

The next was addressed to Father Leverette:

My dear friend and spiritual advisor, I know there is no negotiating with God, but I truly believe that my actions meet the letter of the Catholic law. I am not shortening my life by much; my passing may provide a benefit for all residents of South Carolina if my son defeats that pompous bag of wind, and I know God doesn't need me to suffer these last few moments. I realize I may be placing Isabelle in some jeopardy, and I wish I could debate with you the logic of assisted suicide or mercy killing. Unfortunately, I'll just have to wing that part knowing the church has tolerated euthanasia in extreme cases, and I believe this to be one of those. I'll wait for you in heaven to continue our talks. Until then, bless me, Father, and say a prayer to speed my cleansing before I meet our creator. Ethel

The final letter and the briefest was addressed to her grandson:

My dear Ronald, whenever you are lonely or down, think of me, and I'll be there for you, your own personal angel. You are our future, and I know you know and respect the sacred trust our family has with the community. Continue our traditions. Always remember that no one loves you like your Grams loves you, no matter where I may be. Ciao, baby.

Reading all the letters capped what everyone had said about Ethel Chapman Bowen during Dane's investigation. He could sense the remarkable woman she had been. He remembered what Father Leverette had said at her funeral, "She was always challenging us to do the right thing, to support a cause in which we believed, to reach our full potential. And she did it in such a way that we wanted to do it for ourselves, never dictating, never forcing, but leading us to our own desire for action."

He wished he had known her through his own eyes rather than through the eyes of others. He felt it was truly his loss, but he knew her actions quickly made him a part of the fabric of life in Camden Grove, for better and for worse.

Going into his office, Dane noted the changes in Camden Grove's face and feel resulting from the state and national media attention focused on the murder and South Carolina's hot governor's race.

Mary and friends had begun work to create their Camden Grove Center for Psychic and Paranormal Research, and the on-going debates about managing the town's rebirth were resulting in windows of buildings being un-shuttered for potential reuse.

While Dane was a part of the excitement, he still had one foot in yesterday and today as he focused on Joan, and the other in tomorrow, with the daily growth of Rose and Julia. He was reminded of the opening line of his favorite book of all time, *A Tale of Two Cities*: "It was the best of times, it was the worst of times." That pretty much summed up his feelings.

When Dane opened the paper the morning after the accident, he knew Pat had spoken with Ronnie. The headline read:

Senator Breaks Silence

CAMDEN GROVE, S.C. Senator Ronald D. Bowen (D) talked to press members for the first time since his mother's murder last week saying, "This has been a tremendously sad time for us all. My family and I appreciate all the thoughts, prayers and condolence messages."

When asked what he thought of his opponent's comments during the past week, Bowen responded, "I've been surprised and saddened by comments. My mother and my family have made great contributions to this state, and I believe the governor, for political reasons, has trivialized those contributions. Mother felt strongly about integrity, especially in politicians. I learned those lessons well. The governor said that my mother did not support my candidacy. His facts are wrong. She made many sacrifices to help me see how I must fight for the office I seek."

Asked to expand on the comment, he said, "The basic differences between Governor Baxter and me are character, ability, the advisors with whom we surround ourselves, our policies, and our actions that are right for South Carolina. My Mother challenged me to address these differences head on, and I intend to do so."

When asked if he planned to release the contents of his mother's letter to him, the senator hesitated, saying the contents were better left private. "My Mother always spoke her mind and was never one to beat around the bush. In her last letter to me, she gave good counsel on the race for the highest office in the state. Needless to say, some of that counsel does not speak highly of the governor; thus it would be inappropriate for me to release it."

The next day, as Pat had predicted, Governor Baxter challenged the senator to release the letter, saying there was nothing in his record to hide. Ronnie acceded to his wishes. The release of Ethel's final correspondence to her son changed the tone of the campaign, stirring debate, creating investigations, and resulting in a steady increase in her son's poll ratings. Following the release, Senator Bowen called Pat and offered her a job during the rest of the campaign and his administration, should his bid for governor be successful.

Pat answered, "Senator, as much as I have enjoyed my short time here, I love my life in Washington. Now, if you ever decide to run for a national office, remember me."

He assured her that he would.

Joan's parents, Dave and Barbara Cox, arrived the morning after the accident, having driven down from Maryland. They and Dane had a good cry session and spent time talking to Joan. Their arrival gave Dane some time to keep up with work at the office.

Dave stayed for a week and her mother, two weeks beyond that, but then she too went back home when doctors suggested that they may want to look at different facilities specializing in long term care should Joan stay in a coma for longer. They decided to make the decision in ten days and Barbara promised to come back after settling things at work and stay as long as Dane, Rose, and Julia needed her.

Dane slipped into a routine. Up early, an hour with Joan at the hospital, to the office for the morning's work, lunch, an hour with the girls who were staying at Mary's, back to work for the afternoon, dinner with the girls, then back to the hospital where he stayed at Joan's bedside, holding her hand and quietly talking to her until the staff forced him home to get some rest around midnight. The days all seemed to run together.

Mary asked Dane's permission to add her skills to what the medical professionals were doing for Joan. He readily agreed and asked her to drive up with him that evening.

She explained that in addition to her mother and grandmother's instructions, she also had attended classes in Reiki that helped her access greater sources of healing energies. "People have different reactions to Reiki. I always feel like I enter a weightless force field, nothing around me enters that field, just me and the person I am working with, or me and the person who is working on me. Much like what Audrey did at the start of your session, I start off with a prayer that God will surround us in the White Light of Christ so that nothing but good comes into us and nothing but good flows from us. It is God's energy, we are just conduits.

"I start by sweeping the energy above the body three times," she said, talking him through her actions, "and then position myself at the person's head, cupping my hands across their forehead. Sometimes I can feel the 'static.' Next, keeping my hands cupped, I roll them up and down over the nose and mouth. Then hands still cupped I cradle the back of their head in my hands. You can feel the energy pulling away and they begin to relax. Some people even go to sleep while I do this. I can sense the sluggishness in Joan's brain, both from the injury and swelling, and the drug induced coma.

She continued moving her hands and manipulating parts of the right side of Joan's body, explaining what she was doing as she went. Ending with the right foot, she said, "I always work on their feet. Some energy workers don't do this part but I feel like it really is one of the most relaxing steps. Then I start over at the shoulder on the left side and do the same thing. If they are able to turn over on the table I work on their back, starting at each shoulder. You can start at the top of the spine and lay both hands flat and work down the spine, then lay one hand at the top and one at the bottom and let the energy flow. Since we cannot turn Joan over today, know that the energy works through from the front anyway. But, so many people have back problems that I like to work on their back if I can.

"I end the session at the head and run the energy mentally up and down their body three times. One thing I've noticed is that some people's energy field is close to their body while others extends way out. My hands do get very warm and sometimes hurt over areas where they may have problems. I do feel the benefits of the energy when I work on someone just as much as when I am being worked on. What is really great is if you have two people working and doing the same steps simultaneously on either side. The more you work on people the more you are able to feel when something isn't right. There may be a heaviness or it may feel warmer or colder. Some energy workers have what I call "cold energy", some warm. I've been told my hands feel like little heating pads," Mary said.

As she finished up, Dane was surprised to see that almost an hour and a half had gone by.

Mary and Dane agreed that Mary would come as often as she could while Joan was in the hospital.

As the days went by, Dane did his job, always thanking people when they asked how his pretty wife was doing, and everyone he saw asked. He had lunch with Mary, who, as she'd predicted, was his staunchest friend. He didn't know how he could have managed life without her.

He made sure, every day, to spend high-quality time with Rose and Julia. They were talking, laughing, and playing like normal children, while at the same time learning so quickly about their gifts with Mary and her "girls" and visiting scientists and researchers. While it made him happy, he was also sad that his Joan was missing all of it, and, he'd have felt much better with her input in setting limits of researcher access to their daughters.

Before returning to Washington, Pat agreed to help Mary with all the public relations needs of the new research center, gratis. While Dane knew she would never leave Washington, her short time in Camden Grove had a big impact on her, and she wanted to stay involved. An appointment to the research center's board of directors assured she would be part of the community. She was also contracted to consult for Chapman Farms. Pat called Dane every day, telling him it was just to keep him grounded until Joan was well, and remind him to take care of himself.

Dane was also surprised to hear that there might be a bit of a budding romance between Pat and Harvey. He never saw that one coming, but did notice how much she had impacted Harvey's behavior. He was slowing slipping out of the persona he had created to protect himself, and had a very intuitive and capable mind behind the exterior he had shown to the world.

At the office, Dane set about training Harvey, as promised, so Harvey could become what he called "a real police officer."

Sadly, nine days after Joan's accident their little three-legged tooth-less, blind Bichon, Winston, sickened and had to be put down. He and his brother Dakota had rarely been separated, so poor Dakota was suffering such separation anxiety that he cried and howled when he was alone. It broke Dane's heart. At night Dane put him on the bed, as much comfort for him as they missed their companions.

Three weeks after her confession, Isabelle was found dead in her room at Myrtle Hill. An autopsy revealed no reason for her death. It was as if she'd just willed her heart to stop, and it had obeyed. Few other than the Bowen family, Mary, and Dane mourned her passing. Many thought it was a good thing to spare her and the community a trial.

In one of their morning chats, Wayne told Dane that he had decided to sponsor Steve Adams in making a change in his life. "I'm going to let him work here while he takes a few college courses to see what he wants to do. Ethel gave me an opportunity to reach for my dreams, and I'm going to do the same for Steve."

"What does he think of it?"

"Well, he isn't very trusting. Whenever anyone's done anything nice for him since he was very young, it seems it was because that person wanted something from him, and according to him, it usually involved sex. In the beginning he thought I was looking for 'special privileges.' We've worked through that, and I believe he's excited about the chance to create and control a better future for himself."

"Seems like the whole town is moving on and better," Dane observed. "Becky and Doug are both working harder on resolving their issues, and have a lot of help doing it. Charlotte stayed put. Robin's become an active part of the senator's campaign, and is exploring a leadership role in Chapman Farms. Even Ronald has become involved in politics. Life in Camden Grove is good."

Getting serious, Wayne said, "Only you, my friend, are forced to stay in limbo."

In Camden Grove, life just flowed through the November fourth election day. Dane began that day with the newspaper before leaving for his morning visit with Joan. The headline read:

South Carolina Governor's Race too Close to Call
By Sally Anderson

COLUMBIA, S.C. The latest poll indicates that South Carolina's Republican Gov. Adam Baxter is fighting for his political life, with his race with Democrat Ronald Bowen too close to call.

Baxter is running on a booming economy, in a state that is largely Republican, with big-name Republicans in Congress and the White House backing his record, and his bid for a second term. But in the past four weeks, Bowen, a state senator, has steadily closed the gap, helped in large part by a bizarre twist of events after his mother's murder and a sitting governor who may have spoken when silence would have been the best course of action.

The governor's margin over Bowen was forty-six percent to forty-four percent in the most recent election poll released yesterday. Not good news for Baxter who has watched his lead dwindle from sixty-five percent in the poll conducted six weeks ago. With a margin of error of three point five percent, Bowen could already be ahead.

Despite his fall in the polls, Baxter says he's confident that he'll emerge the victor, stating that South Carolina voters want a man with family values and a success in managing the state's finances.

Bowen sees things differently. "Voters are becoming more savvy every day. They look beyond the rhetoric and see the record. I'm an honest man, I cannot be bought and will have the citizens' best interests in the forefront of every decision I make for South Carolina. Always have, always will."

Both candidates continue with the heart of the battle that emerged from implied accusations made by Gov. Baxter that Bowen could have been implicated in the murder of his mother, Ethel Chapman Bowen, a well-known figure in South Carolina politics and a generous philanthropist. While Baxter claims he was misquoted and misunderstood, the release of a letter from Mrs. Bowen regarding Baxter's character stalled his runaway campaign and leaves the winner of today's election uncertain.

The one thing that is certain is that win or lose, Gov. Baxter will be tied up in investigations for years to come.

Dane smiled. It seemed like Sally Anderson changed her loyalties. He was glad Ronnie was doing well, and the picture of him with Robin by his side on the campaign trail would have made his mother proud.

As Dane prepared for his drive to Greenwood to visit Joan, he promised himself he'd get to the polls in time to cast his vote.

At the hospital, Joan looked as she had since the day of the accident. The respirator raised her chest awkwardly, and Dane had to tune out the sounds as the machine took each breath for her. He'd also become a master at blocking out the sights of all the tubes and machines to which she was hooked. As every other day, he took her hand, focused on her face, and told her everything he'd done since he'd left her the previous night. He told her about the election, and that he was going to try to get to the polls to vote Democrat, something they always laughed about in the past, with Dane a Republican and Joan a Democrat. Joan always told Dane he would come over to the "good side" someday and they would stop canceling each other's vote.

When it came time for Dane to go, he kissed her forehead and told her he would see her that evening.

Dane voted for Ronnie before going to the hospital that night and was happy to hear on his way home that Ronnie was the projected winner, leading with an unofficial sixty-five percent of the vote based on exit polls and the counties where all votes had already been tallied. Dane knew the vote for Ronnie Bowen was great for Camden Grove and great for South Carolina.

Dane fell asleep feeling much was right with life, but woke from a dream, tears running down his face, vibrations running through his body. He was at peace, even though he knew with a strong sense of certainty that something was very wrong with Joan. He was sure, even without a phone call. He rolled into a sitting position, planting his feet on the floor, wiping his eyes with the back of his hand. He stood, went to the kitchen, and turned on the coffee pot before going in to shave, shower, and dress.

He knew he should call the hospital, but the coward in him told him that until he got the call, it really could've been just a bad dream. The coffee wasn't even finished dripping when the phone rang and Mary invited him to come down for a quick breakfast. Going in her kitchen door, he observed, "You're up early, Mary. Are the girls sleeping?"

"I made you some breakfast and you need to eat before you go to the hospital. Lucy and Audrey are on their way over. Audrey will stay with the girls, and Lucy will come with us to add her energy to mine this morning."

Dane wasn't surprised that she seemed to be expecting him. Four places were already set. As she poured steaming coffee, Dane began talking. "I had the strangest dream this morning, and you were in it. I was in the house sleeping when Joan came in and woke me and said we had to talk. She talked about dying and told me that I had nothing to fear. She said she was initially frightened, but that immediately she had soothing hands to calm her fears. She said she was encouraged to let go, but she didn't think she could leave me, even though she felt that her time was up and my place was still here. She said that I should never move away from Camden Grove. In my dream, I took all this in stride while she talked.

"She asked me to walk with her. We were out of the house and walking on a high mountain road with drop-offs on each side, filled with mist. We walked for a long time, holding hands, and finally turned a corner, and we were in a room filled with people. Everything was bright, white, and calm. The sense of complete peace encompassed me, totally comforting.

"Joan said, 'These are my family and guides who are here to encourage me home.' I accepted that. There were three clear, musical gongs. I heard your voice, Mary, saying 'Hold her; don't let her go. What happens next is up to you.' I wrapped her in a strong embrace, and she started vibrating. Everyone in the room vibrated and then came in and out of focus until my arms were empty one minute, then Joan was there the next. I saw you in a doorway, and you were trying to tell me something I couldn't hear. At that moment, I woke up. My face was wet with tears, and I was desperately sad," Dane said, looking down at his coffee mug.

"There are many things we haven't had an opportunity to talk about, but we will," Mary said. "I will tell you that for now, Joan needs you, needs us. I think she is losing the strength to stay in this world. She is at a crossroad where it is easier to slip away than to continue fighting. I think you have a decision to make, and I'd like to help you help Joan fight to stay."

Dane elected to fight.

At the hospital, the nurse was in Joan's room and said she would get the doctor to explain the current status. Joan looked much the same as she had since the accident, but the doctor told Dane that she had a brain bleed and they weren't sure what the next few hours would bring. He said Joan was being kept alive by the machines. He explained that one option was to take her off the respirator and see what happened. Hearing this, Dane took her hand, unable to hold back a sob, tears flowing, and knew he could not do it.

He nodded to Mary, and she and Lucy took up positions across from each other at Joan's head and began their work. Two hours later, Mary said, "We have done what we can. Now talk with her, tell her everything that is going on and how much she is needed."

Dane talked non-stop for the next few hours before the doctor came back in to find Joan in a peaceful sleep.

"Let us run some tests to see what is going on."

Dane left the room as more equipment was brought in. Thirty minutes later, the doctor came out and said that there was good news. The brain bleed was stopped and swelling seemed down considerably. "Let's follow her today and maybe tomorrow, try to bring her out of the induced coma and see how she does."

Dane decided to drive Mary and Lucy back to Camden Grove and bring the girls back for a visit.

Looking at the blinking message light, he hit the play button. The first message was from the governor-elect, followed by many more people who had become integral parts of Dane's life since he moved to Camden Grove and since Joan's accident. Word spread quickly about Joan's potential recovery.

With purpose, he opened the front door of his house for the short walk to Mary's house to get his daughters for the drive to Greenwood. He knew that his family, with Joan included, had found their home in Camden Grove.

The End

A Dane Hunter Mystery

Death Dive Ripples

Robert Ray

If you enjoyed the cast of characters in *Murder at Mrytle Hill Plantation*, prepare for their further adventures in:

DEATH DIVE RIPPLES
A Dane Hunter Series Mystery
by Robert Ray

LAS VEGAS, NEVADA

Two thousand pairs of eyes, drawn by spotlights from stage level, were fixed on the high-dive platform. The red-robed men in platinum wigs atop their wooden carousel horses rode into the distance as they completed their tableau, and the audience was ravenous for the next visual feast in the first act of the aquatic cirque performance. This was the second performance of the night at its permanent theater in the Bellagio Casino and Hotel in Las Vegas.

Four well-muscled young men stepped into the light, their toes feeling for the edge of the platform some thirty-two feet above the glowing water of the pool. The hard surface of the stage began moving, reducing the amount of exposed water surface. On the platform, Gregor Androv stood on the far right, his twin brother Alexi to his left. Two of their fellow Russian divers were positioned to Alexi's left. The four performed this particular dive only once in each of the two performances, Wednesday through Sunday. Music began to build as the sounds of the moving of the stage stopped with an amount of water visible so small that spectators were led to believe that the four bodies could never fit at the same time.

As one, muscles tightened as the four divers readied to spring into the air. On musical cue, they left the platform, their bodies twisting and turning as they plunged toward the postage stamp span of water below. The collective intake of air from the audience was audible.

Louder than the music, one of the divers spat, "Chyort."

Shocked gasps rose from the darkened room as Gregor's hands, positioned to slice into the water, hit the hard surface of the stage, snapping his fingers back, shattering his arms, and driving his head into his shoulders. He died instantly.

In the Casino, at a table in the Player's Club, Roxy Hunter dealt the last hand of her shift and joked with one of the gamblers as she pulled in the chips for the house's winning hand. She had been dating Gregor for seven of the sixteen weeks he had been in America. Her shift over, she rushed to get out, wanting to be home and get dinner made before he came over for the evening.

As she neared her car, she was lost in thoughts of all she needed to do and didn't really notice the man fumbling to put his key in the trunk of the car beside hers. As she leaned to unlock her door, she was grabbed from behind, an arm tightening around her neck and a hand clamped over her mouth muffling her surprised scream. The arm expertly pulled one way while the hand pulled the other, twisting violently and breaking her neck. The man released her, letting her slide lifeless to the ground as he walked off, unseen.

CHAPTER ONE

The phone rang three times in the Camden Grove, South Carolina, bedroom of Police Chief Dane Hunter before he realized it wasn't part of his dream. He squinted to bring the glowing numbers on the clock into focus. It was 3:37 as he picked up the phone.

"Hunter." He knew it had to be some kind of bad news. Most sane people know that good news can keep until normal morning hours for people to be awake, but for some reason feel bad news must be delivered immediately.

"Mr. Hunter, this is Detective Ed Bryant of the Las Vegas Police Department. I am sorry to call you in the middle of the night, but you are listed as the next of kin for your sister, Roxanna Hunter."

"Is Roxy in some kind of trouble?" Dane asked.

"I'm afraid not, Mr. Hunter. Your sister was found in the parking lot where she worked. She was apparently the victim of an attempted robbery and was killed in the process. I'm very sorry."

Dane was silent for a moment as he tried to gather his thoughts. He had just talked with Roxy five days earlier and she was so happy, telling him she had found the "love of her life." "You know you always said there was someone for everyone, I just had to wait for my soul mate to come to America from St. Petersburg, Russia, to find me," she had joked. Dane couldn't believe his sister, two years younger than he, was dead.

"Mr. Hunter," Detective Bryant said.

"I'm sorry. I'm not fully awake, and I'm processing your news. Is there any chance there could be a mistake?" Dane asked.

"Unfortunately, no. Her purse with her driver's license and credit cards were found with her. We got your number from her work personnel files. The Bellagio has designated one of their staff members to be your point of contact. Do you have a pen and piece of paper handy?"

"Give me a second," Dane said, turning on the lamp and picking up a pen. "Go ahead."

Detective Bryant gave him the name of Alice Skinner and her work number, along with his own.

"Detective Bryant, I'll make arrangements to get out there today. I'm the police chief here in Camden Grove and I would appreciate meeting with you and going over everything you have while I'm there."

"Please know we will afford you every professional courtesy. I am really sorry."

"I appreciate that. I'll let you know when I get in."

Dane hung up the phone, stunned, as he let the news sink in. Sitting on the edge of the bed, a million memories ran through his head. It suddenly hit him that if the purse with credit cards was found with Roxy, then something or someone must have interrupted the robbery and may have seen the person who did it. He ran his fingers through his hair.

CHAPTER TWO

In Las Vegas, Alexi was finally back at the house he shared with six other members of the cirque cast, all Russian. The house was quiet, but instead of going into the room he and Gregor had shared, he quietly opened the door next to it. There was enough light to see Stephan asleep on his back. One of his pillows was on the floor. Alexi picked it up with both hands and shoved it hard down onto Stephan's face cutting off his air at the same time he straddled his body, pinning Stephan's arms with his legs. He sat down so hard he knocked the wind out of Stephan who started frantically struggling to free himself.

While Stephan was strong, Alexi was stronger and had surprised him in the attack. When Stephan's struggles started to weaken, Alexi threw the pillow off and quickly covered Stephan's mouth with his hand to prevent him from calling out and bringing other housemates to the room. He could see terror in Stephan's eyes as he greedily tried to suck in enough air through his nose to fill his starving lungs.

"Don't think I am stupid enough to believe you pushed me accidentally. You will pay for Gregor's death and for my having to live with knowing my brother believed in his last moments that I caused his death."

Calmly, quietly, Alexi explained, "Because we have been friends, I am going to give you a choice. I am going to move my hand. When I do, you can either explain to me what is going on, or you can call for help. If you choose to call for help, you better plan to kill me too. Otherwise, you should always be looking over your shoulder because when you least expect it, you will find yourself having accidents. You will experience a million times the moment of fear Gregor felt before he hit. The only difference will be that I will be responsible for what happens to you, not a coward like you were. Nod your head when you have made your choice and I will remove my hand."

Stephan nodded immediately.

As the Alexi's hand was lifted, Stephan took a gasping breath. "That was so unnecessary, my friend. The accident was a surprise to me, too. Peter and I have already had this confrontation and he told me he was just following orders. You know Gregor was weak emotionally. He was only with us because you insisted. He was becoming more and more involved with that American girl, and Peter said those above us believed he was about to betray us."

"Do you believe that?"

"I don't know what I believe. But you have to admit that he has been spending less and less time with us and has seemed more distant from our goals."

"Whether or not he became distant, he would have never betrayed us."

"I'm not sure I agree with you. When we became successful, he would come under suspicion. The deeper the American pulled him in, the more he would hate being forced to go back home. His memory was not long like ours. His anger was no longer fueled. He has forgotten that Mother Russia was ruined by the American capitalists. He has forgotten that we lost everything when the walls came down. All our dreams gone because arrogant Americans think everyone has to live and think as they do."

"In my heart I know Gregor would have never betrayed us. Never have betrayed me."

"Not everyone believed that. I swear to you that I knew nothing before I was pushed into you. You must know, though, that you are going to be watched now. I do not want to lose you too, my friend."

"Think about it Stephan. If our friends are willing to kill even one of us if we don't believe as strongly as they do, then are our friends any better than the Americans we vow to hate? Is the act we plan going to make a difference in this world or are we just fooling ourselves? Are you ready to be a martyr for someone who finds you so expendable?"

"You ask too many questions. Questions that are better left unasked. We are in this too deep, Alexi. We believed that we needed to strike America in the heart, just as they did us. What better place than here? It is too late to turn back."

"I have no intention of turning back. But if you know who did this, I would know it. I will not die beside someone willing to stab me in the back."

"I have told you all I know. I've said more than I should have already."

"And what will you say to Peter of this conversation?"

"Nothing. I swear it to you on the memories we have together. I swear it on our friendship and Gregor's life."

Without another word, Alexi left Stephan's room, went into his own, and got into bed without even glancing at the bed where Gregor had slept. He hadn't been in it for weeks already—since he found this girlfriend. But he knew his better half was gone. Gregor hadn't been weak, just too good. Gregor hadn't gotten any of the angry or cold, hard side of the personality the twins shared. Alexi had it all. He vowed to himself and quietly to the spirit of his twin that he would discover who else to add to the list of those who would pay for the loss he experienced this night.

Acknowledgements

This first book was a long time in coming. Thanks to *Ed Bryant* who carried many of the duties of running our B&B, *The 1895 Inn*, in Savannah, GA, while I wrote and edited my work. A special thanks to two English gentlemen: *Bob Middlemiss*, author and editor, who encouraged me to give myself the chance to write commercially, and *Christopher Scott*, author and writing coach who provided tools to manage and hone my skills. Thanks to: my former son-in-law *Dane Hunter* who loaned his name and knowledge of police procedures to the lead character; my support group team, *Britton Hammett-McCurry* and *Pat Lambe*, who tirelessly discussed plots, flow, obstacles, and all the elements that go into a story line; critical readers *Nancy Brant, Marian Ladner, Caroline Myers*, and *Alice Skinner*, who identified rough spots and cheered me on; and friends and family who lent their names (and perhaps some parts of their personalities and or characteristics) to the fictitious characters in this book. And finally, a huge thank you to editor and author *Erica Orloff* of **Editing for Authors** for her collaborative editing services and rewriting process. I couldn't have gotten to the two main goal words— The End—without all of you.

Photo by Judith Kessler

Robert D. Ray

Murder at Myrtle Hill Plantation is Robert's first novel. He lives in Savannah, GA, where he owns and operates The 1895 Inn, a small Victorian Bed and Breakfast in Georgia's first city's historic district. A graduate of Saint Leo University, Robert is currently working on the second book in this mystery series, *Death Drive Ripples*, featuring many of the characters introduced in this first novel.